One ROGUE TOO MANY

SAMANTHA GRACE

sourcebooks
casablanca

Published by Sourcebooks Casablanca, an imprint of Sourcebooks,
Inc.
P.O. Box 4410, Naperville, Illinois 60567-4410
(630) 961-3900
Fax: (630) 961-2168
www.sourcebooks.com

Printed and bound in the United States of America.
VP 10 9 8 7 6 5 4 3 2 1

For my darling girl

Prologue

Late October 1811

"WHAT ARE YOU DRAWING NOW, BUG?"

Gabby's hand stilled and she turned toward Anthony with a wide smile, setting her sketchbook and charcoal beside her on the garden bench. "That's *Lady* Bug to you, my lord."

She wasn't sure when she had begun to consider his nickname for her a term of endearment rather than the insult she was sure he had intended years ago. Perhaps her attitude toward him was a recent change, a transformation that had come over her during this break between school terms, but affection for him swelled within her chest.

He swept up her drawing and plopped beside her on the bench. "Your nose is red, little bug. Why are you sitting in the cold?"

She made a show of pulling her pelisse tighter around her, but she no longer sensed the chill with him near. "My muse cares little for my comfort. Inspiration strikes when it is least convenient."

"Would you like me to speak with her on your behalf?" He playfully bumped her shoulder then held her sketchbook up to scrutinize it. He glanced up and turned his head one way then the other, his lovely blond brows forming a V over his glorious blue eyes.

Gabby sighed softly, melting inside. Anthony had returned from his second year at Oxford, no longer a boy, but a handsome prince. She'd had plenty of time to revel in his perfection since he resumed posing for her not long after his return to the country. Her favorite sketch rested between the pages of her journal, hidden beneath her mattress.

No matter that she was thirteen and likely was viewed by the adults around her as too young to know her heart. She loved Anthony Keaton, the Earl of Ellis. Besides, she would be fourteen in a month. She was on the verge of becoming a woman.

Anthony's gaze landed on her and flared.

She blinked and quickly looked away as a burst of heat consumed her. He had caught her in the act of pining for him.

He cleared his throat, shifting away from her.

Her stomach took a dive, but she refused to believe his movement held any significance. Only weeks earlier he had grasped her hand when they'd stood side by side at his mother's grave site, his stoic expression ripping Gabby apart when she sensed the tremors coursing through him. He'd held on tighter while the men shoveled every last spade of dirt on his mother's resting spot and refused to relinquish Gabby's hand until their small group of mourners had reached Ellis Hall. He was reluctant to leave her now, too, which was the reason he'd sought her out before her father's coach carried him and her brother back to school. She sensed it deep within her bones.

He tapped her drawing. "Where, pray tell, do you see a lady in dance?"

"Right there." She nodded toward the aged oak standing sentry at the edge of the garden. "Can't you see it?"

"The tree?" He squinted. "The *tree* is dancing."

She rolled her eyes, hopped up from the bench, and marched toward the oak. "The tree isn't dancing, you dolt. Look at the lines of the bark." With a pointed finger, she indicated the outline of the figure that jumped out at her. It was as plain as the pleasing nose on his face. "Here is the curve of her arm and her side. And see how her hip is rounded here and then the length of her leg."

Anthony set the sketchbook aside and came over to examine the bark. He dragged his finger over the grooves in the tree. "How did you see it?"

She warmed at the awe present in his tone. "I see it. I don't know how."

He glanced down at her, his blue eyes alight with something that made her stomach quiver.

This wasn't how he typically looked at her. His admiration was becoming an uncomfortable fit. She scoffed to hide her true reaction. "How do you *not* see it?"

He grinned. "I do now." He patted her shoulder, his touch branding her as his. "Thank you, bug. There is no telling the number of extraordinary things I miss when you aren't around to point them out."

She barely contained her happy sigh. Clasping her hands behind her back, she swayed, debating on whether to give him the gift she'd found earlier in the summer. Perhaps it would seem childish to him. Or it might be seen as one of those extraordinary things he had mentioned.

She held a finger up. "Wait here." Then she dashed for the house. At the French doors, she stopped and turned toward him. "Promise you won't go anywhere?"

"I promise, but hurry. The coach will be leaving soon."

Gabby ran inside and up the staircase, grateful she didn't cross paths with anyone who would scold her for unladylike behavior.

In her chambers, she hurried to her vanity to retrieve her simple treasure from the jewel box before rushing back to the garden. Anthony was still there, his cheeks pink from the cold air.

Her fingers tightened around her gift, the edges digging into her palm.

His smile seemed sad and unsettled her. She came forward slowly, doubting her decision to lay her feelings out to him.

"I am sorry about your mother," she said. "You mustn't ever think you are alone now."

"But I am. I'm an orphan with no family."

She shook her head. "We are your family. You have us."

Anthony had spent more time at their home than his neighboring estate for as long as she could remember. He had to know she spoke the truth.

"I'm fond of your family, Gabby, but that doesn't make them mine."

She came forward on a rush of emotion and grasped his hand. "We are yours. *I* am." She shoved the heart-shaped stone into his hand.

He uncurled his fingers and stared down at her offering. A shadow fell over his features. His lips turned down. "Gabby, I—"

Her brother flung the outside door open. "Ellis, what are you doing out here? It's time to go." Drew sauntered into the gardens, either oblivious to the fact he was interrupting or uncaring. Like Anthony, he was dressed in travel attire.

Anthony trapped the stone in his fist and tossed a jaunty grin toward her brother. "I wanted a breath of fresh air, and I stumbled upon the bug doing her sketches."

There was no endearment attached to the name this time, and Gabby shrank back. She had been the target of their taunts too often to lower her guard.

Drew gestured toward Anthony. "What's in your hand?"

Anthony snorted. "Nothing. Let's get out of here."

His derision drove a spike into her chest.

Drew was not easily distracted, however, and grabbed for Anthony's hand. "Come on. Give it over. You're holding on like it's a piece of gold."

"I am not!" Anthony stopped resisting and opened his fist.

Drew laughed. "A rock? What use do you have for a rock?"

Anthony's gaze lingered on her, his expression grim.

"I told you it was nothing." He walked to the edge of the garden, drew his arm back, and flung it so far Gabby couldn't see where it landed.

Her heart seized and her throat burned. She drew a deep breath to keep from crying.

Her brother came forward and gathered her in an awkward hug. "Now, don't start crying again, princess. I will be back again before you know it."

A soft sob escaped her despite her determination to keep her tears inside.

Anthony shoved his hands into his pockets and studied the ground. "I'll wait by the coach."

And then he walked away without even saying good-bye, leaving her trust and love for him trampled and broken on the ground.

One

Corby wagers £2,000 that when Lords Ellis and Thorne come to blows over a certain duke's sister, Ellis will throw the first punch. Ledbery accepts the bet and wagers Thorne will strike first.

From the betting book at Brooks's

April 1819

When Anthony Keaton, Earl of Ellis, entered the gentlemen's club, there was a spring to his step and a song in his heart. Well, he was whistling anyway. Nothing could spoil his fine mood this evening, not even the prospect of crossing paths with Sebastian Thorne.

The porter met him at the entrance and offered to take Anthony's hat and walking stick. "Good evening, milord."

Anthony sported a wide smile. "Good is an understatement, Harry. This evening is splendid."

"Yes, milord. It's much improved with your arrival." Harry, who had been employed at Brooks's for as long as Anthony could remember, maintained his stony grimace. After all these years, his face would likely crumble if he attempted a change in expression.

"I believe I detect a hint of sarcasm, my good man. Don't tell me my absence has gone unnoticed these past months."

"Not at all, milord. Lord Thorne has found no one accommodating enough to accept his challenges with you gone. As of late, he has stopped coming 'round as often."

"I'm certain that is no hardship for anyone."

Least of all, Anthony. His last encounter with Thorne had left him hugging the chamber pot for the better part of a day, thanks to a wicked bottle of gin and Anthony's inability to back down from one of Thorne's challenges. He chuckled to himself. Perhaps he *had* missed the thrill of besting his rival, but not as much as he missed Lady Gabrielle Forest.

Life was good. No, *very* good. Amazing! And perfect. Or it would be once Gabby's brother granted permission for Anthony to marry her. Unfortunately, he had arrived to Town too late in the evening to call, but tomorrow their secret betrothal would cease to be a secret.

Laughter echoed off the domed ceiling as he entered the great room. Groups of gentlemen were clustered around tables lining the walls, each crowd engaged in a different game of cards.

"Look what rubbish the wind blew in," Mr. Smyth called out in greeting. Anthony wandered to the table to exchange a few friendly words with the men before he was called to an adjacent table and encouraged to join in their game of whist.

"Another time, gents."

He scanned the area, hoping to encounter one of Gabby's brothers so he could at least inquire into her well-being. Four months apart had been unbearable, but there had been no help for it. Once they became husband and wife, he would make certain they were never apart that long again.

None of his childhood friends were among the crowd, not that he'd really expected the Forest men would be in attendance. His friends had become domesticated as of late and spent evenings in the company of their families.

A bittersweet pang originated deep within his chest. *A family life.* The one thing he had always wanted and thought he would have with his first wife.

He shook off his melancholy. He'd not waste another moment grieving the loss of his dreams. His daughter, Annabelle, was safe under his roof now, and he would have the wife he should have married long ago.

On the long journey back from Wales, he had passed the time imagining evenings at home with his two ladies, Annabelle dressing her doll's hair and Gabby sketching whatever caught her fancy.

His grin returned. Damn, he couldn't wait to be domesticated himself.

He spotted Lords Corby and Ledbery sitting away from everyone else with the betting book lying open on the table before them. Corby elbowed his companion and nodded in Anthony's direction. Anthony scratched the back of his neck and looked away.

There was a reason the two men sat apart from everyone else. Corby and Ledbery were young, wealthy, and bored. No better combination for trouble existed. More than one gentleman of Anthony's acquaintance believed the gents fed information to the gossip rags. He didn't know if it was true, but one thing was certain—often when he had a problem, those two were involved.

Turning on his heel, he pretended not to see them and headed for the billiard room. The clack of balls knocking together greeted him as he entered. He grabbed a stick and claimed one of the crimson tables to practice, since everyone else was already in pairs.

Lining up his shot, he leaned over the table, his concentration keen. He drew back his cue, bumped into something, and sent the ball careening to the left.

"Bollocks," he muttered.

A hand clamped down on his shoulder. "Bad luck that, Ellis."

He gritted his teeth. "Corby."

Ledbery circled the billiards table like a mongrel preparing to attack. Anthony moved to line up his next shot, hoping they would take their leave if he pretended they didn't exist.

Corby plopped the betting book on the felt and tapped the page. "You'll want to get in on this wager."

"I'm not interested." Anthony lined up the next shot. "Kindly remove the book."

Corby scooped it up with a frown. "Aren't you curious as to the terms?"

"No." He slammed the cue stick into the ball. It dropped into the pocket.

"We're taking bets on Lord Thorne's wedding," Ledbery said.

So Thorne had gotten caught in the parson's noose. Anthony grinned. He wasn't a betting man on most occasions, although Thorne—aptly named given he was a pain in Anthony's side—had a way of goading him into taking the most ridiculous bets. He looked forward to a little friendly goading himself when they next crossed paths.

"What are you betting on?" Anthony drawled. "How many steps his bride takes down the aisle before she comes to her senses and runs?"

Ledbery scratched his head. "Yes, I suppose that *is* a scenario we hadn't considered. It happened to his sister, only it was the groom to escape in the nick of time."

Anthony waved him off. "No need to drag his family into this discussion. The lady was misused, and she didn't deserve it." He laid down the cue stick and retreated to a table along the wall. Pulling out a chair, he slumped into it. He knew he was going to regret this. "What is the bet?"

The men exchanged matching leers, and Anthony cursed his curiosity.

Corby slid the book in front of Anthony and sat. "We are betting on how long it's going to take for Thorne to woo the lovely Lady Gabrielle."

"Foxhaven's sister?" Anthony snatched up the book. He blinked several times in case his eyes were fooling him then glared at Corby. "You said four days?"

"I think he'll never win the lady's heart," Ledbery piped up.

Anthony thumped the table and pointed at him. "Never is the correct answer. This is balderdash. Lady Gabrielle Forest wouldn't give Thorne the time of day."

Corby smirked. "She allowed him to take her for a ride down Rotten Row today. They seemed cozy from my point of view. In fact…"

A loud buzzing in Anthony's head drowned out the rest of the gent's comment. What did Corby mean Gabby had gone for a ride with Thorne? She was engaged to Anthony. Even if nothing had been formally settled between them, she had given her promise.

"This is a mistake. You have the wrong lady in mind."

Corby shook his head. "I know Lady Gabrielle when I see her. She stands out like an orchid among roses. Thorne's a lucky gent."

"No, he isn't." In fact, the baron's luck had run out if any of this was true. It was one thing to steal the affections of Madame Beaudry—the prima donna had become too demanding for Anthony's tastes anyway—but Gabby was another story.

Anthony sank against the seat back with a mild smile. Corby and Ledbery were trying to rile him. Thorne had no interest in courting a lady. "And what does one carriage ride prove?"

"It wasn't the carriage ride as much as the dancing," Ledbery said as he took up position beside his friend, his expression grim.

Corby nodded, his lips set in a thin line.

Perhaps they weren't joking after all. He sat up straighter. "What dancing?"

"Thorne claimed the supper dance and a waltz at the Finchley ball last night, and he is sure to try the same at Lady Chattington's tonight."

Anthony slammed his palms against the table and surged to his feet. "The hell he will!"

The gentlemen exchanged a glance. Corby smiled slyly as he grabbed up the quill and began to scribble something in the book.

"What are you doing?" Anthony spotted his name scrawled across the page. "Stop writing at once. What do you think you're doing?"

Corby passed the book to his companion and displayed every tooth in his head. "Welcome back, Ellis. London was dull with you away."

"I'll take this bet," Ledbery said.

Devil's bollocks! There had to be some mistake. Gabby wouldn't toss him over like that.

Spinning on his heel, he stormed toward the door.

"Where are you headed, Ellis? Don't you want to take the bet?"

"I have yet to call on Lady Chattington since my arrival. I'm certain she will be pleased to see me."

"Offer our regards to Lord Thorne."

"Go to hell."

❦

If Lady Gabrielle Forest had learned anything in her twenty years on this earth, it was that her heart couldn't be trusted. Her parents' happy union had filled her head with silly nonsense.

There were no such things as perfect matches, true love, or destiny for everyone. And if by chance there were love matches for the undeserving, she had proven a poor judge of who that person was for her. *Twice.* She wouldn't make the same mistake a third time.

Her only destiny involved a smart marriage to a decent fellow so her two younger sisters could finally have their coming out. Liz and Katie had been more than patient with her, but the delay had become a heavy burden to shoulder.

She suppressed a sigh. Here came her destiny now, his dark gaze focused on her. Gabby forced a smile, for no matter how certain she was that the handsome Baron Sebastian Thorne would make a suitable husband, she didn't know whether she could accept a proposal if he offered one. Her heart still belonged to Anthony, even if she'd given up hope of him returning to claim her.

"Anthony," she muttered. His name was a bitter taste upon her tongue.

Lord Thorne reached her, his grin dazzling. "It's almost time to collect the waltz you promised."

Her brother Drew took up position by her side with his arms crossed. "Not until the next set. Move along."

Gabby shot him a scathing look then smiled politely at the baron. "How lovely to see you again, my lord. I can't recall if I thanked you for the drive this afternoon."

"You did, my lady, but I should be the one offering my gratitude. Your company was most pleasant."

Drew grumbled something insulting under his breath about insincere popinjays, but she ignored him. Her brother was of a mind that she was a ninny for considering a rogue like Lord Thorne, but if she wanted his guidance, she would ask for it.

Her brother didn't understand her decision to make a match based solely on a list of qualities she deemed important for a gentleman to possess. Drew believed the heart should guide these types of affairs, but Gabby had followed her heart in the past and it had gotten her in trouble. This time she would apply logic. *Reliability, steadfastness, frankness.* These were the traits she sought, and Lord Thorne had all three.

Besides, *he* was in London courting her while her betrothed had yet to return after months out of the country.

She faked a happy smile. A compliment for her suitor was on the tip of her tongue, but a slight commotion at the ballroom entrance distracted her. Her gaze locked on the new arrival as he ignored the footman's protest that he wasn't on the guest list. Her heart tumbled end over end.

Blast her heart! The dreadful thing always led her to trouble. And trouble's name was Anthony Keaton.

His face lit as he spotted her and headed in her direction, but his step faltered and his eyes narrowed on Lord Thorne at her side. The baron was still speaking, his voice droning on and on, but she couldn't hear a word he was saying. Her thoughts skittered around in her head like ants caught in rain.

Anthony was back. Her hands shook as elation coursed through her. She turned her back to him to gather her thoughts. Why hadn't he returned at Easter as he'd promised? She'd heard nothing from him for months, and here he was as if he'd never left.

Her brother's rigid stance shifted, and he grinned. She knew Anthony was approaching.

"Ellis, I didn't expect to see you at the Chattingtons' ballroom this evening," Drew said.

"I only just arrived to Town."

Gabby glanced at him, quickly assessing his dress.

His coat was free of dust and his boots polished to a high shine, but he was inappropriately attired for a ball. She didn't know how she had missed it upon his arrival. "Only arrived as in moments ago?" Her voice hitched slightly, betraying her hope he had come straightaway to see her.

"I returned a bit earlier," Anthony said pleasantly.

She silently berated herself. Of course he hadn't contacted her the moment he'd arrived in London. Those were the actions of a man in love, and nothing in Anthony's behavior since the day of his proposal had suggested he loved her. Doubt crept into her thoughts again. During his absence, she'd begun to suspect he had asked for her hand out of duty that day rather than any sense of affection for her.

"I didn't know I would be attending Lady Chattington's ball until I had a chat with Lord Corby."

Lord Thorne crossed his arms, the beginning of a smile making his lips twitch. He nodded to the far side of the ballroom. "There is our hostess now. Please, don't allow us to deter you from a reunion with the lady."

Anthony's cool-as-winter eyes assessed the baron. "You've never deterred me from anything that matters, Thorne."

The baron arched a brow, his dark gaze assuming a feverish gleam. "Is that so?"

"That it is." Anthony squared off with him, mirroring Thorne's challenging stance.

It was the oddest exchange she'd ever seen. She looked to Drew to translate.

Her brother rolled his eyes. "Behave yourselves, gents. My sister is here to dance, not watch you two peacocks arguing over who has the prettier tail feathers."

Gabby's face was suddenly too hot as her mind conjured an image of Anthony's backside from the time she'd stumbled upon him swimming one summer. He winked as if he knew the path her thoughts traveled. Embarrassment consumed her.

Lord Thorne scowled. "When was the last time you were in the presence of a lady, Ellis? You have the manners of a goat. And you're no better, Forest, with your talk of peacocks."

Drew just shrugged, flashing his dimpled grin.

The baron bowed toward her. "Forgive us, Lady Gabrielle. I'm afraid all three of us have been absent from the ballroom long enough to forget how to behave like gentlemen."

She took a deep breath to calm her jitteriness and smiled. "Apology accepted, my lord, and thank you. I look forward to seeing you again when the next set begins."

The muscles at his jaw shifted and his returning smile was tight. Still, he bid her a gracious farewell then went to speak with another guest.

Anthony was watching her, his eyelids hovering at half-mast. When she was younger, she'd thought his eyes gave him a bored air, but she had once overheard a widow refer to them as bedchamber eyes. She hadn't understood the reference until after their steamy encounter months earlier. An image of his mouth tenderly at her breast set her body afire again.

She cleared her throat. "Was your journey pleasant, Lord Ellis?"

"I accomplished my aims."

"Oh? And what aims would those be?"

A hardness set in his jaw. "Do you really look forward to dancing with that scoundrel?"

Drew nudged her with his elbow. "See? You won't listen to me, so listen to Ellis." He turned toward Anthony, likely pleased to have found an ally. "I don't care for Thorne sniffing around Gabby's skirts."

"Neither do I." Anthony had an edge to his tone. "How long has he been bothering her?"

They were speaking around her as if she had no say in the matter. "I'm not bothered."

Drew ignored her. "He danced with her last week, then sent flowers thanking her the next day. Every day since, he has been underfoot. I don't know his aims, but you can bet his intentions are not honorable."

Her hands landed on her hips. "Really, Drew. You know nothing about the man or his intentions."

"But I do," Anthony said. "I'm well acquainted with Sebastian Thorne, and he is not honorable. It shouldn't take much to shoo him away."

"Now wait one moment—"

"Splendid." Drew clapped Anthony on the shoulder. "It's good to see you back in Town. Lana and I would be pleased if you joined us for dinner this week."

"My pleasure."

Insufferable oafs! This was just like when they were children. Drew and Anthony would join alliances and tell her what to do. Well, she was no longer a child.

"I have something to say."

Drew chucked her on the chin. "Later, princess.

I've finally spotted Lana. You'll be in good hands with Ellis while I dance with my wife."

Her brother sauntered off without waiting to see if she consented to being left in Anthony's care. She stared daggers at his back before swinging toward Anthony, daring him to try to run roughshod over her now.

He offered an enigmatic smile in return. The air crackled with awkwardness as silence dragged on. He had never been one to engage in polite chitchat, but after four months apart, did he have nothing to say? Frustration brewed in her chest, the pressure building inside her.

"I'm still waiting for an answer," he said at last. "Do you look forward to dancing with Thorne?"

Her chin lifted. He hadn't answered her question either. "As Drew said, I'm here to dance."

"And do you have a spot on your dance card for me?"

In her first Season, there wouldn't have been an unclaimed dance, but she was no longer the most-sought-after debutante. There were prettier, younger ladies on the marriage mart now, and they were more willing to play the ridiculous games involved with collecting many suitors.

She gripped her card, tempted to lie. He owed her answers, but one touch from him and she feared she'd forgive and forget with no effort on his part.

"Let me dance with you, Lady Bug." His voice caressed her injured pride.

She sighed and reluctantly passed her card to him. He scribbled his name and returned it without blinking. She glanced down to see he had claimed the empty slot before Lord Thorne and laughter bubbled up inside her. "The quadrille?"

He had always complained about dance lessons when he was a boy, and in truth, he had never been good on the ballroom floor. She had found that out the hard way when he had volunteered to practice with her when she first began lessons herself.

His lips inched up and a spark of warmth lit his blue eyes. "It will be like old times."

"I certainly hope not. You were abysmal."

He laughed, melting the last of her resistance. Drat, but she was hopeless when it came to him.

"I have missed your directness, Lady Gabrielle."

"How kind of you to say so, my lord." She refused to admit she had missed anything about him. He already held the upper hand.

When it was time to take position on the dance floor, Anthony offered his hand. His intense study of her made her flush again and her legs tremble. "Your brother needn't fret about me keeping close watch. I can't take my eyes off you."

Two

ANTHONY WAS CERTAIN OF THORNE'S INTENTIONS, BUT his boldness surprised Anthony. Gabby's brothers were known for their fierce protectiveness and skill with blades and pistols. What he didn't understand was Gabby's defense of Thorne, and he wanted to know where her mind was, but the quadrille required most of his attention to avoid colliding with the other dancers. He'd forgotten how blasted fast the steps were. Gabby twirled with him for half a breath, then skipped away to her corner.

Questioning her on the dance floor had been a bad plan. Even if he could manage more than a word or two with her before being dragged away by the overzealous Lady Marwick, there was no privacy on the crowded floor. He could barely cavort without treading on the ladies' skirts.

What was it ladies did not understand about men and frolicking? Men were not built to be graceful. At least he'd never been.

When he and Gabby finally came together, they sashayed around the circle, following the other couples.

With her at his side, his suspicions faded. She would never betray him as his wife had. Gabby's heart was too pure.

Thorne stood on the sidelines, his scowl a flash as they passed him. Anthony's irritation flared to life again. He may trust Gabby, but he didn't trust Thorne. Or Gabby's ability to ward off the baron's advances. Thorne could charm even the dourest matrons, making them blush like schoolgirls. Anthony should know, since he'd lost that particular bet. Gabby's innocence would make her an easy target for a man like Thorne.

"How could you have allowed Lord Thorne to take you for a carriage ride this afternoon?"

She gasped and missed a step, but recovered quickly. "Were you spying on me?"

"No!"

They faced each other and turned a circle. She glowered the whole time. "How long have you been in Town?"

"As I said, not long."

"Just long enough to see me in Hyde Park."

The dance required them to switch partners before he could correct her assumption. Lady Marwick snatched his hands and swung around in a wide circle, her head tossed back with a gleeful laugh. He'd never seen anyone dance with such abandon. It was no wonder Lord Marwick usually hid in the card room.

When Anthony and Gabby came back together, he started to explain he hadn't seen her in the park, but she was too quick.

"Obviously, you have been back long enough to have sent me word."

"I sent word to your brother."

Behind her gray eyes, a storm was brewing. Experience had taught him to keep his mouth closed when she was in a temper. Her anger would blow over soon enough and he could speak reasonably with her again.

"I had expected you to be eager to see me after four months apart. I see our separation has been easier on you."

That was unfair. Not to mention untrue. "I came as soon as I could. And I did miss—"

The last strains of the quadrille faded and he swallowed his response. It wouldn't do for everyone at the Chattingtons' party to be privy to their affairs. He escorted Gabby from the floor and led her through the promenade.

"It wasn't easy on me, love," he murmured. "I'll call on you tomorrow and set everything to rights. I promise."

She drew to a halt, her mouth falling open. "Is that what this is about? You feel there is a wrong to make right?"

"No!" He urged her to a quiet corner. "This isn't the place or time for this discussion."

Her eyes filled with tears.

Damnation! They were drawing enough attention with their sudden exit from the dance floor. If anyone suspected what had happened between them, her reputation would be ruined. He pulled a handkerchief from his pocket and passed it to her. "People are looking our way."

She dabbed at her eyes before forcing a detached

smile for their audience. "Please, tell me the truth now and spare me a restless night. Why didn't you come back when you said you would?"

"I had no choice," he said under his breath.

"Why not? What business kept you away?" Her voice was beginning to rise again.

Across the room, Lady Ibberton whispered something to their hostess and Lady Chattington tossed a curious look over her shoulder. Two ladies joined their group, not bothering to hide their stares.

"This isn't the place, Gabby. Please, just trust me. We can discuss it tomorrow."

"You're avoiding me once again. Why am I not surprised?"

Her bottom lip quivered and he longed to pull her into his embrace. Instead, he covered her hand resting on his forearm and gave it a small, reassuring pat.

He should have foreseen how his absence would hurt her. Gabby would have needed more reassurance of his feelings while she awaited his return, especially since the loss of her father. Had Anthony not been scouring the countryside of Wales in search of his missing daughter, he could have written. He also would have been home long before now and gained her brother's permission to marry her. Yet he couldn't explain the reason he was delayed without going into the entire tale, and there were facts he never wanted the *ton* to know about his daughter.

He leaned close to whisper in Gabby's ear, her floral perfume bringing back their last moment alone together. She had possessed him that day in his study, and he'd lost all sense of right or wrong. He'd had no claim to her, but he had nearly taken everything she trustingly offered.

"Everything will be better tomorrow, I swear it," he murmured.

He hesitated to release her, but she jerked away. "You must think me the biggest fool in London."

She stormed off, likely unaware of how enticingly her derriere bounced with each angry step. It was enough to make him want to keep her in a fit of pique.

‿✺⁀

Gabby slipped behind a pillar and sank against it. Her breath came fast and hard; her hands shook. She needed a moment to gather her wits before she danced with Lord Thorne, but the baron was already weaving through the crowd, headed in her direction.

Thorne's brown eyes glittered in the candlelight, and a grin that should have her swooning, as it did with every other lady he turned it on, slowed her racing heart. She never felt out of control with Lord Thorne.

"Here you are, my lady. Hiding from Ellis, I take it?" He held his arm out to her, his smile expanding. "Not that I blame you. The man is a terrible bore."

She hesitated before linking arms with him. "I wasn't hiding. I simply needed a moment to catch my breath."

He led her to the dance floor and they took position for the waltz. His palm against her upper back was soothing and tension flowed from her on a slow exhale. *This was what she needed in her life.*

Serenity.

Control over her feelings and control over her behavior. With Thorne, the wild creature lurking inside her never reared its head to make her behave like a lunatic. He was good for her, but like it or not, she was forever bound to Anthony.

A violin began its romantic call, and the baron swept her backward. As they circled the ballroom floor, she noted the looks of longing some of the debutantes aimed his way.

She studied Thorne with a detached air. He was quite stunning, with his high cheekbones and a straight nose. He hadn't been saddled with the unfortunate features associated with many members of the nobility, but he wasn't of noble birth, was he? His father had been granted a title with a letter's patent for his service to the King. His family was only one generation from being unacceptable in the eyes of the *haut ton.*

Not that she cared a whit about his lineage. Her mother was of Italian descent and far from aristocratic.

Thorne lifted an eyebrow. "I often wonder what it is you are thinking when that tiny line appears on your forehead."

Heat rushed to her cheeks. He might mistake her meaning if she admitted she had been contemplating his family. "Lord Ellis isn't a bore, at least not always."

Thorne's muscles twitched beneath her fingertips, but his lighthearted expression didn't alter. "Now I'm sorry I asked what was on your mind."

"I wasn't thinking of him until this moment." That wasn't a complete lie. "I feel obligated to defend him since he is an old family friend."

The baron's dark gaze seemed capable of seeing into her mind. "Is that all he is?"

Her lips parted, and she bit down on her lower lip. She didn't know what Anthony was to her anymore. His promise to set things to rights fed her fears that he was following a sense of duty rather than his heart.

Thorne frowned. "Please, don't answer. Just know this, Lady Gabrielle. I don't intend to step aside and allow him to win your hand without opposition."

"What is that to mean?" Did he think she was a prize to be won in a competition? That she had no say in which gentleman she married?

He pulled her closer, which should have stolen her breath away, but merely caused her to issue an annoyed huff.

"I know you are meant for me and me for you, Lady Gabrielle. Can you not see it?"

She wiggled to create space between her and Lord Thorne. "I—I'm uncertain of our suitability."

His smile was strained as he scanned the crowd, avoiding eye contact with her. "Then allow me a chance to convince you," he said softly.

A glimpse of Anthony standing vigil at her brother's side sent her emotions awhirl again. Blast him for abandoning her and placing her in this position. She had been unable to provide her oldest brother with a good reason to avoid the marriage mart when the start of the Season arrived. Anthony hadn't returned as he'd promised, and she was still an unspoken-for female relying on her brother's generosity.

"Lady Gabrielle," Thorne whispered. "Allow me one chance to win your love. That is all I ask."

Looking into his eyes, she sensed the storm brewing inside her dissipating. Wasn't this what she wanted: the ability to rule her emotions? To ensure her impulsivity never hurt anyone again? She would never be at Thorne's mercy as she was Anthony's, because he didn't possess the key to unlock her passion.

She closed her eyes and nodded once, a brief and almost imperceptible movement.

"Yes?" Lord Thorne sounded pleased.

"Well…" She felt slightly sick to her stomach.

His smile was glorious, and she tried to ignore her misgivings. Perhaps she owed it to *herself* to give him a chance. If Anthony only wanted to marry her because he'd compromised her, she would be doing all of them a favor.

"I cannot mislead you, my lord. I am conflicted and don't know my heart."

He leaned closer, his breath warm against her ear. "I believe you are worth the risk."

The dance ended and he ushered her from the floor. She couldn't meet Anthony's gaze as Thorne returned her to her brother's care. He bid her good evening, then strolled away with a bounce to his step.

Her brother reached out to take her arm, a deep line forming between his brows. "You look pale, princess. Are you ill?"

The way her head was pounding and her stomach roiling, it was a possibility.

"I don't know. Maybe." She waved her fan to create a breeze, but it did nothing to relieve her heated skin. "Would it be too much trouble to take me home?"

"I could take you," Anthony said.

Drew shook his head. "You have my gratitude, but I wouldn't be able to sleep tonight without knowing she is all right. Allow me to retrieve Lana and we'll go."

Her brother cut through the crowd lining the dance floor, leaving her alone with Anthony.

"How am *I* to sleep without knowing if you are sick or well?" he mumbled.

Anger flew over her. How many nights had he slept with no knowledge of her welfare while she had tossed in her bed and worried for him? "It is simple really. Just close your eyes and forget about me. You seem to be good at it."

He lightly grasped her elbow. His body heat saturated the scant space between them, and his familiar scent made her head swim. When his thumb caressed the skin above her elbow-length gloves, shivers raced along her nerves.

His smile turned her insides to jelly. "I know a better use for that sharp tongue, my lady. Perhaps I'll show you, if you ask nicely."

"That—that's not very likely." She tried to sound harsh and uncaring, but her voice came out breathy.

He shrugged and released her arm. "Very well. Perhaps I won't make you ask."

Before she could form a coherent response, her brother and sister-in-law returned. Lana fussed over Gabby as she led her from the ballroom. Gabby looked back over her shoulder and found Anthony grinning. Her heart floundered in her chest. God help her for hoping he wasn't teasing her about what he could teach her. Their last lesson in kissing had been amazing.

As she and Lana walked outside into the cooler night air, Lana touched Gabby's forehead. "You are flushed, but you don't appear to have a fever."

Yet, Anthony *was* a sickness, and she had little hope of finding a cure.

"I will survive." At least she hoped she would.

Three

As Gabby climbed into bed that night, memories of her first kiss with Anthony flooded her mind and senses, transporting her back to five months ago...

She hadn't known where she was going when she left the gardens. She'd only known she had to get away. Away from her thoughts, her crushing guilt. Away from the knowledge she had stolen her mother's happiness.

Papa had been gone a year, but Gabby's remorse was unrelenting, especially at night. She hadn't been able to shake it this morning among the autumn flowers, so she was seeking peace in the meadow.

Sweat dampened her brow as she crested a hill. She paused to loosen her cape and push back the hood. The air had been cool when she'd stepped outside, but the late morning sun at her back and exertion heated her through. Her breath escaped in forceful exhales.

Ellis Hall stood in the distance, solid and unchanged since she had last sat in this spot and sketched its stone walls and cathedral windows. Anthony had come to attend her father's graveside service. Even through her haze, she'd noticed the deep lines of his face as he'd fought against tears. She hadn't known if his sorrow was all for her father or the wife he'd buried the previous summer. Perhaps he'd been mourning for both.

After the service, he'd returned to London immediately, and she had come to the hillside. Her heart had still·ached from his rejection, but she missed him terribly. She hadn't been able to bring herself to sketch Anthony, so she'd sketched his home, concentrating on drawing precise lines instead of acknowledging the hollowness inside her.

When she'd crossed paths with Anthony again at her brother's wedding, she fought the urge to fling herself into his arms. He had made his feelings known when he'd chosen Camilla over her. Gabby couldn't make a fool of herself again. They had spoken of the beautiful day and their happiness for Gabby's oldest brother. She had even partnered with him for a dance.

Then he had done something that upset her tidy life and revived her hope. He had followed her family to the country. Perhaps he'd sensed the loneliness behind her smiles. She liked to think he possessed special insight when it came to her, but likely she was just being fanciful.

With Luke on his honeymoon and her mother's companion, Miss Truax, married and gone, Gabby had no one to talk to about her father. Her sisters were too young yet, and she worried that bringing Papa up to her mother might make her too sad. In the beginning, her mother's crying had penetrated Gabby's walls at night, ripping her heart to pieces. She had done that to her mother, taken the love of her life and left her shattered.

Gabby closed her eyes to steel against the onslaught of guilt. She needed to see Anthony. He had become her confidant of late, visiting Foxhaven Manor daily, listening when she needed to pour out her heart, and distracting her when she needed a reprieve. But he hadn't made an appearance yesterday, and she feared he might not come again today.

Longing invaded her heart. Anthony had become as essential as breathing.

An unseen force pulled her down the slope toward Ellis Hall. She didn't stop to consider the logic or impropriety of calling on a gentleman. Nothing mattered except seeing him.

Before she reached the bottom of the hill, she was running, heedless of the grassy knolls. The ground evened out, and she pushed herself harder. Dashing up the front steps, she slammed her palm against the door.

"Anthony!" She struck the solid oak and called his name repeatedly until the door flew open.

His butler's jaw hung slack when he recognized her.

"Rupert, what's all the fuss?" Anthony was descending the staircase, his cravat hanging loosely around his neck. "Lady Gabrielle, is everything all right? Is it your mother?"

She shook her head, unable to catch her breath.

He rushed forward to put his arm around her shoulders and guided her in the direction of the drawing room, as best as she could recall. She hadn't visited Ellis Hall often even though Anthony and his mother had been their neighbors since before Gabby was born. Lady Ellis had been something of a recluse. The last time Gabby had been in his home was after he had buried his mother.

"Bring tea for the lady," he called over his shoulder.

"Yes, milord."

Anthony escorted her to the settee, then knelt beside her to draw her cloak around her shoulders. "You are shaking. I'll have a fire started."

"I'm not cold."

The drawing room was chilly, but she welcomed the cooler air on her damp skin. Her heartbeat was slowing and her breathing had evened out, but her emotions were churning and threatening to burst loose. If she started crying now, she feared she'd never stop.

He rubbed her hands between his, warming her fingers. "Has something happened to one of your sisters? Should I send for the doctor?"

"Everyone is well. I—" *Lud*. What was she to say? She decided to tell the truth. "You didn't come to Foxhaven Manor yesterday and I thought you might have returned to London."

He rocked back on his heels and regarded her with an unreadable expression. "I intended to call this afternoon."

"Oh. I didn't realize." She fiddled with the tie of her cloak, her body growing even hotter. Only a fool would burst into a man's home and all but shout out she wanted him.

Anthony stood and put several paces between them. "Let's get you warmed up, then I'll see you home."

"I shouldn't have come." She pushed from the settee, but before she could move for the door, he captured her around the waist.

"Stay. I'm pleased to see you."

His touch crumbled the wall restraining her emotions and her tears flowed.

"Gabby, what is it?" His arms went around her. She snuggled against his chest, her eyes closed on a half sob. He held her together with his embrace, whispering soothing words. His lips brushed her temple. "Shh, my love. I've got you. You are safe."

Her shaking slowed as his warmth broke through the shield she'd erected around herself. It had been so long since she'd felt connected with anyone, and never like this. Her tears continued for a moment, but she no longer worried about being at their mercy with him holding her.

"Anthony," she said on a breath. His name was like a soothing chant.

He brushed the hair from her forehead. "I'm here. I'm not going anywhere."

She melted against him, clinging to his promise. She had lost too many people already. "I miss him so much."

"I know." Anthony continued to stroke her hair. "Your father was a good man."

Her throat began to ache again. How was it Anthony understood every wound to her heart without her having to explain? It was a relief to let everything out, but she reluctantly eased from his embrace. Why should she receive comfort when her mother had lost the love of her life?

She sniffled. "I wish I could go back and do everything differently."

A knock at the door startled her. For a moment, she'd forgotten where she was. She retreated to the settee, removed her cloak, and folded her hands on her lap while the footman wheeled in a tea cart, then left them alone again.

She followed Anthony's movements as he poured, the cup and saucer too dainty for his masculine hands. He dropped two sugar cubes into the tea, stirred with the small silver spoon, and then offered it to her.

"Just how you like it." He sat beside her on the settee. "Drink. It will warm you through."

He had never cared for tea, so he'd ordered it just for her. His thoughtfulness already warmed her heart.

He shifted on the furniture and propped his arm on the seat back. "What did you mean when you said you wished you could do everything differently?"

Her gaze narrowed on the gold filigree rim of the china as heat swept across her cheeks again. He had never brought up the incident in Hyde Park, and she had been beyond grateful. Yet, now she had steered the conversation in that direction without realizing what she'd been saying.

What did it matter? Anthony already knew of her shameful behavior even if he was tactful enough to pretend he didn't.

She set the tea aside and cleared her throat. "I think of Lt. MacFarland all the time."

One golden eyebrow lifted. "Oh? I hadn't realized. Has he written to you?"

"No! Heavens, no. I haven't seen him since that

day." A new concern came to mind. "Do you think he's all right?"

"I suspect he has had a tough go of it, the same as all the soldiers. India is not the most civilized area."

He needn't add "how could you have been so stupid?" She knew how naive she had been.

"I wish I had never met him," she said.

Anthony smiled and eased back against the cushions. "Then my father would still be alive."

"Gabby, what makes you think Lt. MacFarland had anything to do with your father's bad heart?"

"He didn't. I did." A severe gouge formed between his brows, and she held up her hand to stop his argument. "Dr. Campbell said there was too much strain put on his heart. When Papa learned I had tried to elope, it was too much."

"That's not what the doctor meant."

"Maybe not, but Papa said I would be the death of him, and I was."

"Gabrielle, listen to me." He gently took her by the shoulders. "Every man has said that at one time or another, but it doesn't make it true. If so, we'd all be dropping like autumn leaves."

She shook her head.

"Yes, Gabby. The strain on your father's heart was physical. His body stopped working like it should, and it's no one's fault."

"I know I did it to him."

His lips set in a tight line. "Then I'm responsible too. You wouldn't have confessed everything to Drew if I hadn't kissed you after I ran the lieutenant off."

A new heat invaded her body and she wiggled from

his hold. They had never talked about that kiss, and she wasn't sure she wanted to now. "Lt. MacFarland was rather eager to leave after your arrival, wasn't he?"

"Well, one seems to find many excuses to be on his way when threatened with a sound thrashing."

She laughed, relieved to discuss something else. "I could have thrashed you for chasing him away."

His smile faded. "Are you still angry with me?"

Lt. MacFarland had been so dashing in his officer's uniform, and she had been instantly infatuated. But now she knew infatuation wouldn't keep her warm and well fed. She had to be practical.

"I think you saved me from making a huge mistake."

He chucked her on the chin. "And you, my dear girl, saved me from coming to blows with my best friend. I would have kept your secret, you know. You didn't have to tell Drew about the lieutenant."

"I know."

When her brother had burst into the clearing and saw Anthony's arms around her, murder had flared in his eyes. She'd done the first thing that came to mind to protect both of them. She'd pretended to swoon.

Perhaps her performance hadn't explained the reason Anthony had been holding her *before* her knees buckled, but it distracted her brother long enough to derail his attack on his best friend.

"Drew once accused me of being too melodramatic," she said. "Obviously, I've learned a few tricks over the years. He believed I really fainted."

Anthony drew back. "Didn't you?"

"Good heavens, no! It would take more than a kiss from you to make me light-headed."

"Is that so?" A sinful smile eased across his lips, setting off butterflies in her stomach. "Maybe I was doing it incorrectly."

She notched up her chin. "Maybe you need more practice."

"Maybe I do, you impertinent minx." He leaned closer and the butterflies intensified. He cupped the back of her neck; his thumb traced her jaw. "Tell me when I have improved."

His lips were unexpectedly tender and caught her off guard. His last kiss had been bruising, a punishment for goading him.

He pulled back far enough to meet her gaze, his fingers massaging her neck. She began to dissolve under his touch. He softly nipped her mouth. "Kiss me back." His whisper brushed across her skin and sent chills racing through her.

She pressed her lips firmly against his, kissing him the only way she knew how. When she tried to pull away, he gently held her in place.

"Like this, sweetheart." He claimed her mouth again. Parting her lips, he feathered his tongue across hers. She sighed, her breath flowing into him. She had no idea kissing could be like this.

He teased and coaxed until she mimicked his movements, awakening a fire in her too long lying dormant. It flared and burned hotly as she scrambled to get closer to him.

Anthony hugged her against his hard chest, her hand lying between them. Her fingers trailed through the sprinkle of soft hair where his shirt parted. She drew back to see him. Tentatively, she explored the contours of his chest and shoulders, memorizing him to draw later. She was being too bold, and yet she'd known and loved him for so long.

"Will you remove your shirt so I may see you?" she asked, her voice breaking.

His hooded gaze, so intensely centered on her, stole her breath. For a moment, she thought he would deny her, but then he grabbed the hem of his shirt and pulled it over his head.

Her heart beat in a frenzy as she tried to reconcile that this masculine body belonged to him. He'd filled out since she had stolen a peek at the lake. She touched her fingertips to his taut skin, her eyes drinking him in.

"Amazing," she murmured.

A low growl sounded in his throat and he pulled her beneath him, his mouth on hers again. The armrest cradled the back of her head as his feverish kisses muddled her thoughts. His lips were everywhere: her mouth, her chin, her neck. Her breasts tingled and grew heavy as he kissed his way down her body.

He untied the sash of her apron-front gown and peeled the muslin down. Trailing his finger over the swell of her breast, he smiled. "You're amazing."

Before she could respond, he lifted her breast from her corset and took it in his mouth. She sucked in a breath. His lips and tongue were gentle, but the pressure building in her core was disconcerting. And exciting.

When she moaned and grasped his shoulders to hold him tightly, he answered with a low groan. She grew restless beneath him and he returned to kissing her, covering her breast with his hand. She arched into his touch. Lightly, he pinched her nipple as he plundered her mouth, his hips pressing her into the cushions.

The harsh rush of their breath filled her ears as she eagerly returned his kisses. Grasping a handful of her skirts, he jerked them up to expose her drawers. He stole inside her undergarment and caressed between her legs. She cried out in surprise.

Anthony drew back, his blue eyes burning. She couldn't look away even as he swept his fingers over her again. Never had she felt anything so intensely. She stared at him, her lips parted, breathing unsteadily. Something frightening churned behind his darkened eyes. Something bound to consume her if she allowed it, but she didn't care.

"God, you are too tempting," he said with a sigh, then pulled his hand away. She missed the warmth immediately.

"Please, don't stop."

He caressed her again. "I don't want to, but I should."

She bit her lip and shook her head as another pleasurable wave washed over her. A soft cry burst from her.

He chuckled breathlessly before returning to her breast. She sank into the settee with a sigh and closed her eyes. The things he was doing to her made her head fuzzy and she tingled in the most delightful places. But also she sensed she was approaching some-thing…something powerful that caused her to breathe in sharp, short gasps. His fingers drove her forward into an unknown world, barreling so fast she could never stop.

Never wanted to stop.

When she reached the end, it was as sudden as slamming into a wall, but glorious. She cried out repeatedly as his hand pushed her further and further. At last, he stopped. She was both relieved and disappointed as she drifted slowly back into the world she knew. A sleepy haze settled over her. She lazily opened her eyes to find him unfastening his trousers. She jolted awake. "Anthony?"

He froze, his clouded gaze clearing slowly. He fell back against the settee and scrubbed a hand over his face. "Good God. What was I thinking?"

She couldn't move. How unfair of her to stop him now.

He readjusted her skirts and slanted a sheepish grin in her direction. "You look frightened to death. I hope you can forgive me."

She licked her lips nervously. Should she try to sit up? When the armrest became too uncomfortable, she wiggled into an upright position.

"I didn't intend to take things that far," he said. "I'm sorry."

She avoided eye contact as she retied her gown. What must he think of her, arriving on his doorstep and writhing beneath him like a heathen?

He took her hand as he slid off the settee and lowered to one knee. "Gabby, I realize this must seem sudden, but I want to marry you."

"What? Why?" She tried to pull away, but he held on to her hand.

"Because I want to marry you."

Gads, she knew what he was doing. He was trying to take the honorable path.

"I—"

His smile widened as he waited for her answer. "Say yes, Gabby."

She hadn't dared to dream of this moment, but she wanted it too.

"Please, say yes."

Pushing any reservations aside, she nodded.

"Yes?"

"Yes," she whispered.

⁂

Anthony arrived at Brooks's the next morning earlier than usual. Sebastian Thorne was known to break his fast at the club, and they needed to have a little chat. He didn't know what the baron was about pretending interest in courting Gabby, but it was a dangerous game.

Anthony didn't think Thorne was foolhardy enough to do anything that would compromise her. Any man would have to be cork-brained to risk her brothers' wrath. But it would be equally dangerous to make her the object of one of his bets. Anthony glanced around the packed club, wondering which daft gent would accept one of Thorne's challenges.

Besides yourself? He grimaced. Well, maybe he had been stupid in the past, but his days of indulging Thorne were over.

He found the baron sitting alone at a table with a cup of tea and the morning newssheet unopened beside the saucer.

He grinned over the rim of the cup as he took a sip. "Missed me while you were away?"

"As much as one would a bloody case of indigestion." Anthony dropped into the chair across from him. He nodded at the newssheet. "You never read your copy. Why do you bring it?"

"If I leave the house early enough and snag the paper on my way out, Mother and Eve never run across an ugly piece of gossip."

"Ah." Anthony nodded. It was a shame people had nothing better to do than spread tales about Thorne's family. Anthony had always held a bit of sympathy for him, not that he'd dare let on. The baron was meaner than a badger if he thought someone pitied him.

A footman approached and set a plate of eggs and sausage in front of Thorne.

Anthony sat forward, leaning his elbows on the table. "You're either brave or very stupid."

"Come now, the sausage isn't all that bad." Thorne shook out his napkin with a smirk.

"I think you know my meaning."

The baron cut into his eggs. "Am I to assume this has to do with Lady Gabrielle?"

"You're smarter than you look, but still a numbskull. Don't come begging me to be your second when the duke issues a challenge."

"And why would Foxhaven call me out? I'm properly courting the lady."

Anthony scoffed.

"You think I'm lying."

"Not completely," Anthony admitted, thinking of Thorne's respect for his own sister. "But you have a talent for walking the line between proper and debauched."

Thorne popped a piece of sausage in his mouth and waved his fork at Anthony. "What's your interest in the lady? Isn't she like a sister to you?"

"I hardly have brotherly inclinations toward her," he drawled and hooked an elbow over the seat back. "She's to be my wife. I'm on my way to make an offer."

"Is she now? Do you plan to club her over the head first then drag her to the altar? I can't see her going willingly."

Anthony didn't bother answering. "Just stay away from her. Besides, she's not your type. She is a romantic."

"Egads," he groaned in mock distress. "Not one of those." He raised a hand to summon a footman and ordered two plates piled with sausage.

"Yes sir." The footman shot a quick look at Anthony, grinned, then hustled away.

"You'll have to loosen your corset if you eat all that," Anthony said.

Thorne pushed his half-eaten meal aside. "I have a way to settle which of us will continue courting the lady."

"There's nothing to settle. By this afternoon, she will be my betrothed."

The footman returned with two plates quicker than Anthony expected and set one in front of him and one in front of Thorne. A low rumble began in the club as men began looking their way.

Thorne's eyes gleamed with mischief. "A contest to see which gentleman will step aside. Whichever man can shove the most sausages in his mouth—one end out, mind you—becomes the winner of the fair lady's hand."

There was a shout for the betting book and a few men inched closer.

Anthony shoved the plate away. "I'm not allowing a sausage to decide my fate."

Thorne's dark eyebrow arched as if to counter his claim. "Very well. Then I refuse to back down. Either a plate of sausages decides the matter or the superior wooer takes the prize."

Lord Ledbery came over with the betting book and men began calling out their bets. Soon a crowd gathered around their table, someone bumping Anthony's chair. Thorne met his gaze across the table and smiled.

Bollocks! Once the baron set his mind to something, he wouldn't quit. He'd be dogging Gabby's heels morning and night until Anthony had her down the aisle.

"Fine," he growled and jerked the plate in front of him, upsetting the pile. It was the most ridiculous way to settle a matter, but Anthony would win and be done with it.

Thorne grinned. "You may go first. Once you set the number, I will exceed it."

Anthony scowled, picked up a link, and defiantly shoved it in his mouth. Then another and another until his lips felt stretched to capacity. He paused to take a breath. The spices were already making his tongue tingle.

Thorne slowly picked up a sausage from his plate and wagged it. "Done already? After only three?"

"Just wait," Anthony managed to grumble.

The baron gestured for Anthony to continue. He slowly wedged two more sausages into his mouth and nearly choked on the grease sliding down his throat. His eyes began to water, but he held his ground.

Anthony wiggled his tongue along the slippery casings, wondering how he would fit any more in his mouth. It seemed impossible, but he wasn't going to let Thorne win. The sixth sausage was tougher than he'd anticipated, however. He eyed Thorne's plate, trying to calculate the odds of the baron being able to beat five.

"Come on," Thorne goaded. "This is for the lovely Lady Gabrielle."

Anthony glared at him then continued the task with renewed determination. He did his best to shove one more sausage between the others, and he almost had it too when the sausage burst. Grease dribbled down his chin and plopped on his cravat and waistcoat.

Damn!

Thorne threw his head back, laughing so hard he almost fell out of his chair. Their audience also hooted with laughter, making Anthony feel like the butt of a joke. Well, let Thorne see how funny it was to have grease down his front. Anthony dislodged the links, dropped them on the plate, and snatched Thorne's napkin from the table. He smacked his lips, trying to get rid of the horrible taste.

"Let's see you beat that number." Anthony held up his cravat and cursed. He'd have to change and get rid of this disgusting taste in his mouth before he called on Gabby.

Thorne was still laughing. When he sobered, he

looked across the table, his eyes still shining with amusement. "Congratulations, Ellis. You are clearly the better man."

Anthony frowned. "What do you mean? Aren't you going to try to win?"

Thorne shrugged. "You know how to handle sausage. How am I to compete?"

The gents in the club howled. Anthony's face heated. Was this nothing more than a joke? Had Thorne intended to step aside the whole time? He couldn't help laughing at himself. He pushed back from the table and pointed at the baron. "*You* are evil."

The baron grinned. "You have no idea."

Four

WHEN FOXHAVEN'S BUTLER ANSWERED ON ANTHONY'S first knock, he couldn't help but see it as another sign of victory. Gabby must have told the old man to expect him today.

"Good afternoon, milord."

"Yes, it is, Wesley."

The servant moved aside to allow Anthony entrance without observing the usual custom of taking his calling card. Anthony had been a frequent visitor to Talliah House for many years, and he knew Foxhaven's servants almost better than his own.

When Wesley spotted the flowers in Anthony's hand, his brows came together like two woolly caterpillars knocking heads. "Are you here to see His Grace, milord?"

He laughed. "What is the matter? Isn't His Grace fond of dahlias?"

"I couldn't say, sir."

"No, I don't suppose you could. Very well, perhaps Lady Gabrielle would like them instead. Could you have them placed in a vase for her?" Anthony surrendered the bouquet to Wesley, noting that the man's frown lines deepened.

He signaled to a maid who was passing through the foyer. "These are for Lady Gabrielle from Lord Ellis. Deliver the bouquet to her ladyship's chambers."

"Yes, sir." She curtsied, then bustled away with Anthony's gift cradled in her arms.

"This way, Lord Ellis. His Grace is in his study."

Anthony followed Wesley above stairs and waited outside the door while his presence was announced.

"Show him in," the Duke of Foxhaven said. Luke sounded happy to receive him.

His old friend was rounding his colossal desk when Anthony entered and met him halfway to exchange a hearty handshake. "Ellis, it's good to see you, my friend. I haven't seen you since the wedding."

Although Anthony hadn't come to engage in chitchat, he thought it mannerly to ask after his friend's honeymoon.

"It was more than satisfactory," Luke said and gestured toward the seating area.

Anthony selected a wingback chair, prepared to get to the business of asking for Gabby's hand, but apparently Luke wasn't finished.

"Vivian had never been out of the country prior to our trip. It was invigorating to see the continent through her eyes. It was like I was seeing everything for the first time again."

"How novel." Anthony was trying to feign interest. *Trying* being the key word.

"Our first stop was Vienna."

Anthony suppressed the urge to groan and smiled

politely. Luke had a tale for every stop he and his wife had made. And there were many. He had never known his friend to blather on about anything like he did his bride and their little adventure.

When Luke finally stopped to take a breath, Anthony pounced before he gathered a second wind.

"That's fabulous. Splendid indeed. Uh, could we speak of something else now?"

Luke laughed. "By all means, and my apologies for boring you."

Anthony grinned sheepishly and leaned back against the chair. "Sorry. That wasn't my meaning. I'm eager to discuss a matter, but I am also happy for you. Congratulations on your marriage."

"Thank you." Luke propped his foot across his knee and began to jiggle his foot. Anthony fought the urge to tell him to be still. After all, he'd sat through Luke's boring tales with patience.

"What is it I can do for you, Ellis?"

"You must have some idea of the reason I have requested an audience."

"Can't say that I do." Luke pulled his watch from his jacket pocket and grimaced. "Damn. I promised Vivian I would complete my business no later than one o'clock. Is this important, or could it wait until tomorrow?"

"Of course it's important!" *Egads.* Why else would he be requesting an audience? He sure as hell hadn't come to Talliah House for an accounting of the duke and duchess's honeymoon activities.

Luke frowned and slipped his watch back into his pocket. "Go on, then."

Anthony exhaled, stirring the hair on his forehead, then forced a friendly smile. He needed to temper his impatience before he risked alienating his future in-law, which wouldn't do at all since Gabby was rather attached to her family.

"As I was saying, it's a matter of great magnitude. I am here to ask for your blessing in marrying Lady Gabrielle. You have known of my regard for some time, and now that she has left off mourning, I want to offer for her hand."

"Oh." Luke formed a steeple with his fingers and his frown returned. "Is my sister aware of your intentions?"

"I wouldn't be here if I didn't have her consent."

"I see." Luke nodded thoughtfully. "Well, this is a bit of a pickle."

"How so?"

"Let's have a drink." Luke bolted from his chair and strode to the sideboard. He poured two fingers into crystal tumblers and brought one back to Anthony. He remained standing as he sipped his brandy. Slowly.

"Tell me about this pickle," Anthony said through clenched teeth.

Luke tapped his glass, the click of his nail driving Anthony to distraction. "Do you think perhaps you misunderstood Gabby? She can be unclear at times."

When Anthony had had her beneath him months earlier, her black hair falling around her ivory shoulders and plump breasts, she had been perfectly clear. She had wanted him, and he'd wanted her. But one didn't tell that type of thing to a brother who could hit a target better than a sharpshooter in the Light Division.

"I don't believe I was mistaken."

"Hmm..." Luke took another drink. Another long-drawn-out one that had Anthony scooting to the edge of his seat. "I'm not sure how to tell you this, my friend, but I fear you might have misread my sister. I know she is fond of you, just as she is of Drew and Richard."

"Are you implying she thinks of me as a *brother*?"

Luke gritted his teeth in the semblance of a smile, then cursed under his breath. "Maybe. There *is* someone else."

Anthony shot out of the chair. "Who? I know Lord Thorne has been pursuing her, but I swear her heart belongs to me. I saw her last night at the Chattingtons' ball. She has feelings for *me*. Summon her. She'll tell you herself."

Her brother set his drink down. "Gabby isn't available at the moment."

"But she is expecting me."

Luke checked his watch again. "Perhaps it's better for you to return later. Join us for dinner this evening, and I'll allow you a moment alone to speak with my sister. If she is agreeable, we can discuss the matter of a betrothal."

Then Anthony's friend, a man he'd known for most of his six and twenty years, clamped a hand around his upper arm and lugged him toward the exit. Anthony recovered from shock when they reached the double-hung doors and dug in his heels.

"Are you tossing me out on my blasted arse?"

"Pardon?" Luke chuckled and released him. "No, I'm not tossing you out. I invited you for dinner tonight, didn't I?" He shoved a hand through his hair, leaving it standing on end.

Anthony's eyes narrowed. Raking his fingers through his hair had always been a sign that Luke didn't have the cards he needed when they played loo, and Anthony was willing to bet it meant the duke was lying now, too.

"There is something you aren't telling me. Where is Lady Gabrielle?"

"My sister's affairs are her own. If she is amenable to your suit, you must know you have my support. But if her interests lie elsewhere, I won't try to influence her decision."

"Some bloody friend you are." Anthony crossed his arms and glared. "You know I love her. I will be more than generous with her."

Luke sighed. "I'm not the one who needs to know how you feel. Come back this evening and tell my sister."

Anthony allowed Luke to usher him out of his study, but he couldn't believe his friend was dismissing him. It was like Luke couldn't get rid of him fast enough.

Fists formed at his sides and a growl rumbled in his chest. "She is with Thorne, isn't she?"

The bloody trickster had beaten him to Talliah House.

"We will expect you at eight." Luke grinned, then closed the door in Anthony's face.

"Count on it," he shouted to be heard through the thick doors.

Muffled laughter floated from the study followed by what might have been the word "splendid."

Bollocks! This hadn't gone as planned, but then

again, nothing had since his proposal to Gabby. His trip to Wales should have been without complications, which would have placed him back in London long before Easter. He should have been married by now. He should be happily trying to fill his nursery. But no. He was back to trying to win the favor of the minx who had stolen his heart long ago. And she had already agreed to marry him, for God's sake!

Grumbling, he spun on his heel and stalked toward the staircase. He was still complaining under his breath when the butler handed him his hat and walking stick.

"Good day, milord."

"According to whom?" Anthony shoved the hat on his head. He was halfway down the steps when a carriage drove through the gates of Talliah House. An invisible fist slammed into his gut.

It was that damned scoundrel Thorne, and he was with Anthony's woman. After he'd promised to give up his pursuit if Anthony beat him this morning.

Anthony sauntered down the remaining steps, then leaned on his cane as if he hadn't a care. He even forced out a smile when the curricle rolled to a stop in front of him. It wouldn't do to allow Thorne to see his weakness, or he would be even more determined to pursue Gabby.

"Lady Gabrielle, how nice of you to arrive in time for our audience."

Thorne's lips curled as his tiger, a slight boy with much energy, hopped from his seat to secure the horses. Thorne alighted from the curricle before reaching up to assist Gabby. When the man's hands circled her waist, a red haze engulfed Anthony. There was no need to touch her so familiarly. Anthony jerked up his cane, testing the weight.

Gabby's eyes rounded and his impulse to pummel Thorne died away, although it was a slow death. He placed his walking stick back on the ground and exhaled, counting to ten.

Then twenty.

And finally, forty, for good measure.

Once her feet were on the ground and Thorne had released her, Gabby arranged her skirts. "Was our appointment today, Lord Ellis? I hadn't realized I should count on a set date."

"I did say I would call today."

She shrugged. "One never knows whether to take you at your word, my lord."

Anthony's teeth ground together. He wouldn't be surprised if steam was rising off his head. She had a way of heating his blood, whether it was from anger or passion. Since he preferred the latter, he refused to show his rancor and provide her with a reason to refuse to speak with him. After her brother's proclamation that Gabby must choose him in order to earn Luke's blessing, his confidence in settling the matter quickly was faltering.

"Perhaps your mind will be at ease now that I have proven capable of keeping my word," he said.

"Perhaps." She smiled sweetly and linked her arm with Thorne's. "Unfortunately, I fear I must postpone our audience. I'm tired after the lovely ride with Lord Thorne."

Tired? What type of ride had the baron given her?

Thorne smirked at Anthony. "Allow me to see you safely inside, my lady."

"That is kind of you, sir."

Anthony's jaw dropped when Gabby and Thorne swept past him and disappeared into the house. Dismissed twice in one day? What the hell was going on?

❧

Gabby's stomach fluttered and her knees knocked together—the aftereffects of seeing Anthony again. Her heart had nearly bolted from her body when she and Lord Thorne had driven past the gates to find Anthony waiting in the drive.

By early afternoon, she hadn't known whether to believe he would actually come. She hadn't wanted to sit around any longer hoping he would, so she had accepted the baron's invitation for a spin around Rotten Row.

She had been happy to see Anthony at first, but then she'd remembered his promise to kiss her, and it had scared the daylights out of her. When Anthony kissed her, she lost control of *everything*. Her thoughts, her ability to breathe normally, her hands…

She almost groaned aloud, recalling how sculpted and firm his buttocks were.

Lord Thorne glanced down at her. "Is everything all right?"

"Yes." She bit her lip and looked around for Wesley. Being alone with Thorne seemed unwise, as if they had an understanding. "Thank you for another lovely afternoon."

He took her hands in his. His dark gaze caressed her and he smiled softly. "When will I see you again?"

"I—" She cleared her throat and eased her hands from his grasp. "I will be at Lady Dewhurst's musicale tomorrow evening. Perhaps we will cross paths then."

There was a troubled flicker in his eyes, but it disappeared so quickly she thought she might have imagined it.

She suppressed a sigh. Why couldn't she care about Thorne like he seemed to care for her? He was kind and attentive, and so far, reliable. There was no reason to reject his suit.

No reason but one.

"Lord Thorne, I think it's only fair—"

"Shh." He held a finger to her lips. "As you said, we had a lovely time together. Allow me to savor it."

He wasn't making this easy. "But you should be aware—"

"That I have competition. I understand and I'm undeterred." He lightly grasped one of her curls to rub between his thumb and finger. "My parents didn't love each other when they spoke their vows, but a short while later, they were inseparable. Love can grow over time, Lady Gabrielle. And it can be the type to last forever."

Love sounded so logical when he spoke of it. And he was correct. Many people married without love, and some grew to care deeply for each other.

She reached up to hold his hand, hoping he wouldn't see her move for what it truly was. She wanted him to release her hair.

"I don't know if I can become one of those people," she admitted.

"You will only find out if you allow me into your life." He pulled her hand to his lips and placed a kiss on her knuckles. "And if you discover you cannot, I will love enough for both of us."

Her heart softened. When he looked at her so earnestly, she thought perhaps he really did hold some affection for her. If only she could return it.

"I can't make promises, my lord." She carefully extracted her hand from his hold.

A slow grin inched across his face. It was the smile of a man celebrating victory. "And yet you haven't tossed me out."

She chuckled. "An oversight, I assure you. Good day, my lord."

Five

ANTHONY PACED THE FRONT DRIVE, HIS BOOTS CREATING an angry staccato against the cobblestones. It was taking Thorne a blasted long time to say his good-byes to the lady. When the door finally swung open, Anthony advanced on him.

"Gabby is mine. I won."

Thorne simply smirked and stepped around him. "I thought you weren't going to allow a sausage to determine your fate."

"But you convinced me otherwise."

Tugging on his gloves, the baron continued toward his vehicle. "Now, now. You couldn't really think I'd allow a bet to decide my future wife. That's ridiculous."

"But you *are* ridiculous. Come back here," Anthony called to his retreating back. "We will settle this now."

Thorne stopped beside his carriage and slowly turned to face him. "Very well, Ellis. If the lady is yours, as you claim, why did she spend the afternoon with me?"

Anthony gripped his walking stick so hard, it was

a wonder it didn't splinter. Damned if he knew the reason Gabby had agreed to a ride in the park, but she belonged with him. Thorne had agreed to leave her alone.

His teeth gnashed together. "She. Is. Mine."

Thorne sauntered toward him with that bloody smirk Anthony wanted to knock from his face. "But I plan to make her *mine*."

Anthony growled and swung his fist. Thorne ducked. Infuriated by his miss, Anthony charged, but the baron was too quick on his feet. Momentum drove Anthony to slam into the carriage. Pain shot through his ribs like a spear.

Thorne laughed.

"Damn you!" He came at him again. His opponent jumped back, but this time he wasn't fast enough. Anthony's fist connected with his chin. The baron's head snapped back.

"Damn *you*, Ellis!" Thorne rubbed his face, a severe frown aimed at Anthony. "What has gotten into you? Two suitors resorting to fisticuffs on her front drive is likely to make her swoon."

Anthony scoffed. Gabby wasn't some fragile dove. Her father's death had tested her strength and not broken her. Thorne knew nothing about her.

But he was right about one thing. Fighting was below him. He lowered his fists. Gabby and Anthony loved each other, and they were better suited. She wouldn't choose Thorne over him, no matter how angry she might be with Anthony for being gone.

"Set your sights on someone else. Lady Gabrielle is marrying me."

Thorne shook his head as he climbed into the curricle. "You really are dicked in the nob."

"You have been warned. When she becomes my wife, you will be left looking like a fool."

The baron grabbed the reins and signaled to his tiger. "That sounds like a challenge, Ellis."

"I already won the challenge, remember? Now, be gone, you bloody mongrel."

"I'm not the one foaming at the mouth, my friend." Thorne flashed a jaunty grin and snapped the reins. The curricle lurched forward with a loud creak, gained momentum as it sped through the gates, and turned onto the boulevard.

Anthony dusted off his hands. Well, that was settled. But if Gabby's brother thought he was going to wait until that evening to speak with her, Luke was mistaken. They had been apart long enough, and she wasn't likely to forgive him if he gave up so easily.

He reentered the foyer without knocking and thankfully found it abandoned. Pausing inside the threshold, he considered his next move. His gaze locked on the stairwell. Her chambers were situated on the second floor. But he couldn't, could he?

Before he could attempt anything too reckless, a maid swept into the foyer with charcoals and a sketch-book hugged to her chest. The same young woman who had taken care of the bouquet he'd brought for Gabby. She afforded him a curious glance but didn't allow his presence to disrupt her mission.

When she disappeared through a doorway leading to the conservatory, he forced himself to stay put. He couldn't follow and expect the chit wouldn't notice.

Several moments later, the maid reappeared empty-handed. This time she gawked as she slowly crossed the marble floor.

Anthony readjusted his hat and reached for the door handle. "I must be off now. Good day."

He opened the door as if he was leaving, then quietly closed it again when the servant was gone. Before anyone else discovered him skulking about, he strode toward the conservatory, where he was sure Gabby was practicing her art.

Her back was to him, her head bent over her drawing as he entered. Her hand flew across the page in fast, graceful strokes. His throat suddenly felt tight. When had he last watched her sketch? Perhaps around the time his mother had died.

Gabby was so intent on whatever she was drawing she hadn't realized he was there. Sunlight streamed through the windows, igniting the auburn in her dark hair. The color was always subtle and unexpected.

"Beautiful," he murmured.

She gasped and twisted around on the settee. Her rosebud lips were parted and all he could think about was kissing them until they were swollen and pliable.

"Anthony." Her voice was little more than a whisper. She tossed her sketch aside and shoved it under a pillow. "I thought you'd left."

He pulled the door closed, then sauntered toward the settee. Her fingers clutched the charcoal as she looked up with wide gray eyes. Corby had been correct. She was an orchid among common roses, exotic and intriguing. God, how he had missed her.

He smiled. "I came to see you. Why would I leave

before I've accomplished my aim? It is good to see you again, my love."

He sat beside her and she quickly scooted over to create a sliver of space between them. He could still feel her body heat, however, and revel in her lingering perfume. Lavender. The scent was fiery and soft all at once. It suited her.

Her knuckles were turning white from gripping the charcoal.

He affectionately bumped her shoulder with his as he'd done many times. It was his way of telling her everything was all right.

"Cat got your tongue? I've never known you to be this quiet."

She pursed her lips. "You seem uncommonly concerned with my tongue, my lord. First it is too sharp and now you insinuate I've become a mute."

"Well, you just disproved the latter, but I maintain you have a sharp tongue," he said with a wink.

"The better to give you a proper dressing-down for stealing into the conservatory when I am not properly chaperoned. What are you doing here?"

"Aren't we beyond the need for a chaperone?" He reached for her hand, but she pushed to her feet and hugged her arms around her body.

"And why is that, Lord Ellis? Correct me if I'm wrong, but we are not betrothed. You missed your appointment with my brother weeks ago."

He winced. Although he had known he would have to answer for his prolonged absence, he hadn't expected to be scolded. "I promised to return, and here I am."

"You promised to return *before* Easter, and there was no word from you. Did you expect me to read your mind to know you would be late?"

"I expected you to trust me."

"Trust you." She shook her head and walked to the window, presenting her back. "It wouldn't have been the first time you misled me."

He sighed. "Not this again. We aren't children any longer. When are you going to stop holding me accountable for things I did as a boy?"

She glared over her shoulder, then turned back to the window. Well, *one* of them was no longer a child.

His gaze slid down her narrow back and tapered waist, and feasted on the roundness of her hips. No, she was definitely all grown now. The realization that she was a woman and no longer a little girl had hit him at her father's birthday celebration three years earlier. A forbidden desire he had buried had resurfaced.

The day he had received her letter expressing her love and imploring him not to marry Camilla, he had known he loved her too. But it had been wrong. Gabby had been too young, their age difference too large. To love his best friend's little sister was depraved. Besides, he had been engaged to a woman he thought would complete him.

He'd been wrong, because that woman stood before him now. Walking away from Gabby had been a mistake he wouldn't make again.

He went to her and wrapped his arms around her waist. She stiffened in his embrace, but he didn't allow that to deter him. His lips grazed her ear, then trailed loving kisses along her neck. "I missed you, Gabrielle."

She melted against him, her back molding to his front.

"You must have known I wanted to be here with you," he said.

"How?" she whispered. "You were gone so long and you sent no word. I don't even know what you were doing in Wales."

He pulled back, his lust cooling by degrees. He had planned to share his secret today, but her cool reception gave him pause. What if she refused his offer? He must protect Annabelle above all others. If there was any doubt in Gabby's mind...

He urged her to face him. Perhaps if he looked into her eyes, he would see that she still loved him, that he could trust her. He studied her in silence, searching for a flicker of anything to reassure him.

Her expression began to harden again, and she crossed her arms. Her eyes became like shards of ice. "Aren't you going to tell me anything? I want to know why you were in Wales."

He released her, disconcerted by her coldness. "What happened to your promise to wait for me? What is this nonsense with you being on the marriage mart?"

"That isn't an answer."

"Neither is *that*."

She flung her hands in the air. "I had no excuse to give my brother when he insisted it was time to return to London. What would you have had me tell him?"

She had a point, but that didn't explain Thorne.

"Attending balls is one thing, but taking carriage rides with the baron was unnecessary. Your brother didn't force you into accepting his invitations, did he?"

"Luke would never force me into accepting anyone's suit."

"I'm fully aware of that, thank you. Why didn't you tell him I was coming today?"

"Why do you get to ask all the questions?"

"*That* was a question."

"And you didn't answer again. Really, Anthony. You are too frustrating by half. Do you truly want to know why I didn't mention you? I couldn't count on you showing up."

He balked. "How can you say that? I realize I wasn't back by Easter, but you were aware I intended to ask for your hand. When have I ever let you down?"

Her mouth dropped open as if she had a retort, but she snapped it shut.

"Go on. You seem to have something to say."

She shook her head. "It's nothing. Perhaps we should forget about that day at Ellis Hall. I showed up on your doorstep unannounced and my emotions were high. You were just trying to comfort me. I don't blame you for—for…you know."

"Almost making love to you?"

She blushed and backed up a step. "I understand. You did the honorable thing by asking for my hand."

There had been nothing honorable about his offer. Once she was his wife, he wouldn't have to stop himself from taking her on the settee, or any place they damn well pleased.

"I'm releasing you," she said with a dismissive flick of her wrist. "Lord Thorne has made his intentions known. You needn't worry about me anymore."

His blood shot to boiling. "I didn't ask you to marry

me because I was worried about your future." He'd been worried about his own. "I refuse to be released."

"What? Why? Even before you left, you avoided me like the plague. I know you don't really want to marry me."

"You know nothing, you little fool."

She cried out in outrage. "A fool? You call me a fool and I am supposed to believe you love me."

Damn. He was mucking this up badly. "I didn't mean to call you a fool. But not realizing I needed to keep my distance to remain a gentleman makes you seem kind of foolish."

She cried out again. "And *you* seem kind of like an overbearing jackanapes who has no sense of how to woo a lady. Fool, indeed. I would have to be one to marry you."

"What are you saying?"

"I've changed my mind. See yourself out."

He caught her arm before she stormed away. "Well, change it back."

"Change what back? My mind?" She tried to jerk free, but he wouldn't allow her to run without talking this through fully. "Let me go!"

He released her as the door opened, and Gabby's sister appeared in the threshold, her brow furrowed. "Is everything all right? I heard yelling."

Gabby swung toward her sister. "Oh! I— uh… We—"

"I was just leaving, Lady Elizabeth." Anthony bent over Gabby's hand. "Forgive me, my lady," he said under his breath. "I have been an unpardonable arse."

He placed a kiss on her bare fingers, then smiled.

"I shall endeavor to change your mind in a less high-handed manner when we next meet."

But change her mind, he would. He'd learned while he was away that he didn't want to live without her.

Anthony offered another smile to Gabby's younger sister and bid her farewell. "Until tonight, ladies. His Grace has graciously invited me to dine at Talliah House this evening. I look forward to furthering our discussion, Lady Gabrielle."

Lady Elizabeth batted her lashes. "Perhaps you could *both* raise your voices next time, my lord? It makes eavesdropping much easier."

"Lizzie!"

Gabby's sister smiled cheekily in response to her rebuke. "We look forward to this evening, Lord Ellis," she said.

"As do I, Lady Elizabeth."

Six

As soon as the conservatory door closed, Gabby collapsed on the settee. "What did you overhear?"

Lizzie performed a graceful pirouette then plopped on the settee, her deep blue eyes sparkling. "Not enough to satisfy me. Why were you arguing with Lord Ellis?"

"It's a long, uninteresting story."

"I doubt it's uninteresting. Ellis is the most fascinating gentleman I know."

Gabby couldn't help smiling at her sister's enthusiasm. "You don't know many men."

"Just because I haven't had my coming out yet."

When Gabby flinched, her sister's smile faded and she took Gabby's hand. "Katie and I will have our chance. Enjoy your Season."

"But this should have been yours."

"Well, next Season is soon enough." Lizzie's smile returned. "And then I will become acquainted with a slew of gentlemen, all of them eager to sign my dance card. I shall have so much fun choosing between them."

Gabby chuckled and squeezed her sister's hand.

"You're not likely to become acquainted with that many gentlemen. Our brothers have a tendency to keep them at bay."

In truth, their brothers would have their work cut out for them. Lizzie was a beautiful young lady, as was her twin, Katie. But Katie tended toward shyness and Lizzie seemed to have none.

"Why do you find Lord Ellis fascinating?" Gabby asked, unable to deny her curiosity.

"He is mysterious, wouldn't you agree? I never know how to read him, with his hooded eyes and reticence." She sighed. "But how lovely it would be to unravel his secrets."

Gabby rolled her eyes. "What you see is exactly how he is. He has no secrets." She sounded confident in her assertion, but she felt a twinge of doubt. Why wouldn't he tell her what he was doing in Wales, or the reason he was gone for nearly four months? "I find him as interesting as a tangled ball of yarn."

"Like I said, he's a mystery to unravel. What's this?" Lizzie leaned across Gabby's lap and snatched the edge of her sketchbook.

"Wait!" Gabby grabbed for the book, but it was too late.

Lizzie sat back against the settee and held the drawing up to examine it. "Hmm... It's very nice." She tipped her head to one side and then the other as she studied the unfinished sketch.

Gabby held her breath, hoping her sister didn't recognize her subject.

"Impressive." Lizzie dropped the drawing to her lap.

"Thank you." Gabby retrieved the book and hugged

it to her chest. "I should lie down if I'm to be rested for this evening."

Her sister smiled, displaying an adorable set of dimples. "Yes, that is likely wise."

Gabby excused herself and hurried toward the exit, but before she reached the door, her sister cleared her throat.

"Sister?"

With a soft groan, she turned toward Lizzie. "Yes?"

"You've captured Lord Ellis perfectly, but I've never seen that look in his eyes before. It makes me shiver in the most delicious way."

Lud. Gabby's cheeks flamed as she glanced down at her sketch, mesmerized by Anthony's smoldering gaze. She had seen that look once, and it had been branded into her memory forever. "Yes, I see what you mean. I have depicted him wrong. I will have to work on the eyes more."

She swept from the conservatory before her sister could offer any other commentary. Embarrassment engulfed her as she reflected on her behavior. What was wrong with her that she lost all reason when he was near? There was nary a ripple in his comportment, while her emotions crashed like waves upon jagged rocks.

"Cursed man," she grumbled as she let herself into her chambers.

"Whom are you talking to?"

Gabby jumped at the sound of her sister's soft voice. "I didn't see you. What are you doing in here?"

Katie was curled up in a chair by the window with a book. "The lighting is better."

"But it's my chamber. You should ask permission first."

A pink flush invaded Katie's cheeks and she closed her book. "I'm sorry."

Gabby playfully tugged her sister's toffee-colored curl. "You don't have to leave, Katie Cat. Just ask next time."

Her sister's face blazed red at Gabby's use of her pet name, and Gabby's heart swelled with affection. She loved all her siblings, but she shared a special bond with the youngest family member.

Gabby walked to her desk to set aside her sketch and charcoals. She would finish the drawing later. A fresh bouquet of flowers sat on her desk, their subtle fragrance pleasant.

"What did you draw today?" Katie asked as she rose from the chair and came to look.

"Anthony again." She sighed. Katie didn't know what had transpired between them, but she had guessed at Gabby's feelings long ago. Her sister was sensitive in that way and never teased her like Lizzie. "He paid a call earlier."

"I know." Katie picked up her sketch. "I was here when Magda brought in his flowers."

"These are from Anthony? How thoughtful." Light pink dahlias. She had always preferred feminine and romantic flowers to the starkness of orchids or lilies. Had she ever mentioned her preference to him?

"Your drawing is wonderful," Katie said and placed it reverently back on the desk. "It appears Lord Ellis returns your feelings. I'm very happy for you."

Gabby nibbled her bottom lip as she considered the

validity of her sister's assumption. "Maybe, but I don't want to get my hopes up too high. I have been disappointed more than once by the gentleman."

Her sister hugged her. "This time could be different. At least keep an open heart."

Tears misted Gabby's eyes as she hugged her sister back. Katie was as much a romantic as Gabby had been long ago. How she missed the optimistic young girl she used to be. Could she ever be that girl again?

"I promise to try."

Seven

ANTHONY STOOD OUTSIDE THE NURSERY LISTENING TO his daughter's chatter drifting through the cracked door. Her voice was so sweet and foreign to him that he couldn't help eavesdropping. Once Annabelle saw him, she would clamp her lips together tightly and stare at him with large green eyes that reminded him of her mother.

Odd that his anger with Camilla never reared its head when he looked at his daughter. He only felt angry with himself.

More than once, he'd berated himself for the choice he had made to leave his daughter in her aunt's care. He was little more than a stranger to Annabelle now, but he'd thought he was doing the right thing. After all, Miss Teague was Annabelle's true blood and the only mother she had ever known.

"Lady Poppy likes cream in her tea, Mama." He could picture Annabelle hugging the tiny doll. Even if she didn't care for him, she loved his gifts. He supposed he could be proud of that at least.

"Oh, dear," Miss Teague said with mock distress. "Why do I always forget? Allow me, Lady Poppy."

Annabelle's delighted squeal made him smile. "Not on her *hat*, Mama." She expressed her mirth as only a child could, with deep belly laughs. His heart swelled and made his chest feel full. He'd missed out on much of her four years of life with visiting no more than a handful of times a year. But she'd obviously been well cared for by Miss Teague, and Annabelle was happy.

Just not around me.

That did seem to be his lot in life. He was the thief of happiness for every female unfortunate enough to be associated with him. At least that had been his mother's recurring lament when her mind was fuzzy with brandy. He simply assumed his wife, Camilla, had felt the same since she hied off with her lover a few months after marrying Anthony.

He hated to interrupt his daughter's play, but he wished to say good night before he returned to Talliah House for dinner. He knocked lightly on the door then eased it open.

Miss Teague and Annabelle were seated at the miniature table he'd bought after his return from Crickhowell, where he had found his daughter residing with her aunt. Part of him must have hoped Annabelle would live with him one day.

Miss Teague smiled. "My lord, how kind of you to visit us this evening."

"Miss Teague. Annabelle." He bowed toward the doll in Annabelle's arms. "Lady Poppy. My, but you look fetching in your new bonnet, my lady."

Annabelle inched closer to her aunt, her eyes round and fearful.

The gut-punch went all the way to his spine. Ah, well. It had been too much to hope she might like him a little more today.

Miss Teague nudged Annabelle. "Say good evening to your papa."

She snuggled against her aunt, crushing her copper curls.

"Go on, now. Mind your manners."

"Good evening, Papa," Annabelle mumbled.

When Anthony looked at Annabelle and Miss Teague together, their fiery locks the same brilliant shade, he had no doubt the woman had been telling the truth about his daughter. Annabelle wasn't really his.

Miss Teague's brother—Camilla's lover—had sired Annabelle. But that didn't make him her father.

Anthony had loved his daughter before she was born, and he would love her as long as he lived. She was his child by heart if not blood. And if that lousy blackguard James Teague ever tried to take her away again, Anthony would see him swinging from the gallows. He was lucky Anthony hadn't crossed paths with him in Wales or he would already be dead.

Thank God, Miss Teague had possessed the wherewithal to send word to Anthony and go into hiding when her brother had come around threatening to take Annabelle unless she paid off his debts.

Neither female spoke as he rocked back and forth on his heels, trying to think of something clever to say. Nothing came to him. "Well, I will leave you to your

tea party then. I wanted to say good night before I left
for the evening."

Miss Teague squeezed Annabelle to her side. "How
lovely of you to call, my lord. We wish you a good
night as well."

Annabelle was gawking at him as if he were a beast
that might gobble her up.

He sighed and slowly turned on his heel. Perhaps
someday he would cease frightening the wits out of
her. But this evening he needed to turn his attentions
toward charming another young lady.

He had given consideration to his conversation
with Gabby that afternoon and came to an alarming
realization. She truly thought he had asked for her
hand because that was what an honorable gentleman
would do if he compromised a young woman.

He could try discussing it with her, but invariably
he would say the wrong words. That was always the
case when it came to speaking his heart. In truth, a
part of him still feared the rejection he'd known as a
boy, so he held on to his thoughts and feelings tightly.

No, talking might only complicate matters. Instead, he
would do what he did best. He would *show* Gabby how
much he loved her. His quest tonight was something he
should have done long ago. He was going to court her
in the way she deserved. And once he'd won her heart,
he would set his mind on how to win over Annabelle.

❦

Gabby recalled countless times Anthony had dined
at her family's table without incident, but tonight
one disaster seemed to follow another. First, she

had looked up as she was reaching for her lemonade only to discover him staring at her and she tipped over her glass. Next she had dribbled gravy on her newest gown.

And now…

"Oh, dear!" Mama said, her eyes wide with fright. "She's choking."

Gabby tried to suck in a deep breath, but coughing racked her body.

Anthony and her brother sprang from their chairs, but Anthony reached her first.

"Can you speak?"

She couldn't stop coughing long enough to answer.

"Egads! She *is* choking." He spun her around and banged his palm against her back. Hard.

"S-stop," she tried to say, but the next blow knocked the air from her lungs, then set off another round of hacking that seemed to originate from her toes.

More bone-jarring blows followed until Gabby turned on him, having caught her breath at last. "Stop pounding me, you jackanapes! I am not a rug in need of a beating."

Lizzie smothered a giggle with her hands.

"Gabrielle," their mother scolded, sounding rather scandalized. "That is no way to thank Lord Ellis for coming to your rescue."

Anthony's face had changed to scarlet and Gabby immediately regretted her harsh words. He had only been trying to help, even though she might later bear bruises for his good intentions.

She forced a smile, hoping it didn't translate into a grimace. "Mama is correct. That is no way to show my appreciation. I beg your pardon, my lord."

He sketched a bow. It seemed he wanted to say something, but he snapped his mouth closed and resumed his seat across the table.

"Now, Gabby," her sister-in-law Vivian said as she resettled her napkin on her lap, her blue eyes twinkling with good humor. "If you didn't like the lamb chops, you needed only to say so."

Everyone around the table chuckled, Gabby included. Vivian was a nice addition to the family and had a talent for diffusing tense situations.

"You'll forgive me for not asking for seconds, then?" Gabby teased.

Her brother winked at his wife, likely thinking he was being covert. Gabby smiled and returned to her dinner. It was good to see Luke happy at last.

Thankfully, the rest of the meal passed without any other catastrophes, and oddly, she felt more at ease. She was even able to meet Anthony's gaze without feeling she might jump out of her skin.

At least until the last course was cleared from the table and her brother's gaze landed on her.

"Gabrielle, Lord Ellis has requested an audience this evening. Perhaps you could show him to the drawing room and allow him a word."

Lizzie gasped beside her and Katie gawked from across the table.

Gabby's heart clogged her throat. What had Anthony said to Luke to explain his complaisant attitude? She looked to her mother, sure Anthony's request for a private audience had scandalized her, but Mama offered an untroubled smile in return.

Anthony cleared his throat. "Your Grace, if it

pleases you, perhaps it would be best if you were present as I address Lady Gabrielle."

Luke's eyebrows shot up and an odd look passed between them. "Very well, but rest assured my sister speaks for herself."

Anthony nodded sharply. "And I will abide by her wishes."

Gabby's feet felt fashioned of iron and her legs like taffy as her brother escorted her to the drawing room. She glanced over her shoulder at Anthony following behind them, silently praying he hadn't said anything about that day at Ellis Hall. She couldn't bear the thought of her family knowing she had disgraced them once again. He smiled reassuringly and her pulse slowed a smidge.

She and Luke sat beside each other on the settee while Anthony remained standing.

"Earlier today I asked for your brother's permission to marry you, and he was correct in withholding his consent."

Gabby shot a glance at her brother, but his expression revealed nothing. She didn't know how her brothers did it. Everything she felt showed on her face. It was quite unfair.

"In my zeal to become your husband," Anthony said, "I forgot an important step to any union. A proper courtship."

Luke's frigid posture melted and the beginnings of a smile showed at the corners of his mouth. But Anthony wasn't looking at her brother. He was watching her.

Pleasant warmth expanded in her chest.

"Therefore, my lady, I would very much like the opportunity to woo you as you deserve with flowers, rides in the park, and sweet words. May I have the honor of courting you, Lady Gabrielle?"

He wanted to court her, just as she had dreamed of many times. How could she refuse him?

She considered teasing him for his clichéd ideas on how to woo a woman, but in truth, she would welcome every overused romantic gesture recorded if it came from him. She wanted flowers, odes to her composed. She wanted trips to Gunter's and sweet nothings whispered in her ear during the waltz. Most of all, she wanted to feel as cherished as the women who had come into her brothers' lives, even if deep down she worried she didn't deserve that kind of love.

Anthony sighed, reminding her that he was awaiting her answer.

"Yes, Lord Ellis, you may court me. But don't think I will make it easy on you. If you insist upon wooing me, I expect you to be committed to seeing it through to the end."

Luke chuckled and patted her hand. "That's my girl. Well, Ellis. Do you agree to her terms?"

He nodded, a wide smile plastered across his face. "I do."

"You may begin tomorrow." Luke stood and offered her a hand up. She allowed her brother to escort her to the set of double doors but drew to a halt.

"May I see Lord Ellis out?"

"Don't linger. There is no understanding yet." Her brother patted her shoulder before leaving her in the foyer with Anthony.

Wesley brought his hat and cane forward, then discreetly retreated to another part of the house. She knew the butler wouldn't go far, but she appreciated the small amount of privacy afforded them.

Anthony offered his arm, and when they reached the front door, he held her hand.

"Thank you for the flowers," she said. "They are lovely."

"I wasn't sure you had received them."

"I did." Gabby looked down at the marble floor and contemplated the rust-colored veins. She felt unreasonably shy all of a sudden. The urge to ask why he insisted on courting her was on the tip of her tongue. He could have forced the issue if he truly wanted her by revealing what had happened between them at Ellis Hall.

A soft touch on her chin encouraged her to meet his gaze. His blue eyes shimmered with warmth. "I owe you an apology, Gabby. You deserve to be courted, and I missed that important piece. I don't blame you for not wanting to marry me."

"I never—" It was true her desire for him hadn't waned, but she *had* told him she changed her mind. "I'm sorry for turning you out this afternoon. Perhaps a fresh start is wise."

His thumb sketched a slow arc over her knuckles. "I agree. There is, however, one demand I have as we embark on this new beginning."

She raised her eyebrows. "A demand?"

"Yes, a demand. I won't compromise either."

She pulled her hand free of his grasp and crossed her arms. "Let me hear this demand, Your Majesty."

"End any involvement with Thorne. Either you want him or you want me."

She nearly laughed in relief. Discouraging Thorne seemed a reasonable request, one she would gladly grant. Making the baron listen was another matter.

She captured Anthony's hand again and aimed a flirtatious glance at him from beneath her lashes. "Lucky for you, it is *you* I want. Otherwise, you would be in a pickle. Ultimatums are a risky endeavor, Lord Ellis."

A corner of his mouth lifted as his arms snaked around her waist. Her heart leapt into her throat as his lips closed the distance between them. But he didn't kiss her.

"Is that so, Lady Gabrielle? Perhaps I think you are worth any risk."

"More likely you already knew what I would say."

"No. I hoped for the best, though." He touched his lips to hers briefly then pulled away, leaving her wanting. How many times had she relived that glorious moment in his drawing room at Ellis Hall?

She sighed when he released her to open the door. "Where are you going?"

"Another time, my lady. You heard your brother; I may begin my courtship tomorrow."

She followed him to the front stoop. "Well, you'd better be good at it to make up for that lousy kiss."

Anthony chuckled as he sauntered toward his carriage. "Prepare to be wooed."

Gabby rolled her eyes, but she couldn't hold back a laugh. "I shall retire early, though the anticipation may keep me awake all night."

He waved before climbing into the Berlin. "Sweet dreams, Lady Bug."

Oh, she would have dreams, but sweet they would not be.

Eight

GABBY DIDN'T KNOW WHETHER TO GET HER HOPES UP the next morning. Anthony may have promised to court her, but he had disappointed her too many times in the past for her to completely believe him.

That he had tricked her on multiple occasions made her the most naive person alive. Of course, many of those instances were when they were children. It seemed unfair to hold pranks against him, and for the most part, she had let go of her childish anger.

Yet, trusting Anthony with her heart in the past had left her with deep scars no one could see. Those were the wounds she had trouble forgetting, no matter how much she wanted to trust him.

Therefore, she must stop straining to hear every noise from the street in anticipation of his arrival. She had better things to do, such as finishing page three of the gothic novel her brother Drew had snuck her the other night. Mama disapproved of her reading selections, but Drew didn't object to many things, least of all a harmless book. Besides, Gabby had a way of bending her brother to her will. He owed her for helping to win his wife's hand, and Gabby didn't mind reminding him.

She made it to the second paragraph before a noise on the drive caused her to fling the book aside and dash for the window. Her heart tumbled clumsily as she spotted the source of the commotion. Anthony had arrived in a shiny, high-perched phaeton drawn by two white horses.

It was the most ostentatious vehicle she had ever seen. And she loved it. Not because it was the height of fashion so much as he was making good on his promise to woo her in a most impressive manner. Little did he know he needn't try so hard.

She hurried to her dressing table and pinched her cheeks before smoothing a hand over her hair. Pleased with her appearance, she slipped from her chambers. She could hear Anthony asking for her below stairs. His grand arrival warranted a grand entrance on her part. Holding her head high, she floated down the staircase. He didn't notice her at first, so she cleared her throat. When he didn't respond, she cleared her throat again. Loudly.

He turned a lazy grin on her. "Did you swallow a bug, Lady Gabrielle?"

"I did no such thing, you Neanderthal."

Wesley pretended she hadn't said anything unlady-like and made a quiet exit; perhaps he had become accustomed to overhearing her exchange barbs with Anthony after years of him practically living with her family.

Anthony's smile widened as she reached the foyer.

"My, but you look fetching today, my lady. Would you care to make the other gentlemen envious by taking a turn around the park with me?"

She hesitated. Lord Thorne could very well be one of those gentlemen. Although she had made her decision, she owed it to the baron to inform him in private. His family had suffered enough embarrassment over the scandal involving his sister.

"Perhaps another day."

His jaw dropped. "Another day? But I purchased a new phaeton for the occasion."

"Oh, my! I think I might swoon." She covered her heart with her hand and playfully batted her lashes. "Just think how envious the ladies would be if I were to be the first to ride in your fancy new gig."

"Ah, I see," he said with a smirk.

"What do you see?" she asked, struck by the thought he might know she was trying to avoid Lord Thorne. She hadn't been straightforward with Anthony last night. When she had promised not to see the baron again, she had neglected to mention she must speak with him at least once more.

Anthony ignored her question. "Would you grant me an audience in the drawing room instead?"

She allowed her gaze to roam over his body and prayed he couldn't read how strongly he affected her. The sight of buckskins hugging his muscular thighs made normal breathing impossible. "I suppose we shouldn't allow your new waistcoat to go to waste like the phaeton."

The violet satin brought out the blue in his eyes. Gads, how seductive his eyes were, even when he wasn't attempting to seduce. He sauntered in her direction, the embodiment of insolence.

"Shall we?"

When he held out his arm, her hand shook as she reached for him. He left the door to the drawing room open and took a chair after settling her on the settee.

"Even Luke wouldn't deny you the privilege of an ardent pressing of your soon-to-be betrothed's hand," she chided. "There's no reason for you to sit halfway across the room."

He crossed his ankle over his knee. "I beg to differ, Lady Gabrielle. If I were to join you on the settee, an ardent pressing of your hand would be the last thing on my mind."

She flushed, recalling their last encounter on a settee.

"Your brother wouldn't be as forgiving if I forgot myself."

He had a point. She smoothed her hands over her skirts, her palms damp in her gloves. Well, they should get on with it then. Gabby had made her decision, so there was no sense in dragging out the affair. Liz and Katie would be thrilled to learn she had made a match, and they truly would have their Season at last.

"I'm ready," she said.

His brow arched. "Have you changed your mind about Rotten Row?"

"I am not referring to the park, Anthony. You may ask for my hand now. I've prepared my answer."

"Is that so?" He leaned forward with his elbows on his knees, merriment shining in his eyes. "I hate to disappoint you, darling, but I'm committed to wooing you now. You haven't even allowed me to take you for a turn around the park."

"That's not funny."

"I'm not trying to be humorous. I intend to romance you like you deserve."

She crossed her arms. "And if I don't *want* to be romanced?"

"It doesn't matter. You will have flowers, trips to Gunter's, and declarations of love whether you like it or not."

Huffing, she hopped up from the settee and marched to the window to peer at the phaeton again. Perhaps she should just accept a silly ride. "This is ludicrous. I don't need those things."

His hand on her shoulder startled her. "Yes, you do, my love." He slid his hand down to her waist. His mouth touched her ear, sending tingles to her fingers and toes. "You may not think these are important now, but you want a love story of your own. I've known you since you were a young girl. This will only feel right if I try to win your heart."

"I already said I'll give it to you."

"Only if I prove I'm worthy, and I will prove it, Gabrielle. I'll never leave you with doubts again." His arm wrapped around her waist and pulled her back against him. She sank into his chest, soaking up his heat, and surrendered little by little. He placed a soft kiss behind her ear.

It was her family duty to marry a gentleman of means, but loving the man who would become her husband wasn't a prerequisite. Still, she *had* always longed for an epic romance, and in her girlish fantasies Anthony had always been the one.

She nodded slowly. "As you wish, my lord."

"Hmm… I might grow to like your docile side, my dear."

She spun in his arms and captured him around the neck. "I wouldn't get used to it." She planted a big kiss on his mouth, then laughed when he quickly set her away with a mild curse.

"You are dangerous, Lady Gabrielle."

"You don't know how dangerous I can be, my lord, but I expect you'll find out soon enough. Beginning tonight at Lady Dewhurst's musicale, should you choose to meet me there."

⤎⤏

When Anthony had learned of Gabby's plans to attend the musicale earlier that afternoon, he thought he'd hidden his dismay well. While Gabby had heralded Miss Eliza Dewhurst's unparalleled talent, he had nodded and interjected with "ah" or "oh" at the appropriate times. He hadn't groaned, grumbled, or complained even once, at least not aloud.

Cursing in his head didn't count.

He glanced at the mantel clock above the marble fireplace of the Dewhursts' great room. The hands hadn't moved since he last checked the time. Gabby was late. He took up position opposite the door in order to see her when she finally made an appearance.

Guests trickled into the oak-paneled room and began laying claim to the white damask chairs lined up in neat rows. Perhaps if he was lucky, all the places would be taken before Gabby arrived and they would be forced to seek entertainment elsewhere.

He had never been a fan of amateur performances, although in truth he didn't care for the opera either. Still, he kept a box at the theatre and attended on occasion. Therefore, he knew the difference between the voice of a diva who could shatter glass and one of a lady who was intent upon abusing his eardrums. His expectations were low this evening, at least when it came to the musical entertainment. Gabby, on the other hand, could be quite entertaining.

A flash of dark hair and alabaster skin through the crowd made his heart speed up. She was here at last. He moved forward to greet her and came up short when she entered the great room on Sebastian Thorne's arm.

Bollocks! What was she doing with that bloody scoundrel? She had promised to have nothing to do with him. But Anthony's wife had made promises, too, and she had broken every one. He mentally shook the thought from his head. Gabby wasn't Camilla, and his wife had never measured up to this woman he loved so completely.

Small lines formed on Gabby's forehead as her gaze shot around the room. When she spotted Anthony, the lines deepened, and she caught her bottom lip between her pearly teeth. Thorne leaned close to say something in her ear. She tried to angle away from him.

It was clear Gabby welcomed Thorne's company as much as she would a case of the Clap. Gabby's mother stood a few feet behind, chatting with Lady Eldridge, and apparently hadn't noticed anything untoward. Anthony's fingers curled into a fist, and he stalked toward them.

"Lady Gabrielle, I have seats saved," Anthony said and held out his arm to offer his escort.

"How thoughtful, my lord." Gabby slipped her hand into the crook of his elbow, but when Anthony tried to draw her away, she jerked to a halt.

Thorne had tightened his grip on her other arm and looked none too willing to give her up. "Yes, how thoughtful, Ellis."

Gabby's mouth fell open, and her wide-eyed gaze shot back and forth from the baron to him.

Anthony forced a smile so any onlookers would think they were having a friendly conversation. "I only claimed two chairs. You'll have to find another place to enjoy the musicale."

"And there are only two of us," Thorne said. "Again, Lady Gabrielle and I thank you for your thoughtfulness."

"She is sitting beside me," Anthony hissed, trying not to draw more attention to them than necessary. "Release her now."

"Gentlemen, please," Gabby said. "People are looking."

She was correct. Several pairs of curious eyes were glued to them.

"May I suggest we find a place where we may all sit together?" Without waiting for a reply, Gabby dragged them toward a row of vacant chairs in the back.

Anthony glared at Thorne as they both stood, waiting for Gabby to take her seat. Thorne glowered in return. Why wouldn't the baron leave them in peace?

"What are you doing here?" Anthony demanded.

There was a cocky lift to Thorne's brow. "Lady Gabrielle invited me."

Her head snapped up, her gray eyes larger than usual. She whipped out her fan as a pink flush invaded her cheeks. "I believe the concert is about to begin."

Thorne plopped into the chair next to Gabby like an obedient pup.

She had invited him? Anthony narrowed his eyes as he assumed the vacant spot beside her.

"Later," she mouthed behind her fan.

Oh, yes. They would be discussing this later. He crossed his arms and waited for the young miss to take her place on the dais.

Gabby's mother found a seat with Lady Eldridge three rows ahead. Despite allowing her daughter a little distance, Anthony knew the dowager duchess would be watching them like a mother bear.

Miss Eliza Dewhurst scurried toward center stage while her older sister, Beatrix, sat down at the pianoforte. With eyes downcast and hands clutched to her chest, Eliza appeared the very definition of mousy. How she would sing for more than a hundred guests without dissolving into tears was a mystery. She surprised him when her sister played the introduction and she broke into song. She had a lusty voice, larger than she was, and she had adopted a rather good imitation of a Scottish brogue.

At first, he paid no notice to the song as he stewed over Gabby arriving on Thorne's arm. He was eager to hear her explanation. The song went on, telling the story of a blacksmith and a lady. It wasn't until the lady turned herself into a cloud and taunted the smithy with "catch me if you can" that Miss Eliza Dewhurst's song selection caught Anthony's attention.

"So the blacksmith shook his hammer and it turned into a magic stick," Miss Dewhurst sang clearly, "so he became a lightning bolt for to zap into her quick."

Anthony sat up straighter in his chair and looked around to see if anyone else noticed the innocent young miss was belting out a bawdy tune. Everyone around him was smiling politely, pretending to listen.

It wasn't until she sang of the lady changing into a rose bush and the man into a bumblebee to sting her that Thorne gave a small jerk as if snapping out of a trance. He blinked at Anthony, the beginning of a grin lifting one corner of his mouth. Anthony couldn't help it. Suddenly he was smiling, too.

When the lady turned into a horse and the man became a golden saddle strapped on her back, they sniggered.

Gabby hushed them and nailed Anthony with a severe frown.

Neither he nor Thorne could hide their amusement when the lady turned into a man and the smithy became a bonny lass, and she took him where he stood. The applause, however, drowned out their laughter. Gabby's plump mouth formed a tight circle as she stared straight ahead.

"I suppose you gentlemen think you could write a song half as beautiful," she said under her breath.

"At least half," Thorne quipped.

"Very well. You both have until tomorrow to write a sonnet and prove yourselves."

Anthony smirked. "And why would we do any such thing?"

"Because I will be the judge, and the winner shall accompany me to Gunter's for an ice."

Anthony stammered, unable to form a coherent thought.

Thorne took her hand and raised it to his lips. "Challenge accepted, my lady."

Nine

GABBY KNEW IT WAS WRONG TO LAY DOWN THE gauntlet with her two suitors, but she was cross with both gentlemen for laughing at Miss Eliza Dewhurst. She was a sweet girl in her first Season and shy beyond reason, except when she was singing. To have two sought-after bachelors twittering in the back row like silly chits would be mortifying for any debutante.

Irritation rolled off Anthony in waves as they sat quietly through the second song. She chanced a side-glance and noted the muscles in his chiseled jaw working. If he composed a sonnet as she had demanded, she would declare him the winner, but he needn't know the outcome. Let him stew all night.

Lord Thorne deserved punishment as well, but Gabby couldn't encourage his suit. She would pull him aside after the concert and tell him she hadn't been serious about the contest. She would also implore him not to tell Anthony. At least one gentleman would get his comeuppance.

She no longer felt as guilty about entering the room on Thorne's arm. Truly, she hadn't known what to do. The baron had been waiting outside when their carriage pulled up to Dewhurst Place, and there had been no way to refuse his offer of an escort without insulting him.

She tried to steal a glance at Thorne, but he caught her looking and winked. She couldn't help smiling in return. He was a handsome scoundrel. If her heart didn't already belong to Anthony, he would make a good choice for a husband.

"Shall I compare thee to a summer's day?" he whispered.

"No plagiarizing, my lord."

Anthony shifted beside her, his elbow conveniently connecting with her ribs. She frowned at him. He raised his eyebrows toward Miss Dewhurst. Chastised, she straightened, folding her hands in her lap.

Thorne leaned close to her ear. "Killjoy."

She suppressed a chuckle. Perhaps she was being too hard on Anthony for laughing. They managed to make it through the remainder of the concert without any more snickers between the three of them, but it had required Gabby's focused attention. She had never realized the baron was as playful as he was.

The guests began to mingle, and liveried servants swept in to move the chairs to the outer walls of the room while others carried refreshments to the banquet table on large trays.

She sought a quiet corner out of the servants' way. Her gentlemen stuck by her side like ticks on a dog, as her brother Drew was fond of saying. It was inconvenient, to say the least. She needed a moment alone with Lord Thorne.

Waving her fan vigorously, she regarded the men. "My, but it is stifling in here."

Thorne was quick to pick up on her insinuation. "Allow me to retrieve a glass of lemonade for you, my lady."

"If anyone is going to service the lady, it will be me." Anthony hurried off before Thorne could protest.

Gabby didn't waste the moment alone. "Lord Thorne, please don't write a sonnet. I was only needling Lord Ellis. You won't tell him, will you?"

His smile slipped. "And the contest? Gunter's?"

"I'm sorry. I didn't mean to mislead you."

The sparkle in his eyes dimmed. "I take it you are seriously considering his suit."

Gads, she must be the worst person on earth. Playing the role of rejecter was as bad, if not worse, than being rejected. She wished there was a way to ease the blow. "I don't want to insult you by denying it, my lord. I have great admiration for you, and I cannot play you false."

His grin returned. "Admiration is a start."

She made a sound of protest, but before she could discourage him further, Anthony returned with two glasses of lemonade. He was still in a mood, if she read him correctly. No one else might notice, since his expression was blank, but the only time Anthony's emotions weren't as easy to read as a copy of *The Morning Times* was when he didn't want others to know he was bothered.

He passed a glass to her, then sipped from his own.

Thorne's eyebrow arched like a question mark.

"Get your own drink," Anthony said.

The baron chuckled, his dark eyes glittering. "I can't stay anyway. I have a sonnet to write and a lady to escort to Gunter's tomorrow." He bowed to Gabby. "Good evening, Lady Gabrielle."

"He can barely write his name," Anthony grumbled as Thorne walked away.

Gabby smiled sweetly at him. "You should have the advantage then, I should think. I've seen you write *your* name."

A rapid, red flush climbed his neck and infused his cheeks. "You promised to stay away from him."

"I did and I meant it. It is he who doesn't want to stay away." She held up a hand when he opened his mouth to argue. "I can manage Lord Thorne. Your task is to compose a sonnet to rival Shakespeare."

He grunted and took another gulp of his drink. She allowed herself an unguarded moment to appreciate his form. His black jacket hugged his broad shoulders, hiding the sculpted arms she knew were underneath.

When he and Drew were young men—perhaps sixteen or seventeen—she had stumbled upon them swimming at the family's summer cottage. She hid in the brush, mesmerized by the play of sunlight on Anthony's golden hair and the shadows defining his muscles. The hair on his chest was so light, she wouldn't have been able to see it from a distance, but water droplets clung to him and glimmered. In her fanciful imagination, he had appeared like the god Apollo.

The years had been kind to him, for he still resembled that gorgeous vision she'd held in her head. Only improved. He had lost his boyish looks and possessed the hard-earned edge of a man.

A corner of his mouth quirked up. "Do you like what you see?"

She boldly held his gaze. "Very much, Lord Ellis."

Being close to Anthony all evening without the freedom to touch him was driving her mad. She reached out to caress his arm. His blue eyes darkened, and she had no doubt if they were alone, he would have his strong hands all over her.

Her mother's white-feathered headdress moved at a steady pace through the crowd, headed in their direction. Gabby pulled her hand back with a sigh.

"I look forward to spending tomorrow afternoon with you, my lord."

"Are you implying the winner has already been decided?" he asked with a flash of his heart-stopping smile.

She shrugged one shoulder. "I said you had an advantage, but you must earn the win."

He nodded slowly, his good humor still intact.

Her mother approached, warmly greeting Anthony with a firm squeeze to his hands. "How lovely to see you again so soon, my boy. I apologize for whisking my daughter away, but the time has come to return to Talliah House."

"No need to apologize. I too must be going. I have a difficult task awaiting me this evening."

"Oh? I hope nothing too dire."

He offered his arm to her mother, then waited for Gabby to take his other. "I'm afraid it is extremely dire, Your Grace. I must learn to write a sonnet."

Ten

ANTHONY FELT SLIGHTLY QUEASY WHEN HE WALKED into Brooks's the next afternoon. He had worked on Gabby's sonnet until sunrise and had to admit he had nothing.

No, that wasn't entirely true. His pocket held an elegant sheet of foolscap—for he'd used his best— scribbled with gibberish.

The porter looked on Anthony with the same bored expression he'd given him days earlier. Nevertheless, Harry could never be accused of favoritism for he was equally disinterested in everyone. "Good afternoon, milord."

Anthony mumbled a greeting and handed over his cane and hat. Two hours remained until Gabby was expecting him, and he wanted to earn the privilege of taking her for an ice. His prospects were looking bleak.

He touched his jacket pocket and heard the paper crinkle. Last night he hadn't even been able to recall what a sonnet was exactly, so he had muddled through as best as he could.

The result? Utter rubbish. If she didn't toss him out on his ear, he would be fortunate.

Perhaps a cup of Turkish coffee would chase away his fog, and brilliance would strike him before he was due at Talliah House.

He claimed one of the leather chairs and ordered a coffee from one of the footmen. The gentleman seated across from him lowered his newssheet to his lap and Anthony grimaced.

"Unusual weather we are having, aye, Ellis?"

"Corby." He returned the troublemaker's greeting with a sharp nod. A quick glance around the club reassured him that he would at least be spared Ledbery's obnoxious company.

Corby returned to his newssheet, and Anthony eased back against his seat with a soft sigh. He was deep in thought when the footman returned with his coffee. Anthony had taken only one sip when Thorne rounded the vacant chair and dropped down beside him.

The baron grinned. "Beautiful day for an outing to Gunter's."

"Too bad you'll have no one to take," Anthony said.

Thorne shrugged, his smile growing wider, if that was even possible. He might believe his flash of straight teeth made the ladies swoon, but it made Anthony want to knock a few loose this morning.

Toothy jackass.

Thorne's eyebrow angled upward. "Are you prepared to sweep the lady off her feet with your brilliant words? If I remember correctly, you never earned high marks for penmanship *or* composition."

Anthony sipped his coffee, pointedly ignoring

Thorne's insult. He wished he had a witty rejoinder, but the baron was correct. Anthony had never thought those things were important, until now.

"I suppose you think you can do better," Anthony said. If memory served, Thorne had never been a bard himself.

The baron drummed his fingers against the armrest and cocked his head to the side, his eyes trained to the ceiling. "Let not to the marriage of true minds admit impediments." His voice boomed. "Love is not love which alters when it alteration finds or bends with the remover to remove: O no! it is an ever-fixed mark that looks on tempests and is never shaken."

Damn. That was good. And Thorne's delivery had a certain *je ne sais quoi*. No wonder he could claim success with the ladies.

Anthony grimaced. "Out of every available lady, why are you chasing after her? Are you even interested in matrimony?"

Corby peeked around his newssheet, saw Anthony's glower, and snapped his paper back in place.

Thorne lost his smirk. "One doesn't court a duke's sister unless one intends to marry her. I enjoy Lady Gabrielle's company and she is not hard on the eyes. She suits my purpose well."

"And what purpose would that be?"

Thorne regarded Anthony as if he was dense. "The same purpose *you* have. She will make a good wife and beget me an heir."

Anthony's head felt like it might burst. If Thorne even thought about bedding Gabby, Anthony would strangle him.

Slowly.

And he would enjoy it.

Immensely.

"The lady will not accept your suit," Anthony said.

Thorne winked. "Any lady can be persuaded to change her mind." He pushed to his feet and strode away with a swagger.

Anthony gulped his coffee, barely noting it had grown too cold to be enjoyable. Gabby was too intelligent to fall for Thorne's flattery and eloquent words.

Uncertainty tugged at his heart. She did like beautiful things, however, and Anthony's sonnet was hideous compared to Thorne's. "How did he write something that polished in the little time we were given?"

Corby shoved his newssheet into his lap and gaped. "*He* didn't write that balderdash he was spouting. He was quoting Shakespeare."

Heat swept over Anthony and he tugged at his cravat self-consciously. Thorne likely knew Anthony wouldn't remember the bard's work. It wasn't one of his topics of interest, unlike arithmetic and animal husbandry, which were twice as useful in his estimation. Unfortunately, Gabby hadn't asked them to explain Pythagoreanism or how best to breed Cotswold sheep.

"If you want to win the lady's heart," Corby said, "you will need to do one better than quoting poetry. What interests does your lady hold?"

Perhaps Corby had a point. Gabby enjoyed poetry, but she loved something much more. "She is talented with sketching and watercolors."

Corby nodded. "Yes, that's good. Go on."

"She seems to like all things art related, in truth. Oils. Marble sculptures."

"I have it," the viscount said with a snap of his fingers. "I'm a bit of a collector myself. My father turned me on to it."

"Poetry and art. I wouldn't have guessed you were a romantic, Corby."

His companion's face pinched. "Do you wish for my help or not?"

"Fine." What was the world coming to that Anthony would accept assistance with courting from Corby?

"I will have my mother plan a private showing and make certain Lady Gabrielle is on the guest list, along with you, of course. You may tell her you persuaded me to open my gallery to a few select people because of her love for art."

"That's a brilliant suggestion." Gabby would be thrilled by the opportunity to peruse Corby's private collection. Anthony couldn't wait to tell her. Perhaps she would even forget about the sonnet in her excitement.

Corby was watching him too keenly and a crawling sensation crept up his spine. Something didn't feel right.

"Why do you want to help me?"

A leer broke across Corby's too-pretty face. "I have money riding on you."

His jaw dropped. "You made a bet concerning Lady Gabrielle?"

"Don't look at me like I kicked a puppy. The competition between you and Thorne isn't of my making. I simply saw an opportunity to plump my pockets." He raised his newssheet again, cutting off eye contact. "Truth be told, I feel sorry for the lady. Either way *she* ends up the loser."

"Sod off, Hugh." Anthony thumped the other man's paper on the way out.

"I'll have Mother send 'round an invitation soon," he called.

And damned if Anthony wouldn't accept it. A private showing of a rarely seen art collection was just the thing to give him a leg up on the competition. Gabby would be ecstatic, and he couldn't resist the urge to make her smile.

❧

Gabby pasted on a smile for Lord Thorne and tugged open the double doors to the drawing room. She hadn't expected him to pay a call after their conversation last night, and yet she wasn't surprised. He was as persistent as a case of head lice.

He stood at the window with his back to her. Sunlight poured through the glass and cast his broad-shouldered frame aglow. Admittedly, he was several degrees more appealing than head lice, but the comparison was still apt.

"Good afternoon, Lord Thorne."

He swung around with a grin. "Lady Gabrielle, haven't I implored you to call me Sebastian?"

"You have, my lord, and I have declined."

He chuckled and came away from the window. "I do enjoy a challenge, my lady."

Which created quite the bind for her. The more she resisted, the harder he tried. Her maid claimed a quiet corner of the room and turned her attention toward knitting. Gabby hadn't felt right about asking Anthony to recite his poem in the presence of one of her family members, so she had requested her maid chaperone this afternoon. Magda was slightly hard of hearing after a bout of measles as a child, so he would have no cause to feel nervous. Now she questioned the wisdom in receiving Thorne without someone more capable of making him toe the line.

She took a seat in the wingback chair to discourage him from coming too close. "I didn't expect you after I asked you not to write a sonnet."

With a shrug, he lowered to the settee adjacent to her. "If I follow every direction you give, I'll never win your heart. Ladies may say they like an amenable chap, but I've come to learn a man easily wrapped around a lady's finger is soon tossed over."

"Have you been tossed over then?" This news was surprising. Sebastian Thorne was hardly the type of gentleman a woman would banish from her bed. And she was certain this was the nature of any past assignations.

"I wasn't referring to myself, my lady, but Ellis can enlighten you on the ills of a lady running roughshod over a gentleman."

Gabby snorted, a most unladylike sound. "Lord Ellis is as ungovernable as you. I doubt he knows anything about the subject."

"I wouldn't be so sure."

He was being too cryptic for her tastes, and she wanted to hurry him on his way. Anthony would arrive any moment, and although she wanted to punish him a little for his bad manners last night, she didn't want to do it like this.

"Well, be that as it may, Lord Thorne, I asked you not to write me a sonnet."

Thorne's off-kilter grin reappeared. "I didn't."

"And why not?" she asked, a bit outraged despite not wanting pretty words from him.

"Because you ordered me to write one."

"You are impossible, my lord."

"And *you* are intrigued."

"I am not." She crossed her arms and pressed her lips tightly together. Perhaps she was a *little* intrigued. He was providing her with a glimpse into the workings of the male mind. Did Anthony think this way, too? "I'm afraid I must ask you to leave. You failed your task, and I cannot reward you with an outing to Gunter's."

"You weren't going to choose me anyway, Lady Gabrielle, but now you'll be unable to stop thinking about me. You will wonder why I didn't mind my p's and q's. Why I'm not trying to win your favor. You'll ask what you can do to gain my notice and make me want you so badly I would do anything you desire."

She rolled her eyes. "Does this actually work with some ladies?"

He chuckled as he stood. "Yes, but I didn't expect it would with you." He bowed over her hand, a mischievous twinkle in his eyes. "You become more appealing every moment, my dear."

"Lucky me," she mumbled, but even though she would like to be cross with him, she wasn't. She appreciated his frankness. It was difficult to feel manipulated when the gentleman told her what he was doing. "Enjoy your afternoon, Lord Thorne."

"Take no offense, but I wish you the opposite."

Eleven

WHEN ANTHONY ARRIVED AT TALLIAH HOUSE, THE butler informed him Gabby was already waiting in the drawing room with her maid. He clutched the plain wrapped parcel he had stopped to pick up after leaving Brooks's. He'd promised Gabby pretty words and romance, and he would deliver one way or another.

"This way, my lord."

He shoved his hand in his pocket to check for his lucky talisman and followed. His rapid pulse slowed as his fingers skimmed the smooth edge. It was silly to find solace in a common object, but old habits were hard to break.

Gabby was sitting on the settee with her hands folded primly in her lap. She studied him with the same cautious look he would expect from his childhood tutor, rather than a lady prepared to be impressed by his brilliance.

"Lord Ellis, shall we get to the business at hand?"

"Is that the only greeting I'm to receive today?"

She pursed her lips. "Well, perhaps if you hadn't kept me waiting all afternoon, I would be more patient."

Her haughtiness was revealed as only a charade when
a smile crept across her lips. She patted the seat beside
her. "Come. I'm eager to be on our way."

With her maid in the corner, he didn't hesitate to
sit beside Gabby. He needn't worry temptation would
overcome his self-discipline as long as an audience
was present. His fingers skimmed the pink rosebuds
dotting Gabby's ivory skirts.

"How smart you look today."

"Thank you." Her cheeks flushed the same rosy
color as the flowers on her dress, and her gray eyes
appeared more like lavender. She was the most beautiful woman he'd ever seen.

"Are you ready to read your sonnet?"

A hot, prickly sensation traveled the back of his
neck and he rubbed it to ease the discomfort. "About
the sonnet…"

Her lips turned down so slightly he might not have
noticed if he hadn't been preoccupied moments earlier
by the thought of tasting them.

"You didn't—"

"It's not very—" They spoke at the same time.

"Forgive me. Please, continue," Gabby said.

He grimaced as he reached into his jacket pocket
and pulled out the sheet of foolscap. "I'm afraid it isn't
very good. I hope you're not disappointed."

"You really composed one?" Her voice was filled
with wonder and her smile lit up the room.

"Of course I did. You requested poetry, and poetry
you shall have." But perhaps he should give her his
gift first. He placed the parcel on her lap. "Open it."

She unwrapped the slim volume of Shakespeare's

sonnets he had chosen for her at Hatchard's bookshop. Her delicate brows lifted in question.

"You have proven your point twenty times over, Gabby. It isn't easy to write anything worth a pence, so I'll leave it to the masters in the future. Perhaps you can read a sonnet or two later to strike from your memory the rubbish I'm about to spout."

Her face softened and she reached for his hand. "You don't have to read it if you don't want. It's enough that you made the attempt."

"Oh, no. I was awake all night working on this sonnet. I'm *going* to read it." He shook out the paper and cleared his throat. Gads, this was harder than he'd thought it would be. "I'll begin now."

She nodded solemnly, as if expecting a disaster. So be it. He had nothing to lose, aside from his pride.

"Your radiant smile feeds my soul. I bask in your attention like flowers turning toward the sun."

He looked up quickly to find her studying him with an odd expression. He barreled on. If he stopped to wonder what she was thinking, he might not finish.

"You see beauty where I once thought none existed, and suddenly, through your eyes my mundane world becomes extraordinary. How I long to hold you until my days should end, for you are the only paradise I have ever known."

When he glanced up again, her eyes were shimmering with tears.

"Egads. Was it *that* awful?"

"Those were the most beautiful words I have ever heard."

She was being kind.

He tucked the paper away. Perhaps he would burn it when he returned home. "It's too short, and I'm certain I mucked up the rules."

She captured his face and caressed his clean-shaven jaw. "I loved it, Anthony. Truly I did."

When she pressed her lips against his, the sweetness of her mouth nearly undid him. He stopped her retreat and held her close. His breath churned heavier as his fingers curled around the base of her neck. Soft hairs at her nape tickled his wrist. Her lips were still parted, so plump and ripe for the taking. He leaned toward her, eager to taste her again.

Gabby's maid yawned loudly and broke the spell. Magda lowered her gaze to her sewing. "Pardon me, milord."

Bloody chaperones. He reluctantly released Gabby. The brief kiss hadn't been enough, but such was the curse of courtship. Perhaps he should just make an offer and forget about flowers and sugary words. But he couldn't. Deep down, he knew Gabby longed for romance. It was closely woven into the fabric of who she was, a woman he adored.

He stood then assisted her to her feet. "And now, my lady, I owe you a fruited ice."

⁓

Gabby didn't want a man who wouldn't try to please her. Thorne had been wrong. Anthony's heartfelt poetry had proven what she had known long ago and had tried to deny.

He had always been the love of her life, and they belonged together.

But do you deserve him? Gabby attempted to silence the guilty voice in her head. She was deeply sorry for her part in her mother's loneliness, and that would remain unchanged. But must she sacrifice the one thing she most wanted in order to make amends?

She squeezed her eyes closed to banish the memory of her mother's tears.

Anthony brushed against her knee. "Are you all right, Lady Bug?"

Her eyes flew open and she forced a smile. "The cold made my head hurt for a moment."

He slanted a look at her. "I'm not surprised, with the way you've been gobbling that bergamot. Doesn't your brother feed you?" He shifted his weight where he was leaning against the carriage and chuckled as he spooned a heaping bite into his mouth.

"There's nothing wrong with a lady enjoying a treat, you jackanapes." She discreetly swatted the back of his head from her perch still inside the carriage.

He turned and grinned up at her. "I like a lady with a healthy appetite. It bodes well for other indulgences."

"I don't eat too much."

His gaze slowly traveled her figure, his smile still in place. "Just the right amount, I'd say."

Heat rushed into Gabby's cheeks, and she was grateful she hadn't been forced to bring Magda along. Gunter's was one of the few places she could enjoy Anthony's company without a chaperone.

"You are taking liberties, Lord Ellis. I should be cross with you."

"And are you?"

She licked the citrus-flavored ice cream from

the spoon. "What I *should* do and choose to do often differ."

This wouldn't be news to him, however. A proper lady didn't correspond with an unmarried gentleman and pour out her heart, nor did she arrive unexpectedly at his home and allow him to kiss her senseless.

His blue eyes glowed softly. "I appreciate that you take risks, Lady Gabrielle. It is but one of your many assets."

"Are there others, my lord?"

He chuckled. "You are never satisfied with one compliment, are you, love? Perhaps I will dole out more when I escort you to the private showing of Viscount Corby's gallery. You should expect an invitation from his mother soon."

Gabby's heart did a triple flip. "But how? No one has been allowed to view the Corby collection. The former viscount was very protective of his oils and marbles, and his heir isn't rumored to be any different."

"I have connections," Anthony said with a shrug of his broad shoulders.

He knew just the thing to make her blood run hot.

"Good heavens, Lord Ellis. If we were not on display, I'd demand you take all kinds of liberties right now."

He nearly choked on his ice cream, but once he'd recovered, a smile eased across his lips. His eyelids returned to half-mast, his wispy blond lashes giving his blue eyes a smoky appearance. "Let's find a way to be out of the public eye."

Oh, yes. Lord Thorne had been completely wrong. A man who knew her desires and wanted to please her was arousing beyond words.

Twelve

DESPITE ANTHONY'S BEST INTENTIONS, HE HADN'T managed to steal anything more than a courteous kiss on Gabby's hand when he'd returned her to Talliah House after their outing to Gunter's. The duke and his duchess had come strolling through the gates the instant his carriage had rolled to a stop in front of the massive town house, thwarting his plans to whisk Gabby away to a secluded spot.

He had been paying call for the past three days, and he still hadn't been spared a moment alone with her. It seemed her damned brothers would always be underfoot. At the moment, Richard and Drew were taking turns interrupting them in the drawing room. He and Gabby could barely speak a sentence without one of her brothers popping in to ask a question or retrieve an item.

Gabby didn't seem to notice in her excitement. "Do you think the rumors are true? Could Lord Corby truly have a Rembrandt?"

Her eyes shone brightly, their color an iridescent shade similar to her lavender gown.

"We'll soon find out." He pushed a strand of hair

behind her ear, his fingers lingering on her ivory cheek. She would rival any artist's masterpiece, but to speak this sentiment aloud would make him feel awkward. He allowed his hand to communicate for him and brushed his thumb over her ample bottom lip. She pressed a featherlight kiss to the pad.

A groan sounded deep in his throat. "Gabby."

Bang!

They jumped apart, their heads whipping toward the sound. Drew stood in the threshold with a book at his feet. "How clumsy of me." He bent to retrieve the book, but his eyes didn't stray from them. If Anthony didn't know better, he would swear his friend was glaring at him.

Gabby huffed. "Why are you still here? Doesn't Lana usually keep you on a leash?"

Drew strolled to the chair opposite the settee and plopped down. "What my wife does or doesn't do is none of your concern, princess."

Gabby lifted a haughty brow. "And what I do is none of yours, so stop spying on me. His wife should put him in a cage," she said confidentially to Anthony.

Anthony chuckled, but Drew didn't crack a smile. It wasn't like Gabby's brother to be so serious. When he continued to glower, Anthony sighed and scooted a little farther away from her on the settee. His best friend was becoming a blasted nuisance.

The dowager Duchess of Foxhaven swept into the drawing room like a petite tempest, smiling broadly. He and Drew stood. "Lord Ellis, I've come to understand you are responsible for this lovely outing today. Gabby has been beside herself with excitement."

"Mama," she demurred.

"And rightly so," her mother said. "No one has ever been invited to view Lord Corby's collection."

"I've seen it," Drew said with a chuckle, his good humor returning at last.

Gabby blinked. "You have? When?"

"Long time ago. You'll enjoy it."

The duchess gestured to her daughter. "We should go if we wish to arrive on time."

As Gabby and her mother walked toward the doors ahead of him, Drew detained him. The ladies left them alone.

"If you hurt her, I'll kill you," Drew said through clenched teeth. "You know she was in love with you."

Anthony hoped she *still* was in love with him. He calmly extracted his arm from his friend's grip. "I am courting her, not trying to seduce her."

"It appeared otherwise when I walked in."

"I intend to marry her first, but I will bed her eventually. You should grow accustomed to the idea."

"Egads!" Her brother drew back with a grimace and covered his ears. "Be quiet, man."

Anthony laughed and slapped his friend on the back. "Might I suggest you mind your own concerns if you don't wish to hear anything further about your sister's love life?"

Dimples dented Drew's cheeks. "Fair enough. But don't forget your pledge. Marry her first, and never speak of this to me again."

"You have my word." Anthony straightened his waistcoat and followed the same path the ladies took.

"One more thing," Drew said as Anthony reached the threshold. "Keep her away from the far end of the south gallery."

Anthony raised his eyebrows.

"Let's just say Corby has a secret collection that *should* be kept private."

❧

Goose bumps rose on Gabby's arms as she stood in front of Lord Corby's Botticelli. The artist's subject boasted a face so soft, the woman seemed other-worldly, and yet the detailing was so expertly defined, it kept her from floating off the canvas. The painting appeared effortless, like anyone could do it, which was the hallmark of genius in Gabby's opinion.

She hugged Anthony's arm where they were linked. "If only I had half his talent…"

Anthony tipped his head to the side and studied the painting. "It's nice, but I think your drawings are more lifelike."

She slanted a smile up at him. "Do you remember when I sketched you at Twinspur Cottage that summer?"

"Do you refer to the drawing where you gave me the hind quarters of a mule?"

An unexpected laugh burst from her, earning a few amused stares from the small party perusing the expan-sive gallery. "I had forgotten about that drawing," she said, lowering her voice to match the quiet murmurs around them.

Anthony sniffed. "Well, I obviously haven't, but it's hard to forget your brothers' jibes." He leaned close to whisper in her ear. "Does the name Anthony the Ass sound familiar?"

This time when she laughed, he joined her.

She glanced around the private home gallery and sighed. The space was spectacular with crimson walls and gilded pedestals for the sculptures. Perhaps someday she would have a similar gallery to display her work.

They wandered arm in arm to a tasteful nude painting, her heels a dull echo against the parquet flooring. Gabby found the painting rather tedious given every home she visited had the requisite piece—either in oils or marble—depicting a male or female in a state of undress. She gestured to the painting. "I declare, once you've seen one nude, you've seen them all."

He grinned. "How worldly you are, my dear."

"You know my meaning," she said, wrinkling her nose. She wasn't nearly as worldly as Anthony and her brother, although she was adept at eavesdropping. Drew's warning to keep her from the south end of the gallery piqued her curiosity. What could Lord Corby possibly have secreted away? Something very scandalous, no doubt.

She held her tongue as Lady Corby meandered past with Lady Eldridge and Gabby's mother. The three ladies were preoccupied with some incident from the last Mayfair Ladies Charitable Society gathering, but she didn't want to chance them overhearing her.

Once they had moved far enough away, she whispered, "Do you think Lord Corby's mother knows about his secret collection?"

Anthony smirked. "And you accused your brother of spying."

"I wasn't spying. I just have excellent hearing." She tried to draw him toward the south end. "Let's take a peek."

He dug in his heels. "Absolutely not. Your brothers would have me drawn and quartered. Besides, I'm sure it is unfit for ladies' eyes."

The stubborn set to his jaw told her it was pointless to argue. Therefore she must be clever instead. "Oh, I hadn't thought of that. I assumed he had rare pieces he wanted to protect."

His eyes narrowed as if he didn't trust her. She smiled sweetly. "Thank you for arranging this today. I still cannot believe I'm here. Should we look for the Rembrandt?"

The stiffness in his shoulders melted and his easy smile made *her* melt, leaving her warm and tingly.

"I mean that sincerely, my lord."

"Anything to please you, Lady Gabrielle."

Anything except allow her to view their host's private collection of scandalous art. Of course, she couldn't hold it against him, since he meant well.

Gabby spotted the Rembrandt first and drew him toward it.

"What do you think?" Anthony asked after several moments of her staring at the painting.

She nodded, too overcome with emotion. The work was dark and weighed on her. How amazing that any form of art could alter the feelings of those who stood before it.

She blinked back tears. It was silly to cry over something like this, but the painting reminded her of her father. Anthony's fingers gently curled around her arm where they were still linked. Somehow he understood.

He discreetly passed his handkerchief to her. "Would you like a glass of lemonade?"

She touched the pristine white square to the corners of her eyes. "That would be lovely."

As Anthony walked away, she couldn't help following his retreat with her eyes. He was more to her than a set of well-formed calves and strong back, but she wasn't blind. The sight of his body clad in tight breeches created an odd sensation in her lower belly. It was both delicious and frightening.

Just as he passed the stairs on the way to the refreshments, Sebastian Thorne appeared at the landing.

Drat! Anthony had been in a good mood all afternoon, and the baron was going to ruin everything if he started up with his flirting again. Perhaps if she could avoid Thorne for a bit, he would turn his attentions on one of the other young ladies Lady Corby had invited.

Gabby hurried away from the men, hoping she wouldn't be spotted before she could find a hiding place. When she reached the south end of the gallery, it came to her. Lord Corby's secret room would be the perfect location to dodge Lord Thorne. Now, she just had to find it.

She almost barreled past the massive tapestry claiming a prominent space on the wall, but it moved. Just a little. Like a breeze had disturbed it, and last time she'd checked, solid walls were not breezy.

She looked over her shoulder and with everyone at the far end paying her no attention, she lifted an edge of the tapestry and slipped inside the hidden room. A small window cast dim light over the space, and she stopped a few steps from the threshold to allow her eyes to adjust. There was a relief hanging on the wall in front of her, but she couldn't make out the figures at once. She walked toward it. When the relief came into focus, she gasped.

Thirteen

Anthony sighed as Sebastian Thorne snagged a glass of champagne from a passing footman and approached. "What are you doing here?"

Thorne raised his glass in salute. "I was invited. Generally, this isn't my idea of an entertaining way to spend an afternoon, but when I heard Lady Gabrielle was attending…" The baron flaunted a cocky grin. "Does she like this sort of thing?"

Anthony swallowed his sarcastic reply, which involved a word or two not appropriate for mixed company. If Thorne knew anything about Gabby, he would know of her likes and dislikes. "When are you going to abandon this quest?"

Thorne shrugged. "Not until she signs her name on the church registry, I suspect. The question is which of us will she marry?" He sipped his champagne and gazed around the room. "Where is Lady Gabrielle? I would like to offer my regards."

Anthony looked over his shoulder where Gabby was supposed to be waiting for him, but she was gone. He slowly spun on his heel, searching the massive room, but there was no sign of lavender skirts among the groups of ladies chatting together.

Bollocks. He had a good guess where she'd gone. "She's visiting the retiring room," he said with authority.

His sight landed on Lords Corby and Ledbery standing with their backs to a towering marble statue in the center of the room. They wore expectant grins, their eyes alight with a feverish quality.

Anthony nodded toward them. "They have taken bets on which of us will win Lady Gabrielle's hand."

"I've heard." Thorne didn't sound troubled in the least.

"It's unseemly to drag a lady into their wagers."

"It's what they do. I have found it best to ignore the addlepates. I would wager they have a bet now on whether we will come to fisticuffs today."

"I hate to disappoint them," Anthony said dryly.

Thorne chuckled and sketched a bow to the men. "Perhaps another time, Ellis. I want to look nice for my lady, and your blood on my coat wouldn't do."

"She's my lady, remember?" he said under his breath. "Do yourself a favor and find your own."

He headed toward the south section of the gallery, not finding Gabby with any of the other ladies. He should have known not to leave her alone. When he caught Gabby in Corby's secret room, she was in for a good scolding. The trouble was he didn't know exactly where it was located.

As he passed a tapestry of a maid collecting water from a well, he heard a sound and skidded to a stop. He listened closely and after a while, thought he might have imagined the noise. He started to resume his search.

"Oh, my!" a soft voice squeaked.

With a shake of his head, he yanked the tapestry back and stormed into the hidden room.

Gabby cried out and wheeled around to face him, her hand clutched to her chest.

"Gabrielle Forest, your brothers would line up for a turn to tan your hide. What are you doing in here?"

Her face seemed paler in the dusky light, and she wagged a finger toward a sculpture of a man and woman copulating in a most unusual position. "Is—is that what men and women do?"

He bit back a laugh. "That is but one way."

Her gaze strayed back to the sculpture. She took a deep breath and blew it out slowly. "Will *we* do that?"

The little minx deserved a lesson in listening to her husband-to-be. He rubbed his jaw and studied her. Her wide eyes seemed to be pleading with him to dispel the notion. "Do you know how to stand on your head?"

"No," she said on an exhale.

"Hmm...neither do I. Perhaps we should leave this one to the acrobats."

Understanding flitted across her expression. "Oh, you beast!" She whacked him on the arm, laughing. "You're teasing me."

He captured her around the waist and nuzzled her neck. "Serves you right for disregarding my warnings. I told you this wouldn't be fit for ladies' eyes."

She snaked her arms around his neck and tipped her face up. "It was educational, however."

"Can we agree that any further lessons will come from me?"

"Agreed."

He closed the distance between them, his lips lightly pressing to hers. God, he wanted more.

He pulled her to him, her lush breasts crushed against his chest, and delved his tongue into her sweet mouth. A soft sound in her throat made him hard in seconds.

Denying himself had been taking its toll. He woke every morning with a painful cockstand that left him in such a foul mood that his servants kept a wide berth. And his growly demeanor had done nothing to ease his daughter's fear of him. Gabby was the answer to every ill he had, but she was also the problem. He didn't know whether to further their encounter or send her away as quickly as possible.

That was untrue. He knew what he needed to do, but he was short on willpower. Footsteps outside the tapestry made his decision for him.

"You'll want to see this," Corby said, his voice muffled.

Damn. He directed Gabby toward a tall cabinet that might fit both of them if they crammed together. If not, at least he could hide her.

When he jerked the cabinet doors open, she recoiled. "Ew!"

Primitive phalluses tied with leather strips hung from pegs inside. "Get in," he whispered harshly. "Your reputation is at stake."

She allowed him to deposit her in the cabinet. He barely fit with her, but he was able to pull the doors closed behind him in time.

There was a loud sigh from the room. "This is what was so important for me to see?"

It sounded like Thorne.

"Oh!" Corby's surprise was evident in his tone. He tried to cover it with a chortle. "You seem unimpressed. I have the largest collection of erotic art in London."

"Yes," a third voice piped up, likely Ledbery's, "the largest in all of England, I'd wager."

"Once you've seen one fornicating couple, you've seen them all," Thorne said in a bored tone.

Gabby began to shake, her bottom jostling against Anthony's erection. He wrapped his arm around her waist, thinking she was afraid, only to realize she was trying not to laugh.

"Don't you dare make a sound," he whispered in her ear, her suppressed laughter contagious. "You naughty girl."

The shaking increased until he knew she was going to get them discovered. He would take some lumps from her brothers for ruining her, but there would be no more questioning his claim to her.

"Shh, sweetheart." As much as he looked forward to marrying her, he didn't want her reputation ruined for his gain.

"I have no time for this nonsense," Thorne said. "I'm here to find a wife, not loiter in a dark room with you and Ledbery. I'll leave you two lovebirds to it, though."

"Lovebirds!"

"We aren't like that," Ledbery protested.

"I couldn't care less," Thorne said, his voice fading as he left the room.

Anthony wasn't certain if the other men had followed or stayed behind, so he tightened his grip when Gabby tried to move. Her sweet scent filled his nose, blocking out the mustiness of the cabinet. "Listen."

She held still as he strained to detect any noise outside the cabinet.

They stood that way for a long time, Gabby's derriere snugly nestled against his crotch. Her breathing sounded uneven, or maybe that was his breath.

"Anthony," she murmured, "I think one of those *things* is touching me."

"It's close quarters. Wiggle a bit and maybe that will help."

She shimmied, managing to arouse him even more. This must be what hell was like.

"I can still feel it," she hissed. "On my back."

Heat rushed into his face. "Yes. Sorry, love. I think it's all clear now."

"Is that *you*?"

He pushed against the doors and light burst into the cabinet. They were alone, but he didn't know how long they had before Corby tried to show off his collection to another gentleman.

Grabbing her hand, he helped her climb from their hiding spot and dragged her toward the tapestry. She jerked his wrist to get his attention.

"What is it?" he asked.

She looked up at him with smoky gray eyes. "I don't mind that it was you."

He really couldn't resist. Clutching her chin, he tipped her face up for one more hard kiss. "I don't know how much longer I can court you, Gabby. I want to marry you badly."

She raised a slender brow. "So we can do that?" She pointed to an etching of another couple in a creative, yet reasonable, embrace.

"And several other *thats*," he said, grinning.

He checked the area outside of the tapestry and, finding it vacant, snuck from the room with Gabby in tow.

❦

Sebastian made several rounds of the gallery and drawing room where Lady Corby was serving refreshment before checking the terrace a second time. There was still no sign of Lady Gabrielle. And Ellis was missing too.

As he reentered the house, he spotted Lady Gabrielle on Ellis's arm headed toward the refreshment room. Her cheeks boasted a rosy glow and her normally perfect coiffure was mussed slightly. Flames licked at Sebastian's belly. The damned rogue had been playing a game of slap and tickle with her. She turned an adoring gaze on Ellis, and Sebastian knew he'd been beat.

He hated losing.

Worse, he hated losing to Ellis, but this wasn't a carriage race. Nor was Gabrielle a wide-eyed wall-flower shaking in her slippers when he or Ellis asked for their dance cards in a bid to see who could dance with the most neglected ladies.

That had been Sebastian's idea. He had become depressed seeing the same ladies lined up along the ballroom walls, the hopeful sparkle in their eyes dimming with each unsuccessful ball. The poor girls had reminded him too much of his sister, Eve.

Every inch of him clenched in anger as it dawned on him what was really at stake. Lady Gabrielle had been the path to his sister's salvation. Marriage to a duke's daughter would have smoothed Eve's way back into society, and Lady Gabrielle would have helped her. She was too tenderhearted to do otherwise.

His sister would have had a strong ally and Sebastian, a wife he couldn't help but love eventually. He had been close to having everything he wanted, until Ellis came back to Town. Ellis probably hadn't even wanted Lady Gabrielle until Corby told him that Sebastian was courting her.

Bloody thief.

He spun on his heel to leave Corby Place before he caused a scene he would later regret and jerked back in surprise. "What the hell do you want now?" he growled at Corby and Ledbery.

The two miscreants wore slimy grins that made Sebastian want to wash his hands. They were slipperier than a whore's— Well, he didn't trust them and he would leave it at that.

Ledbery clamped an arm around Sebastian's shoulders. "Come have a drink, Thorne."

Sebastian shook him off. "I only drink with my friends."

Corby faked a sniffle. "Why, Lord Thorne. Now you've hurt our feelings."

"A heart is required for feelings, and rumor has it you haven't a whole one between the two of you."

"Really?" Corby's cheekbones jutted in his face when his smile widened. Everything about the viscount was too sharp, including his cunning gaze. "We heard a more interesting rumor circulating the Den of Iniquity this week."

"I'm not interested." Sebastian pushed Corby's shadow aside, which was no real feat since Ledbery weighed little more than a scrawny rooster. His long, skinny neck and scarlet waistcoat completed the image.

Sebastian stalked for the exit.

"A certain lady would be interested," Corby called.

Sebastian stopped and cursed under his breath. If they were referring to another rumor about Eve, someone was going to pay with his blood. He turned toward them, his own smile dangerous. "Let's have that drink, gentlemen."

"Splendid," Corby said.

He wouldn't be so pleased once Sebastian called them both out for slander.

Fourteen

GABBY STOOD IN THE FOYER OF LORD AND LADY Norwick's second London house, Kennell Place, with close to two hundred other guests. Their excited voices swelled within the massive space and echoed off the marble columns.

Anthony edged closer to her. "This is madness. Are you certain you want to stay?"

A gentleman rammed into Anthony and knocked him flush against her. His arms steadied her when she wobbled. She leaned her body into his while she had the opportunity. Of course, she wanted to stay.

The past few days had gone smashingly well with Anthony, and the opportunity to explore the massive home and all its nooks and crannies with him was irresistible.

"Lana says the countess has the best parties," she said.

According to Drew, some circles considered Lady Norwick's parties to be scandalous. He'd scowled when his wife had reassured Gabby's mother the rumors about the countess were exaggerated. He hadn't contradicted Lana, however.

At the moment, Gabby's brother was glowering at her and Anthony, so she eased from his embrace.

Lana looked up into her husband's face and snorted with laughter. "Drew, you're behaving just like Jake did when *you* were courting me."

Drew's jaw dropped. "I am not. Your brother was a raving madman."

Lana's brows shot up, and she laughed when her brother, Jake Hillary, who was standing close by with his wife, elbowed Drew.

"A madman, am I?" Mr. Hillary quipped. "At least Ellis is *properly* courting your sister, you scoundrel."

Although Gabby didn't doubt Drew had been more than improper in his pursuit of Lana, Mr. Hillary seemed to have forgiven him. The men exchanged good-natured jabs and began telling embarrassing stories on each other until Lord and Lady Norwick climbed the stairs halfway and turned to address the crowd. A ripple of shushing sounds traveled the room, and the roar died down.

Lord Norwick cleared his throat. "Lady Norwick and I welcome one and all to Kennell Place. It is our pleasure you could join us for what is sure to be an enjoyable afternoon, since my clever wife dreamed up the event."

Raucous applause followed along with a humorous suggestion from a gentleman behind Gabby that the earl shut his mouth and let the lady speak.

Lord Norwick's hand flew to his chest as if he'd been gravely wounded, but the smile never left his face. "The masses have spoken, Lady Norwick."

The countess, a tiny woman with a very large

personality, signaled for everyone to quiet down again.
Once she had the crowd's attention, she explained the
rules of the treasure hunt she had organized, waving
her hands for emphasis. There were many treasures
hidden throughout the mammoth house and gardens.
The first couple to find all the items would be declared
the winners.

"Now, pick your partners—one gentleman to
one lady—and gather a list from one of the footmen
around the room. May the best couple win."

Gabby cared nothing about winning the game. She
was simply looking forward to the chance to wander
the corridors and explore rooms. There was no telling
what masterpieces graced the walls of Kennell Place.
People shoved forward, jostling to get their lists first.
Anthony's arm went around her waist protectively and
kept her from stumbling.

"Watch out for her," Drew said to Anthony as he
pulled Lana close to keep an eager young man from
trampling her.

Gabby lost sight of her family members as the
crowd carried them deeper into the house. Anthony
managed to grab a paper, then led her toward the
servants' domain. They stopped in a narrow corridor,
and Gabby leaned against the patched plaster wall to
catch her breath.

He read the list aloud. "A model ship, statue of
Aphrodite—a portrait of the fifth viscount's dog?"

Gabby returned his smile and shrugged.

"A rare specimen of orchid, the family Bible…" He
released a forceful breath. "There are at least twenty
items on the list. This could take hours."

"Hours alone sound lovely to me."

A corner of his mouth inched upward. "Remind me to send a thank-you around to Lady Norwick later."

When he held out his hand, she took it and they hurried toward the servants' staircase. The corridor on the second floor was congested but orderly, unlike how it had been moments before in the foyer.

"I'm surprised the earl doesn't mind having his home invaded by guests like this," Anthony said.

"Kennell Place belonged to Lady Norwick before they married. Lana said the countess never liked the house and compares it to a prison."

"That explains the reason she and her husband reside elsewhere."

Gabby meandered the passageway with Anthony trailing at a leisurely pace. He made no complaints when she stopped to admire a painting or run her fingers over the contours of a marble. How she would love to feel the smooth, cool stone without her glove.

She sighed wistfully as she dropped her hand from the statue. "Such a beautiful piece. It's a shame it is rarely enjoyed."

When she looked up, Anthony was watching her, his eyes deep blue and shimmering.

"What is it?" she asked. "Did I say something wrong?"

He shook his head. "Come with me."

Taking her arm, he led her back to the staircase. They climbed the stairs in silence. Gabby didn't care where they went, so she didn't question where he was leading her. Reaching the third floor, he guided her down the abandoned corridor, checking each room as they passed.

"Yes, this is perfect," he said as he nudged the door open with his boot. Golden light from the windows flooded the sitting room. Leaving her just inside the entrance, he crossed to the double glass doors and threw them open. A burst of fresh air sent the gauzy curtains fluttering, and the light scent of honeysuckle clinging to the stone walls outside infused the room. Beyond the doors was a balcony enclosed with rusted wrought iron.

He beckoned to her. She walked into the sunlight, drawn outside by the intricate pattern of the gardens below. She rested her hands on the railing and studied the manicured hedges and varying shades of green.

Anthony took up position beside her, his arm brushing against hers. "Tell me what you see."

"I see the same thing as you, a garden."

He turned to face her and leaned back against the railing. "There has to be something more. There always has been with you. What is hidden in the garden?"

Prickly heat invaded her body. She felt self-conscious with him staring at her. She hadn't come to Kennell Place to sketch, and yet she couldn't help viewing the garden through her artist's eyes. The hedges curved gracefully, but there were strict limits imposed on nature. She didn't care for the contrived orderliness.

When she glanced at Anthony, her heart skipped. His eyes were clear and unguarded, as if he were allowing her a view into his soul.

She shook off the silly sentiment and smiled. His intensity didn't subside.

"When I was a boy, I came to your home to escape from Ellis Hall."

Part of her had known life at home hadn't been good for him. On more than one occasion, she had overheard whispers about Lady Ellis and her bad nerves, which required increasing amounts of cordial to calm. It seemed everyone had held sympathy for the countess after her husband and oldest son had drowned, all except Gabby's mama.

She had never heard her mother speak ill of anyone, but Mama had once come close when she reminded Lady Eldridge that Anthony's mother still had a son and the countess shouldn't forget it. Gabby hadn't understood her mother's meaning until much later. Anthony had practically lived at their home, because her family was the only one to pay him any notice.

She reached for his hand. "I'm sorry."

"Don't be," he said, smiling softly. "You were one of the few people who made everything better."

"How? I pestered you to no end. You and Drew were always looking for ways to lose me."

He entwined their fingers; his gaze lowered. "I'll admit, you were a pest at times, but you helped me, too."

When he didn't continue, she gently jerked his hand. "*Tell* me. Don't leave me guessing."

His expression softened, the hard lines around his mouth disappearing. "All I had was ugliness in my life, but then you showed me things I was missing. I still can't see animals in cloud formations, and I don't notice a blade of grass has more than one color to it, at least not on my own. But you do, and the world becomes more interesting and beautiful through your eyes."

He drew her closer, their hands still joined in a link she didn't wish to break.

"I needed you, Gabby," he said as he smoothed her hair behind her ear. "I still need you."

Cautiously, she allowed her gaze to travel from their joined hands and up his chest before meeting his bedchamber eyes. Her breath grew shallow. He had looked at her this same way at Ellis Hall that day. And oh, how she wanted to kiss him again.

She tossed her arms around his neck and pulled him to her. His lips slammed against hers as his arms circled her waist. They stumbled back into the room, their lustful urges knocking them off balance. Anthony caught the door frame and spun them around. A soft "oof" escaped her as her back banged against the wall.

He drew back. "Egads! Did I hurt you?"

She shook her head. His body held her trapped against the wall, exactly where she wanted to be. With each exhale he took, his warm breath danced along her neck, sending tingles to every part of her.

"You are so beautiful, sweetheart." He kissed her temple, then her cheek. "Sometimes I can't believe my good fortune."

When he shifted his weight to release her, she tightened her grip on his jacket. "Kiss me again."

Doubt clouded his blue eyes.

"*Please*, Anthony."

He swayed into her and captured her mouth. Gabby sighed as his lips softly nibbled hers. She had never kissed anyone besides him, and she could be content never kissing anyone but him for the rest of her days.

He urged her lips apart and she welcomed the taste of him. He was mint and chocolate. And heady. Her head was becoming fuzzy like the first time she'd had wine with dinner. His hand splayed over her ribs, his thumb sliding along the underside of her breast.

Touch me, she silently pleaded. She wanted to feel the rush of excitement coursing through her veins as she had months ago. The words hovered on the tip of her tongue, yet she couldn't gather the nerve to say them.

Laughter from the corridor floated into the room, still far away. Anthony slowly broke their kiss and rested his forehead against hers with his eyes closed. "Blast," he mumbled.

"I don't want to stop."

"You are doing nothing for my willpower, darling." He chuckled, but it sounded strained. Reaching into his pocket, he pulled out the list Lady Norwick's servants had distributed. "We should at least try to find one or two items, or Drew will wonder what we have been doing."

She frowned. "Surely nothing he hasn't done already. He is a hypocrite."

Anthony stole one more kiss, then gently patted her derriere. "Don't be too hard on him. He only wants to protect you."

She knew he was correct, but her brother was still annoying beyond the pale.

Snagging the list from Anthony, she studied it. "Well, I know where to find Cupid's arrow. I spotted it in the garden."

"You saw an arrow in the garden?"

"Didn't you? It's part of the sundial."

Anthony shrugged sheepishly. "I had a more pleasing view distracting me."

❧

Gabby and Anthony had found a little less than half the list when Lady Norwick called time. Arm in arm, they strolled outside to find tables had been carried onto the lawn and lanterns strung. Music drifted from the terrace where a string quartet had been set up. The Norwicks' garden reminded Gabby of a miniature version of Vauxhall Gardens.

"Would you like a glass of lemonade, my lady?" Anthony asked.

"That would be lovely." She was parched after traipsing around the east wing all afternoon, and she wasn't too proud to admit she was ravenous as well.

While Anthony went in search of a drink, she tried to locate her family, but they weren't in sight. She wandered to an empty garden bench away from the crowd to wait for Anthony when a touch at her elbow made her jump. A shadow fell over her.

Lord Thorne grinned. "I wasn't certain you were in attendance, Lady Gabrielle. Do you mind if I join you?"

Her gaze darted toward the queue where Anthony was stuck behind four people waiting for refreshments. She gave a brief nod and Thorne dropped down beside her.

"I have decided to accept Lord Ellis's proposal when he asks," she said, unable to meet his eyes.

"Hmm…"

"You see, Lord Ellis and I have known each other a long time, and I believe we are well suited. I hope you won't hold it against me. I'm truly sorry."

Thorne pressed his lips tightly together and a worry line formed at his eyebrow. "I fear you're making an unwise choice. Ellis is not everything he seems."

She resisted the urge to roll her eyes. The man did not easily surrender. "Be that as it may, I believe I know Lord Ellis better than you. I trust him."

"Then you misplace your trust."

Gabby was taken aback by his direct manner. "What do you mean? What has you making such bold judgments?"

His dark gaze shot around the area, perhaps in search of Anthony. "He has secrets involving his daughter."

"I'm already aware Lord Ellis has a child from his first marriage."

"The girl isn't from his marriage." Even though he had been speaking quietly, he lowered his voice even more. "She is his by-blow."

Gabby crossed her arms with a huff. "Really, my lord. Who has been feeding you this nonsense?"

"It isn't nonsense. You must know I would never spread rumors. I'm only telling you this to save you from heartache. I investigated the claim myself, and it's true."

"Investigated how? Have you any skills?"

A corner of his mouth twitched. "I've been told I have. I know how to ask questions, to be sure, and seeing the girl put any doubts I had to rest."

"Well, I don't know what you think you were able to deduce from catching a glimpse of the girl. I hardly think you would be able to determine her parentage from a look." She hopped up from the bench, tempted to shake her finger in his face. "And you shouldn't go around goggling young girls. People will start talking about *you*."

She intended to march away, but his hand at her wrist halted her. Thorne gazed up at her with his fathomless brown eyes. "Please, ask him about his daughter. You should know the truth before you pledge fidelity to him."

Her stomach took a dive. He appeared sincere.

"What does her parentage matter?" she asked in a soft voice.

"It's the reason his first wife ran away. No matter what you think, I care what happens to you, my lady. Don't play the fool for Ellis."

But she had played that role many times. She was an expert at it now.

Fifteen

WHEN ANTHONY RETURNED WITH REFRESHMENTS, HE found Gabby seated at a table with her family and the Norwicks. Everyone was laughing together except Gabby. She wore a wan smile and picked at the floral tablecloth. Present, but not there.

Anthony sat beside her, passed her the glass of lemonade, and took a sip of his drink.

"Thank you," she murmured, not looking at him.

She played with her glass as the teasing between Drew, Jake Hillary, and Norwick continued. She had no witty responses when Anthony was drawn into their playful arguments, nor did she have anything to say when the ladies tired of the men's antics and began a side conversation.

Her lemonade remained untouched until it had likely grown tepid. Nothing appeared out of sorts with her family, so he couldn't determine the cause of her sudden change in demeanor.

"Would you care to take a turn about the garden?" he asked.

She met his gaze for the first time since he had sat

down. Her eyes seemed a cooler shade of gray, duller somehow. She nodded.

Anthony assisted her from the chair and led her away from the crowd. As they moved deeper into the garden, the noise of the gathering became muffled. A thread of music from the quartet carried on the air.

He guided her toward a gazebo at the back of the property. "Something is troubling you."

"Yes, but I don't know the reason I'm bothered. It's a matter of little consequence."

They entered the gazebo and Gabby dropped his arm. She wandered to the railing to lean her elbows on it. He took the place beside her and mimicked her stance.

"Perhaps it will help to talk about it."

She pursed her lips and wiggled them side to side as if considering whether to confide in him. It wasn't like her to be unforthcoming with her thoughts or feelings.

"You may speak freely with me, Gabby."

"It's your daughter," she blurted. She turned to face him. "I heard a rumor about her, and I'm troubled by it, even though God knows it is none of my concern."

He stiffened, his body arming itself for battle. Annabelle was the only person he loved as much as Gabby. If it came to a choice between Gabby and Annabelle, however, he couldn't turn his daughter out.

"What did you hear?"

She frowned slightly. "I'm sorry, Anthony. It truly makes no difference to me if your daughter is illegitimate. I can accept her all the same."

Her words slammed into him, making his head reel. How did anyone know of his daughter's past?

He had done everything in his power to keep the secret hidden.

"Annabelle is my child. She has my *name*."

Gabby backed up a step. "I didn't intend to upset you."

He captured her arm when it appeared she might flee. "I'm not upset with you, but I am going to thrash whoever is spreading rumors about my child."

She released a breathy laugh. "Oh, thank heavens it's a lie. I know I said it wasn't my concern, but I wasn't completely honest with you. I would be troubled to some degree by her origins. It's only natural."

Natural? Annabelle was an innocent. Why should she bear the stigma of her mother's infidelity? "Tell me who's spreading this rumor."

Gabby's mouth dropped open, then she snapped it shut.

"Tell me, Gabrielle. I have a right to know."

She licked her lips. "But you said you plan to thrash him, and I don't believe he intended any malice. He was concerned when I said I planned to accept your proposal."

"Thorne," he bit out. Anthony was going to do more than thrash him. In one swift move, Sebastian Thorne had left Anthony's life in a precarious place. His daughter's reputation was at stake, and it was clear Gabby would take issue with his daughter's parentage once she learned the truth. This wasn't a game to Anthony.

He released Gabby's arm to run his fingers through his hair. *Damnation.* He needed time to think.

"I doubt Lord Thorne has told anyone else about

Annabelle," she said, "but I could speak with him. Once he knows the rumor is false, he will forget about it."

"No," he snapped. "I don't want you anywhere near him."

The last thing he needed was Thorne's continued interference. He had to discover the source of the rumors about Annabelle and put a stop to them, then find a way to tell Gabby the truth without losing her.

Another couple was strolling along the pebbled walkway headed in their direction. His discussion with Gabby would require privacy, and they wouldn't have any at the party.

Her arms were crossed and her dark glare was aimed at him. Well, he'd stepped in it bad this time. He feigned a smile. "I apologize for being sharp with you, sweetheart."

One dark eyebrow arched. "Do you have no apology for ordering me about like a hound?"

This time his grin was real. "A good scratch behind the ears ought to suffice." When he reached for her ear, she slapped his hand away and laughed.

"I'll never roll over for you, Lord Ellis. I'm not the submissive type."

"You are the only way I would ever want you."

When she accepted his escort, the spark had returned to her eyes. He only hoped he could keep it there in the end.

❧

Gabby's sisters were waiting in her chambers when she returned from the Norwicks' party.

Lizzie bounded from her perch on the window seat beside Katie and grabbed Gabby's shoulders. "Tell us everything. What was it like attending the notorious countess's party? Was it as scandalous as you thought?"

She gave her sister a censorious look. "Elizabeth Forest, have you been eavesdropping again?"

Lizzie didn't even blush. "How else am I to know what goes on outside of Talliah House?"

Indeed. This would have been her sisters' first Season if Gabby hadn't failed her family. Yet they never expressed any bitterness for their circumstances. She cupped Lizzie's cheek, her heart swollen with love for her dear siblings.

"We should walk in the park tomorrow," Gabby said. "Perhaps you will glean some interesting information to tide you over for a bit."

"Splendid!" Lizzie threw her arms around her and almost knocked them both to the ground. When she released Gabby, she bit her bottom lip. "Oh, dear. I have nothing to wear. I should summon Magda at once."

She rushed from the chamber, mumbling under her breath.

Katie lowered her book and smiled. "You realize she won't sleep a wink tonight."

"Aren't you excited to escape the house, too?" Gabby sat beside her sister, sinking into the plush cushion. No wonder Katie preferred to read in her chambers.

Her sister shrugged one shoulder. "Perhaps if we were to visit the lending library."

"I will do even better and give you what's left of my pin money so you can purchase your own book."

Her sister took her hand and squeezed. "You have no cause to feel guilty, Gabrielle. You don't need to try to make amends."

"I don't feel guilty."

Katie's crooked smile looked so much like their brother's. She was too clever for her own good, just like Drew. When she tried to raise her book again, Gabby reached out to stop her.

"Very well. I might have a bit of remorse, but I want to make life more pleasant for you and Liz because I love you."

"And we love you. You needn't do anything to earn it."

"Thank you, kitten." There was no sense in debating it with her sister. In her heart, Gabby knew she owed Liz and Katie, even if they refused to acknowledge it. "And you will allow me to purchase you a new book."

❧

Anthony and his servant entered the mist-choked alley leading to the Den of Iniquity, Thorne's favorite gambling hell. The jackass had disappeared from the Norwicks' party before Anthony had located him, and a stop by the club had yielded nothing. A matter like this couldn't be ignored, so he would hunt Thorne all night if necessary. Anthony had to make Thorne understand that using his daughter to gain an advantage was unacceptable. Annabelle's future could suffer irreparable damage.

He tightened his grip on his flintlock's handle as they moved farther into the darkness. Remaining on alert, he listened for the presence of footpads, even as they reached the secret entrance of the gambling den.

"State your business," a voice rumbled from the dark.

"Lord Goldfinch sends his regards."

A guard materialized from the fog; gleaming eyes stared out from a shadowed face. "Disarm yourself."

Anthony handed his pistol to his coachman. "This shouldn't take long. Wait with the coach."

"Yes, sir." His man vanished into the dark, his footsteps echoing on the cobbled path.

The door creaked open and a dull river of light spilled down the narrow staircase inside the entrance.

"Welcome to hell, milord." The man sounded bored, as if he'd repeated the same words countless times.

Anthony barreled up the stairs, paused at the top, and made a visual sweep of the room. Pungent tobacco smoke hovered on the air, curling around the gamblers like a giant snake. He blinked against the sting to his eyes.

Thorne had to be here. He hadn't been at Brooks's or any of the taverns he was known to frequent. Eventually Anthony spotted him slumped over the faro table with a thin pile of blunt in front of him. The dealer called out the card as he pulled it from the box then raked up Thorne's money along with all the other men's.

Crackbrains.

Only idiots came to the Den hopeful of leaving with any gold still in their pockets. How could the baron think he was any good for Gabby when he was so careless with his money?

With a renewed sense of indignation, Anthony marched across the room and jerked Thorne from his chair by the scruff of his neck.

"What the hell?" Thorne stumbled back as the chair tipped and banged against the floor. Anthony swung for his nose before he had time to get his bearings.

Thorne deflected the blow. "You mad bastard. What has gotten into you?"

"You know what this is about."

"I know you're a damned thief!" Thorne's eyes narrowed to slits and he pounced, catching Anthony off guard. They slammed into the floor; every bone in Anthony's body shuddered.

With an animalistic roar, Thorne drew his fist back. He'd always fought like a demon from hell, but Anthony was usually pulling him off some poor sap. Not on the receiving end of his temper. He caught the baron's fist before it plowed into his face and wrenched his arm to the side. Thorne toppled to the left, his head rapping against the wooden planks.

Thorne cursed, his eyes flaming black as Anthony scrambled for position. He snatched the baron's waistcoat and drove his fist into Thorne's mouth before he could strike again. A spray of blood splattered Anthony's cravat. He drew back to hammer Thorne again, but someone snagged his arm from behind and roughly hauled him to his feet.

Before Thorne could move, two of the Den's henchmen lugged him from the floor, too. The baron bucked against their hold, cursing and nearly breaking free before the bigger oaf delivered a gut-punch that doubled him over. Thorne rested his hands on his knees as he coughed and spit up blood. Anthony stopped struggling before he received the same treatment.

The owner, Sly Si—referred to as sir within his hearing since he was as large as an oak—frowned at them from the upper floor. He nodded sharply to his men.

They dragged Anthony and Thorne toward the entrance.

"Take it outside," Si's man said before tossing Anthony down the stairwell. He caught his elbow against the wall and gained his feet before he tumbled headfirst.

Thorne's captors took it easier on him—perhaps because he was still wheezing from the stomach blow—and released him with a hearty slap on his back.

"Until tomorrow night, Thorne."

The baron glowered at Anthony, panting. Blood trickled from a cut on his lower lip and he swiped his sleeve across his mouth. Slowly he straightened and jerked his waistcoat back into place. "Bloody Philistine." Thorne passed by him on the stairs, his head held high like he was blasted royalty.

"This isn't over," Anthony called then followed him. He wiggled his fingers to battle against the stiffness setting into his knuckles. Damn, Thorne had a hard head.

Silence hung between them as they left the building. They walked side by side down the alley, the fog surrounding them.

"If we are murdered by thieves, I blame you," Thorne said.

Anthony came to a halt, while Thorne kept walking. "If you had kept your damned mouth shut, we wouldn't be here."

Thorne retraced his steps and stopped in front of Anthony. "Someone must look out for Lady Gabrielle's interests. Were you planning to tell her?"

So he did know what this was about and he wasn't denying his part.

"I'll still tell her," Anthony said through clenched teeth, "but this isn't about Gabby. I can't have people speculating about my daughter's origins. She's an innocent girl."

"So is Lady Gabrielle." Thorne moved closer, his perfect nose begging to be knocked out of joint. "She should be aware of any scandals associated with her future husband."

"That's hypocritical, given your father's history and Miss Thorne's unfortunate situation."

"Don't you dare speak ill of my sister," he growled.

"I have nothing but the greatest respect for your sister. You, however, are despicable."

Blood continued to drip from Thorne's lip, lending him the appearance of a savage animal when he bore his teeth. "You think *I'm* despicable? Well, I have never kept my past a secret from Lady Gabrielle. Can you say the same?"

"My past is my concern. And if you ever spread tales about my daughter again"—he thumped Thorne's chest—"you'll have more than a bloody lip when I'm finished with you."

"I would like to see you try. Without the advantage of surprise, I would make short work of you."

Anthony scoffed and continued the long walk down the alley. Thorne fell into step with him, both of them sullen.

Angered by the other man's presence, Anthony walked faster. The baron stepped up his pace and pulled ahead.

Bollocks! Everything was a contest with the jackass. And Anthony was damned, because he wanted to beat Thorne more than ever. He increased his speed until he was at a walk-run. The baron's head snapped toward him when Anthony came up beside him and broke into an easy jog. So did Anthony. By God, he wasn't going to lose to the ungrateful bastard.

Not for the first time, Anthony regretted the day he'd come to Thorne's defense at Eton. Thorne had become a target for bullies who thought his father had bats in the belfry. Anthony must have been mad himself to intervene. Not only had Thorne been unappreciative of Anthony's assistance, the baron had been trying to prove his superiority ever since.

Thorne broke into a run, his boots slamming against the cobblestones.

"Come back here." Anthony dashed after him.

He grabbed for and caught the hem of Thorne's coat to slow him. Throwing his arm around his neck, he jostled for control. The baron fought back, twisting and bucking, until they banged into a wall. Thorne threw his head back and connected with Anthony's nose. Cursing and wrestling with Thorne, he tried to slam him to the ground.

"Who goes there?" a shaky voice called from the fog. "I have a firearm, and I will use it."

They froze.

"It's only Thorne and Ellis." Anthony released the baron and Thorne snarled at him. "You have nothing to fear. Lower your weapon."

A muted light traveled down the alley. When the gentleman and his footman reached them, he held the lantern high, blinding Anthony.

"Have you been fighting?" a much too cheerful voice asked.

Anthony groaned under his breath. "Ledbery. Fancy meeting you this fine evening."

"There's blood. You have been fighting, haven't you?"

Thorne shouldered past Anthony harder than necessary.

"Who threw the first punch?" Ledbery asked.

Thorne jabbed a finger in Anthony's direction. "He attacked me and I assure you, it was unprovoked. He should be carted off to Bedlam."

Ledbery's smile fell. "Damnation. Were there any witnesses?"

"Only half the occupants of the Den," Thorne spat.

Ledbery cursed again. "What's the matter with you, Thorne? You have the temper of the devil himself. I had money on you throwing the first punch."

Anthony didn't have time for any more of this nonsense. He started down the alley toward his carriage. "Remember what I said, Thorne. The lady wants nothing to do with you. Steer clear of her."

When Anthony reached the end of the alley, Thorne's voice floated from the fog. "She will."

Sixteen

WHEN GABBY AND HER SISTERS LEFT TALLIAH HOUSE en route to Hyde Park the next morning, she purposefully selected the least direct path. There weren't many people about yet since it was still early, which made it the perfect time for them to venture out.

"Isn't the park the other way?" Katie asked when Gabby led them in the opposite direction.

She opened her parasol and kept up her brisk pace. "I believe you are correct, kitten."

Her sisters fell behind with the footman assigned to accompany them. They whispered back and forth.

"But why are we going this way?" Katie said.

"Shh. Let's see where she takes us."

Gabby smiled at Lizzie's eagerness to alter their usual course to the park. She had known her sister would appreciate a chance to see a bit of London on foot, not that they would go anyplace dangerous. Still, Gabby hadn't chosen their detour to please her sister. All night she had been plagued by Lord Thorne's cryptic words at the Norwicks' party.

How could seeing Anthony's daughter lay the

baron's questions to rest? It made no sense. She should dismiss it as balderdash, but that niggling feeling that something wasn't right wouldn't go away. Calling at Anthony's town house was too scandalous to contemplate, but passing by while on a lovely stroll with her sisters wouldn't raise any eyebrows.

It wasn't likely she would catch a glimpse of Annabelle, so it probably would be a wasted trip. But she'd made a bargain with herself. If she didn't see Anthony's daughter, she would put the matter from her mind. Or she would try. Doubting him didn't sit well with Gabby.

Lizzie came forward and linked arms with her. "What is it like to be on the marriage mart?"

Katie came up on her other side, apparently having given up her quest to determine where they were headed. There they were, just three sisters who were also the best of friends. She snuggled them closer, her heart lighter for a moment.

In her first Season, Gabby had been deemed a diamond of the first water. She'd had more suitors than she needed, and she had tossed away a good number of men who would have made a decent husband in favor of Lt. MacFarland.

Lizzie and Katie wouldn't make the same mistake she had, of course.

"It's a little tiring this go around," she admitted, "but you both will have a marvelous time. The gentlemen will line up to sign your dance cards and you'll have suitors galore."

Katie frowned. "I wouldn't think I would care for many suitors. One is all I require."

"Not me," Lizzie said. "I want my choice of hand-some men like Gabby has."

Katie glanced at Gabby. "Wouldn't it be easier if you had but one gentleman, and it was the one you desired?"

"That it would," she answered with a chuckle.

Lizzie flashed her dimples. "I will take Lord Thorne if you plan to toss him aside."

Gabby playfully wrinkled her nose. "How thoughtful, my dear."

She relayed some of the sights she had seen at balls this Season, and answered Lizzie's unending questions about the rumors she had read in the gossip rags. Not that she was supposed to have access to such things, but Mama didn't know and their oldest brother, Luke, often looked the other way if he didn't see the harm.

As they neared Anthony's town house, she slowed her pace, dragging on Lizzie's arm.

"Why are you slowing?"

"I have a pebble in my shoe," she lied and pretended to limp. "I should sit and remove it."

She hobbled over to Anthony's front stoop and sat. It was a bold move, but she couldn't have her sisters rushing her if she hoped to spy a bit. She took her time shaking out the imaginary pebble and listened for sounds from within the house.

The footman who had been sent to escort them leaned against a lamppost with a frown, seemingly disgruntled with his duties that morning.

After a while, Lizzie cocked a hip and sighed. "Will you please hurry? There's nothing interesting here, and you promised Katie a trip to the lending library after the park."

Katie's all-knowing gaze lingered on the house a moment before meeting Gabby's. "I don't mind waiting."

Lizzie didn't miss the silent exchange. Her eyebrows lifted. "Is there something interesting about this town house? Who lives here?"

Gabby felt the blood rushing to her cheeks. Blast her sisters for being too smart for their own good. She shoved on her boot and hopped up from the stoop. "How should I know?"

"Is it one of her suitors?" Lizzie whispered to her twin.

"Likely Lord Ellis."

Gabby tossed up her hands. "Oh, for heaven's sake! Does nothing escape your notice, Katherine?"

The girls giggled.

"Someone's in love," Lizzie said in a singsong voice, setting off another round of giggles.

Gabby tried to appear stern, but she had a hard time maintaining a frown. Even John the footman was smiling now. She linked arms with both sisters. "You two are naughty for teasing me. Let's go."

They had only reached the next stoop when a door slammed behind them. Gabby stopped to look over her shoulder.

A little girl with red curls was hopping down the steps one at a time.

"Annabelle, what did I say about leaving the house alone?" A harried woman with matching copper hair bustled down the stairs in the little girl's wake. "Your papa would be very displeased."

From the set to Annabelle's jaw, it didn't appear she cared what her papa thought. "I want to go to the park."

"I told you to give me a moment." The woman put on her bonnet and tied the strings to secure it. She hadn't noticed Gabby and her sisters had turned to gawk, so Gabby had a moment to take in the woman's appearance.

Her dress was of a good quality, although not as expensive as what Gabby and her sisters wore. Still, the woman's attire was finer than one would expect of a servant. Her physical appearance alone marked her as Annabelle's relation. Perhaps the late Lady Ellis's sister?

Gabby searched her memory for a vision of Lady Ellis dressed in her wedding gown. That had been the only time she had seen Anthony's wife, and that was through watery eyes. She had tried to pass her tears off as ones of happiness, but her heart had been breaking that day.

She had thought Lady Ellis resembled her in many ways, her hair just as dark and their heights similar. Gabby had wondered again why Anthony hadn't thought *her* good enough to marry instead of her look-alike. When she had learned Anthony was seeking a wife on the marriage mart, she had shored up her courage and written to him. She beseeched him to consider her since they had known each other most of their lives, got on well, and she had developed an affection for him. She realized she was perhaps a little too young to become a wife yet, but surely he would be willing to wait a year or two.

He'd sent back a nice letter to her brother with a message for her. *Please give my regards to Lady Bug and tell her to stay out of mischief.*

His dismissal had been humiliating. And weeks

later, when he had become betrothed to Miss Camilla Roth, all of Gabby's dreams were crushed.

Even now, the telltale itch of coming tears tickled her nose.

"We should go," she murmured as the woman looked up with a start.

"Oh! Pardon me," the woman said. "Are we barring the walkway?"

Her accent sounded Welsh. The little girl took her hand and peered back at Gabby and her sisters. "We're going to the park," she announced with a big smile.

When she spotted the footman, however, her smile faded and she inched closer to the woman. "I want to go, Mama."

Mama? The word struck Gabby with the force of lightning. She was stunned. Is that what Lord Thorne had meant? Had Anthony had a child with this woman and driven his wife to flee?

The woman patted Annabelle's head. "Now, now. There is no cause to be frightened, little one." She smiled apologetically at Gabby. "Pardon her, milady. She's a bit skittish around men."

Gabby's mouth was too dry to speak. She sensed her sisters moving closer to her as if to hold her up. It only reinforced her sense of despair. They knew it, too. She hadn't heard the girl wrong. This woman was her mother.

"No need to apologize," Katie said. "We were just on our way to the lending library, so if we could pass…"

"Of course." The woman scrambled out of the way, dragging Annabelle with her.

Gabby's sisters urged her forward. She was walking

through a heavy fog, the ground sucking at her feet so she could barely move.

No one spoke for a long time as they wandered the streets. She hadn't realized where they were going until Talliah House loomed at the end of the block.

"The library—"

"Shh." Lizzie tightened her grip on her arm.

"I promised."

"Another day, princess," Katie said.

She almost laughed at the absurdity of her younger sister using the nickname Drew had given to her. And yet the tenderness in Katie's voice made her want to cry.

They made it into the house and outside her chamber door when a sob burst from her. She dashed into her room and collapsed on the bed. If Anthony had a child by that woman, what did it mean? Did he love her? Why would she be living under his roof?

Her sisters joined her on the bed, each stroking her head and murmuring kind words.

"What exactly has happened?" she heard Lizzie ask.

"I'm uncertain."

Gabby knew. At least she thought she did. Anthony had sired a child with that woman, and he had laid claim to the girl. What if he had forced his wife into hiding so he could say Lady Ellis had been the one to give birth? Perhaps he had expected her to raise his lover's child just as he expected it from Gabby.

"No."

Her stomach pitched. Scrambling from the bed, she landed on her knees and groped for the chamber pot.

Her sisters sat helplessly on the edge of her bed as she tossed up her accounts.

"Oh, Gabby." Katie went to retrieve a dampened handkerchief, then held it against her forehead.

She closed her eyes, savoring the coolness on her feverish skin. "I'm wrong," she mumbled. "I must be."

She had known Anthony her entire life. He wasn't a calculating or cruel man.

Katie helped her to her feet. "Whatever you might think, you must talk to Lord Ellis. There must be a simple explanation."

"His mistress is living in his town house," Lizzie declared. "Any explanation would be a lie."

Katie scowled. "You don't know that, Elizabeth. Do not put such notions in her mind."

"Gabby isn't dense. She already had that idea or she wouldn't be distraught."

She pressed her fingers against her temples where a dull ache had begun. "Please, I need to lie down. I need quiet."

Breaking from her sister's hold, she tugged on the bellpull to summon her maid.

Liz and Katie hesitated, but when she moved to her dressing table without looking at them, they silently left her chambers.

When Magda arrived, Gabby requested her assistance undressing before climbing into bed and falling into a troubled sleep. It was late afternoon when she woke. At first, she felt the same happiness she had been experiencing for the last several days. But then she remembered Annabelle and the woman, and her breath rushed from her as if someone kicked her in the stomach. She curled into a ball and closed her eyes.

Magda checked on her several times throughout the day, but Gabby sent her away each time. It was getting dark when her mother swept into the room with Gabby's maid.

"Good heavens, Gabrielle. Why didn't you send Magda to retrieve me earlier? Are you ill, my darling?"

Magda ducked her head when Gabby looked her way, and went about lighting candles to chase the darkness from the room. It did nothing to dispel the darkness in Gabby's heart.

"I'm unwell, Mama. I don't think I should attend the Bexley Ball tonight. Will you offer regrets for me?"

"Of course you shouldn't attend, dear girl." Her mother perched on the side of the bed and smoothed her hand over Gabby's hair. Worry lines crisscrossed her brow. "I will send both of our regrets."

"I simply need to rest, Mama. You should go. You have been looking forward to Lady Bexley's ball all week."

"You are more important than Lady Bexley."

She captured her mother's hand and smiled weakly. "Please, Mama. I only want to sleep. I promise to send word if I feel too poorly."

Her mother's teeth worked her bottom lip. "Are you certain you don't need me?"

"I'll be fine." It was a lie, but Mama could do nothing to help her anyway.

When her mother reluctantly left her alone, Gabby curled onto her side and tried to fall asleep again to shut off her thoughts and the ache inside.

Seventeen

"HER GRACE THE DOWAGER DUCHESS OF FOXHAVEN." The footman's voice rang out above the crowd's garbled conversations, catching Anthony's attention. He couldn't see Gabby or her mother, but his pulse raced with the knowledge she had arrived at last. He circled the outside of the ballroom floor to intercept her.

His duties at the House of Lords had kept him occupied much later than he'd hoped, so he had been unable to call on Gabby earlier. Eagerly, he weaved through the crowd, intent upon signing her dance card and perhaps stealing a moment alone with her on the terrace.

He located Gabby's mother as he made progress through the maze of bodies, but he still didn't see Gabby. The duchess's smile appeared strained as he approached.

"Lord Ellis, it's always a pleasure to see you." Her greeting lacked its usual liveliness.

"Likewise, Your Grace. Did Lady Gabrielle arrive with you?"

Sebastian Thorne elbowed his way out of the

throng just in time to eavesdrop. Anthony shot him an icy look before ignoring him.

The duchess fiddled with her fan and sighed softly. "I'm afraid she won't be attending this evening, my lord. She's under the weather. I hope I didn't make a mistake in coming tonight, but she insisted I proceed without her."

Thorne stepped forward. "I'm certain Lady Gabrielle wouldn't have you go along without her if she is seriously ill. Your daughter is a sensible young lady."

Gabby's mother turned a hopeful gaze on the baron, then frowned when she noticed his swollen lip. "Are you all right, Lord Thorne?"

He absently touched his mouth. "This? It's nothing," he said, then added under his breath, "I've known misses to hit harder."

Anthony bit back a retort. He didn't want to air their grievance in the duchess's presence, especially when she seemed so troubled about Gabby.

"I do hope you're right about Gabrielle, my lord."

Thorne offered his arm. "I know so. And Lady Gabrielle would want you to enjoy yourself. May I offer my escort, Your Grace?"

Her smile brightened and she linked her arm with his. He tossed a smug grin in Anthony's direction as he led the duchess away.

What did it matter if Gabby's mother liked Thorne? The duchess liked everyone. Besides, she cared for Anthony like a son and had told him on more than one occasion that he held a special place in her heart. Let Thorne spend his time trying to win over Gabby's mother. Anthony was going to see Gabby.

He wouldn't put it past her to minimize her symptoms for her mother's sake. She carried too much guilt for events that were beyond her control, and she would do anything to save her family from further distress, even if it meant her suffering instead.

He ordered his coach and, while he waited, contemplated how he could see her. Calling at this late hour was not exactly proper. When he arrived at Talliah House half an hour later, he had a plan in mind, shaky as it might be.

The butler answered on Anthony's third knock. "Lord Ellis?"

"No need to be alarmed," he said. "I'm here to retrieve a book His Grace said I could borrow."

"The duke is not in, my lord, and I'm uncertain I would be able to assist you."

Anthony released the breath he'd been holding. It had been risky to use this excuse, but he had counted on Luke being out with his wife this evening. "I know where it's shelved in the library. The duke said I could help myself to any books that interest me."

Wesley opened the door wide to admit him as he'd done many times through the years. "Follow me, my lord."

Waving off his offer, Anthony headed for the stairway. "I know the way, Wes." He jogged up the stairs to discourage the old butler from following him.

Gabby's chambers were down the corridor to the left. Outside her door, he lightly tapped against the solid wood and received a muffled command to enter. He pushed the door open and found her sitting up in bed, leaning against the headboard.

"Anthony!" She jerked the counterpane up to her chin. "What are you doing here?"

"Your mother said you were ill. I wouldn't be able to sleep tonight without knowing how serious it is."

She wagged a finger toward the door, making him halt. "You have to leave. Magda will return any moment with a dinner tray."

God, he just wanted to go to her. She looked so beautiful with her dark hair falling around her shoulders. But she was right. He couldn't be found in her chambers.

"Do you promise you're all right?"

She hesitated, then nodded, her eyes closed. "I'll be fine. Now, please go. My family would be crushed if we were discovered together."

"I am going, love."

As he touched the door handle, she called out his name. She was sitting with her knees drawn to her chest, her arms hugging her legs. "When you went to Wales…"

"Yes?" He tried to his cover his unease with a smile, but his lips felt tight. He needed time he didn't have to tell her what had happened in Wales, how frightened he'd been when he had found the cottage destroyed and his daughter missing.

"You went for Annabelle."

"I did." He watched closely for any sign of reluctance. It couldn't be easy for any lady to accept another woman's child into her heart. How would she feel once she knew Annabelle wasn't even his? "Gabby, I love you and so will Annabelle. You'll see she's a lovely girl once you get to know her."

Her eyes filled with tears and she swiped at them furiously.

Anthony was across the room in three strides. He tenderly caressed her luxurious hair. She held herself stiff, obviously uncomfortable. But what did he expect? He had stolen into the chambers of an innocent.

"I'm going," he said with a sigh.

"You brought a woman back, too."

Gads. Mayfair had eyes and ears everywhere. "Miss Teague is Annabelle's nanny. They are inseparable."

Her gaze dropped to the counterpane and she picked at a thread. "I see."

Miss Teague was more than his daughter's nanny, but he couldn't get into their relationship without rehashing the entire tale. "We'll talk tomorrow when I may call on you properly. I promise to answer whatever questions you have." He dropped a kiss on her forehead. "Get some rest, my love."

⌘

Gabby hadn't been able to do as Anthony wished. Even when she slept, her dreams were troubled.

He had lied to her.

Annabelle had called Miss Teague her mama, and Gabby had no doubts about who Miss Teague was to Anthony's daughter. Gabby had been under the care of the same governess most of her childhood, and she had never been confused about who her mother was. The strong physical resemblance just confirmed the relationship.

Still, a small part of her hoped there was an explanation. Her heart couldn't bear to give Anthony up so easily. She would allow him another chance to tell her the truth when he called on her today.

A tiny flicker of optimism compelled her to climb from bed and dress for his visit. She was trying to distract herself with sketching in the drawing room when Wesley approached with his silver dish bearing Lord Thorne's calling card.

Gabby set her work aside. "Please show him in."

"Yes, milady."

The temptation to question Thorne further about his accusations was too great. He hadn't come out and accused Anthony of siring Annabelle with Miss Teague, but his insinuation was clear now. She wanted to know the source of his information, and if he truly believed the person was reliable.

When Lord Thorne entered the drawing room, his grim expression transformed with a smile. "Lady Gabrielle, how relieved I am to find you looking well this morning. Your mother painted a dire picture last night."

"Mama has a tendency to fret, but as you can see, I'm fine. Please have a seat." She gestured toward one of the chairs opposite the settee, but he took the place next to her. He kept a proper distance between them, but his gaze slid over her much too intimately.

"Are you certain you're well? There are circles under your eyes."

"You shouldn't notice such things, sir. And if you do, you certainly shouldn't point it out to a lady."

He ducked his head and gave her a chagrined half smile. "My apologies. I only meant to convey my concern. You must know nothing detracts from your beauty."

She chuckled in spite of herself. "You always have the words to smooth a lady's ruffled feathers, don't you? I should toss you out for false flattery."

All humor faded as he reached for her hand. "There's nothing false about my compliments. You take my breath away."

His eyes glittered darkly like the deepest lakes in Northumberland. Lord Thorne was a man with a passion to match her own. He was free with his emotions and generous with his adoration. He was everything she should want in a husband.

She blinked, breaking his hold over her, and extracted her hand from his. "I'm pleased you called, my lord. We didn't have time to finish our discussion at the Norwicks' party and I have questions."

"I'll answer anything you ask."

There was a dull throb in her chest. Anthony had made the same promise, but would he be this open with her? He always seemed guarded when she questioned him.

"Who is the source of this rumor?" she asked.

"Lords Corby and Ledbery. I don't consider them the most reliable gents, however." He adjusted his position on the settee, propping his arm on the seat back. "You should know I would never spread false tales about anyone. I had to seek out the truth for myself. I have no intentions of telling anyone else what I discovered, but you deserved the truth."

She turned toward him. "What is the truth, my lord?"

He hesitated, his lips parted. Her heart warmed toward him a little in that moment. He didn't want to hurt her. "The story goes Ellis's wife went missing not long after their marriage. After a few weeks passed, Ellis told everyone she was visiting family abroad, but no one acquainted with the lady and her parents had heard them speak of travel plans or relations outside of England. It was rather odd, but her parents left Town abruptly, too."

Before the Season was over? She could see the reason others might find their actions bizarre.

"After Lady Ellis left Town, Lord Ellis would go missing for weeks at a time," Thorne said. "No one knew of his whereabouts. It must have been a year before anyone received word that Lady Ellis had given birth in Wales and died in childbirth."

"Did she have family in Wales?"

"It doesn't appear so, and her parents weren't with her either. They returned to the country upon leaving London and kept to themselves. For a husband to allow his wife to travel abroad alone..." He frowned and shook his head. "Either Ellis was a fool or he lied about his wife's disappearance."

Gabby's nausea returned, and she took slow breaths to quell her sickness. "You—you make it sound sinister."

"That isn't my intention. I don't believe Ellis had anything to do with her death, at least not directly."

"Then what are you implying?"

His dark gaze held her entranced. "I believe Lady Ellis died of a broken heart, and I can't sit back and watch it happen to you, too. I'll do anything within my power to protect you."

She rubbed at the throb in her temple. "Why would she have died from a broken heart?"

She feared she knew the answer, but she needed to hear him say it.

He squeezed her shoulder, massaging her tight muscles. "I'm speculating about the cause of her death, but I've seen what heartache can do. I wasn't sure my sister would ever recover after Benjamin Hillary's betrayal. When I saw Ellis's daughter with her nanny, the pieces started coming together."

He continued to rub her shoulder muscles, and her headache eased but didn't disappear.

"Do you believe the nanny is Annabelle's mother?"

He blinked as if surprised by her question.

"I saw them together yesterday," she said. "The girl referred to the nanny as her mother."

The compassion in his eyes almost made her cry again. "I believe she is the girl's mother," he said, "and I think Ellis may have forced his wife to hide in Wales until the baby was born. There is no one to dispute his claim that Lady Ellis gave birth to his daughter."

Tears blurred Gabby's vision. "What does it all mean? Why did he keep Annabelle hidden away in Wales, and why is she here now?"

Thorne pulled her into his embrace, and she didn't resist. She needed the comfort too badly to turn him away.

He caressed her back just like her papa had when she was little and skinned her knee. "I don't know the answers, love. But I know it's not right to ask you to live under the same roof as his mistress. Ellis is a disgrace. I promise you would never be second in my heart if you married me. I would love you dearly, Gabrielle, if you would only let me."

She came back to her senses suddenly. Sebastian Thorne was a wonderful man, but she didn't love him in return. Allowing him this intimacy was wrong. She tried to ease away from him but discovered her mistake at once.

His eyes were aflame and his mouth too close to hers. Before she could escape, he captured her face and kissed her. He held her head in place as he gently parted her lips and delved his tongue inside her mouth. It felt awkward and terribly wrong. Nothing like a kiss was supposed to be. She flattened her palms against his chest to shove away when she heard a cry of surprise.

Lord Thorne released her and turned toward the noise. Her mother and Lady Eldridge stood inside the doorway. Mama was too pale. Lady Eldridge, Mama's dear friend, slipped an arm around her to assist her to a chair.

Gabby's world tilted off its axis. "Mama—" Her voice broke.

Oh, God. Gabby had seen that same look moments after her mother had discovered Papa the night he died. She couldn't breathe. Pain and guilt crushed her.

"Your Grace, please forgive me," Lord Thorne said as he stood. "This isn't how it seems."

Lady Eldridge crossed her arms. "And *how* does it seem, Lord Thorne?"

"I'm afraid it appears as if I have compromised Lady Gabrielle, and though I deeply regret my enthusiasm, I was overjoyed when she accepted my marriage proposal."

Proposal? The room spun, and for a moment, Gabby thought she was going to be sick again.

Thorne turned to offer his hand and mouthed, "I'm sorry."

"Is this true, Gabrielle?" her mother asked. "Did you agree to marry Lord Thorne?"

Gabby wanted to snatch her hand back, but Lord Thorne was offering her a graceful way out of this mess. Corroborating his story would mean sacrificing her happiness, but disappointing her mother again was unbearable. She tried to swallow, but her throat was so dry.

"Yes," she whispered. "He has asked for my hand."

Lady Eldridge's disgruntled frown remained in place. "Lord Thorne, have you spoken with her brother?"

"Not yet, my lady. I was uncertain if Lady Gabrielle would have me."

"Then may I suggest, young man, that you hop to it? Stealing kisses before you have received her brother's blessing isn't well done."

"You're correct, Lady Eldridge."

"Lud! I well know I'm in the right, Lord Thorne. I don't need your validation." Lady Eldridge continued her diatribe, scolding the baron properly.

Gabby met her mother's gaze and the sadness she saw made her want to sob. So, this was it. Her punishment for being careless and stupid was to be trapped in marriage with a man she might never love. She blinked back tears. Bravery didn't allow for tears, and she *would* be courageous, for she had brought this on herself.

Mama shook her head slowly. "How could you?"

Her censorship pierced Gabby's heart. She had always suspected she was a failure as a daughter, but now she knew it with certainty.

Eighteen

GABBY'S BROTHERS REMAINED BEHIND CLOSED DOORS with Lord Thorne while she had been ordered to wait in the drawing room.

This must be how a condemned man feels.

With her mother's gaze locked on her, she couldn't even allow herself a good pacing of the room. Instead, she forced her hands to lie calmly on her lap, while every other part of her was primed to run away. She took a cleansing breath to battle her nerves.

At least Lady Eldridge had excused herself. Gabby hadn't held out any hope of maintaining decorum with two sets of disapproving eyes aimed in her direction.

Mama shook her head slowly, her mouth puckered with disappointment. "I don't understand you, Gabrielle."

Guilt heaped on Gabby's shoulders, curling her inward.

Her mother sighed when Gabby didn't respond, but she didn't know what to say. "I expected you to accept Anthony's proposal. He loves you, darling. Why did you agree to marry the baron?"

She hadn't, but how could she tell her mother she

had allowed a man she'd had no intentions of marrying to kiss her? She might as well hang a sign around her neck identifying herself as a loose woman. Her hands formed fists and she trembled with suppressed rage. Thorne had made her a disgrace. She hadn't asked for his kiss.

Didn't I? Her face flamed and she dropped her head. She'd admitted him without a chaperone and had sought comfort from his embrace. Was Thorne truly the villain?

"I asked you a question, daughter. Why have you accepted Lord Thorne's offer?"

"He asked me."

Mama made a disgusted sound and Gabby's head snapped up. "What is wrong with the baron? He's handsome, titled, and has the means to support a wife."

"I never expected practicality from you," Mama said.

Gabby's mouth dropped. She didn't have time to recover from the blow before Wesley entered. "Your Grace, the duke has requested Lady Gabrielle's presence in his study."

Her mother nodded. "Of course. And where is Lord Thorne?"

"The baron has been escorted to the door, ma'am."

Gabby's brows shot up. Escorted to the door? That sounded ominous. She rose from the settee and followed the butler. Thankfully, she was spared seeing the baron again this evening, but now she was facing an even more daunting task: being called onto the carpet by her three older brothers.

Earlier, when Drew and Richard arrived only moments apart, her heart had plummeted. She had been in this situation once before and it had ended badly, but at least her family should find Lord Thorne more acceptable than Lt. MacFarland. All except Mama, who found both men lacking.

Gabby felt weighed down, as if she wore several extra petticoats, as she slogged toward Luke's study. Her brothers stood when she entered.

"Have a seat, Gabby." Luke's expression was neutral. She had never been good at reading her eldest brother, but Drew's scowl wasn't difficult to decode. They were not pleased.

Obeying her eldest brother, she selected a place on the masculine couch with lion's feet. She must appear as a child on the oversized piece.

"What in God's name happened?" Drew blurted.

Richard shot him a warning look. "Let the girl get her bearings before you begin hammering at her."

"Richard is correct. We are here to ascertain Gabby's wishes, not to badger her," Luke said as he sat beside her.

Her other brothers followed his example and claimed the matching wingback chairs.

Luke gently patted her shoulder. "There's no need to fret, dearest. We simply want to talk to you."

Her throat shrunk, making it hard to swallow. Her brother was being kinder than she deserved.

"I'm sure you are aware Lord Thorne has requested your hand in marriage."

"Yes." She spoke just above a whisper.

"I have yet to give him my answer."

She looked up sharply. The tenderness in Luke's gaze almost brought her to tears.

"What would you have me tell him? Do you want to marry the baron?"

Richard cleared his throat. "Sorry to state the obvious, but she has been compromised. Had Mother been alone when she discovered Gabby with Thorne, the situation might be different. I'm afraid our sister's choice has been made for her."

Drew's hands slammed the padded armrests as he launched from his seat. "She damn well has a say in the matter. If Thorne took liberties to force her hand, I'll call him out."

And Drew had accused her of being too dramatic. Gabby resisted the urge to roll her eyes.

Luke's gaze followed Drew as he paced behind the chairs. "You may be my second if that's the situation."

"I'm the next oldest," Richard said with a scowl. "I should be your second."

Gabby's breath stuck in her throat. Were her brothers seriously suggesting a duel? "This is insane."

No one seemed interested in her opinion and continued to bicker over which one would act as a second for Luke.

Drew's eyebrow lifted as he addressed Richard. "You couldn't hit an elephant at ten paces, old man, much less Thorne."

Richard shot to his feet and squared off with him. "I'm fair with a blade."

"Fair doesn't make for acceptable odds. Besides, Thorne isn't likely to choose swords."

"I agree with Drew," Luke said. "I'm the best shot, therefore I will issue the challenge and Drew will be my second."

They were talking as if this was a foregone conclusion. Gabby's head spun and she gripped the heavy armrest to steady herself.

"Risking *your* life is unacceptable," Richard argued. "You are the duke."

Drew clapped him on the shoulder. "I'm not trying to insult you, Rich, but the odds of you winning against Thorne are poor. We've buried one Forest too many already."

"No," she muttered. None of them would risk their lives for her. She refused to be responsible for another loved one's death. She had to stop this nonsense. "I—I wanted to kiss him."

They continued to shout over each other.

"Listen to me," she said, surging to her feet and throwing her hands into the air. "I asked him to kiss me. I *begged* him."

Their argument ground to a halt and her brothers gawked.

Well, she had their attention now. She cleared her throat. "As I was saying, I requested a kiss from the baron and he obliged. There's no call to defend my honor."

Drew's lip curled. "Really, princess? You *begged* the man to kiss you? What were you thinking?"

His disapproving tone stirred her temper. She jabbed a finger in his direction. "Who are you to pass judgment? I wanted a kiss from *one* man. I dare say you've kissed half of Britain, you scoundrel."

Her hands landed on her hips, daring them to contradict her. The study crackled with stunned silence.

A corner of Drew's mouth twitched up. "Only

the prettier half, princess. Let's get the facts straight, shall we?"

Luke and Richard were suddenly smiling too.

She fussed with her skirts, her body heating through. "Yes, well. I never said you had poor taste."

Her brothers chuckled and the tension eased.

Richard winked. "You'll keep Lord Thorne on his toes. Perhaps that's punishment enough for his forward behavior."

He was teasing, of course, but his comment still hurt. Now she would become the millstone around Lord Thorne's neck instead of her family's.

Luke sighed. "If this is what you want, I'll have the marriage contract drawn up."

Drew regarded her doubtfully. "Is it what you want?"

She wanted her brothers to be safe. She wanted her sisters to have their Season. She wanted to curl into a ball and weep.

Lifting her chin and hoping her quiver went unnoticed, she said, "I've made my decision."

Luke grimaced. "Very well."

She took a seat and held her tongue while Luke and Richard discussed the particulars of her dowry and how she could maintain a portion for her use only. Drew's gaze remained on her still, but she refused to look up.

He must think her fickle beyond reason after seeing her with Anthony at Lord and Lady Norwick's party. She had been so happy that day, and now...*this*.

A light knock sounded at the door and the butler entered.

"What is it, Wesley?" Luke asked.

Wesley's gaze traveled from Gabby to her brother.

Heat climbed her face as she realized the servants must be aware of her situation. "Lord Ellis is requesting an audience with Lady Gabrielle."

Luke's mouth set in a grim line. "Show him to the plum drawing room."

"Yes, Your Grace."

Gabby's nausea returned tenfold. She couldn't face Anthony, not when she had betrayed him. Even if he had lied about Miss Teague, Gabby had owed him a chance to explain as he had wished. Now it was too late.

Luke took her hand. "Ellis should hear the news from you."

"Are you all right, princess?" Drew asked. "You look like you might swoon."

She grasped Luke tightly. "Please, don't make me receive him. I can't bear to tell him."

Her brother frowned. "I don't wish to cause you distress, Gabby, but Ellis is like family. Eventually, you must speak with him."

"I know." Her voice began to waver. "I just can't do it now. Please."

"I'll tell him." Drew slowly hauled himself from the chair, appearing none too pleased with his task. "It's better for him to hear it from one of us than Thorne."

Tears swam in her eyes. "Thank you."

❧

Anthony had begun to worry now that he'd been kept waiting so long. Gabby hadn't seemed seriously ill last night, but what if she'd taken a turn for the worst?

When Drew stepped into the drawing room looking like the harbinger of death, Anthony's heart seized. He was already headed for the door. "Where is she? How ill is she?"

He tried to barrel past Gabby's brother, but Drew shoved a hand against his chest. "She is fine, but you can't see her."

"Why not?" His friend struggled to hold him back as Anthony resumed his forward movement.

"She doesn't want to see you, Anthony. I'm sorry."

The fight drained from him as Drew's words sunk in. "She doesn't want to see me? Why not?"

Drew released Anthony's waistcoat and raked his fingers through his own hair. "I'm here to explain, but perhaps you should sit."

Anthony didn't care for Drew's tone of voice or serious expression. He warily sat on the edge of the chair and motioned to Drew to continue.

"I'm afraid I have some unexpected news. I doubt you'll be pleased. My sister accepted an offer of marriage from Lord Thorne today."

He blinked, trying to make sense of the words. He'd heard the part where Gabby was marrying Thorne, but now Drew should be laughing and admit he was joking.

He wasn't.

A buzzing began in Anthony's ears. He shook his head to get rid of the noise, but it didn't help.

"So I'm sure you understand why Gabby is reluctant to see you at the moment. We believe she owes you an explanation, but she can't bring herself to face you. Perhaps tomorrow she'll be prepared to receive you."

Drew moved toward the door.

"Wait!" Anthony bolted from his seat. "Wait just one damned moment. You've made a mistake."

He dashed past Drew and was at the stairs before his friend caught up to him.

"Where are you going?"

Anthony jerked free of his hold and barreled up the steps. "Something isn't right. She wouldn't accept an offer from Thorne."

"But she has." Drew was on his tail, but nothing short of tackling him to the ground was going to stop Anthony. "Listen to me, man. You're going to make a fool of yourself."

Anthony didn't care. He would make a fool of himself a thousand times over for Gabby. He stalked toward her chambers and banged against the door with the side of his fist. "Gabby, open the door."

"She isn't in there. Stop making a scene."

He hammered the door again. "Open up this instant."

The door slowly creaked open and a pair of frightened eyes peeked out at him. "Lord Ellis?"

His jaw hardened when he realized it was Gabby's sister answering. "Lady Katherine, I would like to speak with your sister. Please move aside."

Her fingers curled around the edge as if preparing to throw her slight weight against the door if he tried to barge in. "Drew, what's happening?"

"No need for alarm, kitten." Drew lunged and locked his arms around Anthony's, trapping them at his sides. "Close the door!"

Lady Katherine slammed it as Anthony struggled to break free. The lock tumbled.

"Damn you, Drew! I won't leave until I see her."

Anthony threw his shoulders, trying to dislodge his friend. They staggered. Anthony's hip banged into a table and sent a vase crashing to the floor. Drew grunted as he connected with the wall.

Planting his feet, Anthony tried to remain standing while Drew threw his weight against him. He shifted to the side and Drew went down, but he took Anthony with him. Drew's grip broke when he hit the rug. Anthony scrambled to pin him to the floor, but Drew threw a hand up to block him and jabbed Anthony's eye.

Fury escaped him in a guttural howl. "Goddamn your bony fingers!"

He rocked back on his heels, covering his left eye. It throbbed like a sharp stick was lodged in his eyeball.

Drew was propped on his elbows, frozen in place.

The absurdity of their situation must have hit them at the same time, although their reactions differed. The fight drained from Anthony while dimples pierced his friend's cheeks.

"Bony fingers?" Drew said with a chuckle.

Anthony uncovered his eye and blinked to clear his vision. "They are like bloody daggers."

There was a delicate clearing of a throat. He looked up to find Gabby standing in the corridor as if she had just climbed the stairs and stumbled across their mess. "What is going on?"

Drew stood and dusted shards of porcelain from his trousers. "There was a little mishap. Nothing to fret over."

Anthony remained on bended knee, not wishing to scare her away with any sudden movement. "We need to talk."

Nineteen

GABBY STARED DUMBLY AT ANTHONY DOWN ON ONE knee among pieces of a broken vase strewn on the Turkish carpet. It was as if she were viewing the scene through cloudy spectacles. Nothing seemed real.

"We need to talk," he repeated. He was supposed to be in the drawing room receiving news of her betrothal from Drew, not in the corridor outside of her chambers. She had felt cowardly slinking above stairs to avoid him, but she had wanted time to absorb what had happened today. She wasn't getting it.

Uncertain she could speak, she nodded. She led Anthony to the larger drawing room rather than receive him in the same room where she had betrayed him. Drew trailed at a distance, then stopped outside the doors.

"I'll be here if you need me."

Suppressing a sigh of resignation, she closed the doors and turned to face Anthony.

"Why?" His pained voice cut through her calm facade. Violent shaking overtook her. She groped for a chair and dropped into it before her knees buckled.

Why? She still didn't completely know how this had come about herself.

The reason didn't matter, because she was as good as leg-shackled to Lord Thorne. She would never allow her brothers to risk their lives.

Anthony came to stand before her. Her gaze slowly traveled up his lean body to meet his troubled blue eyes. "Gabby, tell me it isn't true. You can't be planning to marry *him*."

She swallowed hard. How had the tables turned? It seemed like only yesterday she had been begging him not to marry someone else, to choose her. Their past should make her want to see him hurting as she had, but she only felt the pain more deeply now. She loved Anthony. She would always love him, but she couldn't put her happiness above her brothers' lives.

Luke was newly wed to Vivian and destined to bring an heir into the world. Richard was deeply in love with his wife, Phoebe, and he had two sons who looked up to him. Then there was Drew and Lana. Her dearest brother had found his other half in his wife, and he was a better man for it.

Still, giving up Anthony was killing her inside. Every instinct told her to fight for her survival. But she wouldn't. She had put herself first two years ago and lost her father because of it.

Her throat was scratchy and her tongue felt coated with sand. She couldn't bear losing Anthony completely. "Y-you told me the day of your wedding that we would always be friends."

He knelt at her feet and clutched her hands. His forehead was scrunched in concentration. "Is this what this is about? Are you punishing me for doing the right thing? You were young and the world was yours for the taking. It would have been selfish to take you as my wife."

She shook her head sadly. "I'm not punishing you." She was punishing herself. That he was injured in the process made everything a thousand times worse, but she too was doing the right thing. By marrying Thorne, she would protect her family from scandal. And most importantly, no lives would be put at stake. "Lord Thorne is a good man. He will make a decent husband."

"Dammit!" Anthony shot to his feet, startling her. "How can you do this? You are promised to me."

"You never asked me to marry you."

His mouth dropped open as if he would argue more, but then he clamped it shut. He simply stared at her, his eyes aflame. She could see the moment he closed down, the tightening of his jaw, his gaze becoming icy and hard.

A sharp pinch in her chest made her breath catch.

"Is that it, Gabby? You wanted the matter settled, and Thorne asked you first."

How much easier would it be if she allowed him to believe that was true? If he hated her, he would get on with his life, wouldn't he? And he would hate her. How could he feel anything but revulsion for a lady who had led him on a merry chase then accepted the first proposal tossed her way? She wanted to tell him yes, it was true, but the ache in her heart wouldn't allow the lie.

"I must marry him. There's no choice in the matter."

"Your brother is forcing you to marry Thorne?"

"No," she said softly, but he didn't seem to hear.

"Luke said he would never do that. We'll just see what he has to say about the matter."

When he stalked toward the door, Gabby leapt up too. She grabbed his arm before he made it to the door. He was too strong for her to detain, but he stopped.

"What's done is done," she said. "*I* made the decision and I stand by it."

He grabbed her upper arms to pull her close. "You still haven't told me the reason. Tell me you love him, that you don't love me."

His nearness made her tremble. This would be the last time he touched her. The knowledge wrecked her. She closed her eyes and drew in a shuddering breath. "You know love is not a factor in deciding one's mate."

It couldn't have been a consideration in his marriage to Camilla. Images of Anthony's daughter with his mistress broke through her numbness. He couldn't have loved Camilla. If he had, he never would have forced his wife to claim his illegitimate child.

Her anger flared and her eyes flew open. "We both know there was no love between you and your wife."

He released her, his body jerking as if she had struck him. The hurt in his expression confused her. "I was trying to fulfill my duty."

"And I'm trying to fulfill mine."

"You're hiding something."

His accusation fanned the flame inside her, consuming her. "You think I'm hiding something from you? That's rich when you've been hiding Annabelle's mother under your roof."

"What did you say?"

She crossed her arms, refusing to be swayed by his wide-eyed bemusement. "I saw your daughter and her nanny yesterday. That woman is no more Annabelle's nanny than I'm a hat."

"And you think Miss Teague is Annabelle's mother."

"Among other things," she said under her breath.

Anthony's jaw jutted forward. "If you are going to hurl accusations, speak up."

"You aren't denying the relationship."

"Because it's ridiculous. My wife gave birth to our daughter, and she died giving life to her. Have some respect for the dead."

His vehemence gave her pause. His eyes were nearly black and his chest rose and fell rapidly.

"I meant no disrespect to Lady Ellis, but I overhead Annabelle referring to Miss Teague as her mother."

"She is the only mother Annabelle has ever known. I was fortunate Annabelle's relation was willing to take her in. I certainly wasn't equipped to care for a baby."

Anthony met her gaze directly, his expression guileless. Gabby's stomach roiled as she realized he was telling the truth. If Miss Teague were related to his daughter, that would explain their similarities. This was his reasonable explanation, the one she would have gotten had she waited for him. Her distrust had destroyed their chance at happiness together.

Her head throbbed as she fought to hold back her tears. For the past year, she had vacillated between her desire for true love and believing herself unde-serving of it. Today her questions could be put to rest. Gabby's only true love stood before her, his heart hardened against her. And she couldn't even blame him for hating her. She was marrying another man.

Twenty

LUKE GROANED UNDER HIS BREATH WHEN HIS WIFE DUG her fingers into his knotted muscles. She stood behind his chair in the drawing room, applying her healing touch. He hadn't had a headache like this for months, but he also hadn't dealt with a mess like he'd had tonight in… He searched his memory and couldn't remember *ever* having a similar situation arise.

"Sisters are an unpredictable lot."

"I'm sure we are," Vivian said with a droll quality to her voice. She squeezed his shoulders, releasing some of his tension. "Perhaps you could think of something else for a bit. Fretting over Gabby isn't helping your head."

"I don't fret."

She bent forward and placed her warm lips against his neck. "Of course you don't. Although if you were to fret like a dotty old aunt over your sister's well-being, that would be perfectly understandable."

He grabbed her hand and walked her around the chair. Every time he laid eyes on Vivian, his heart skipped a beat. Months of marriage had done nothing to diminish his desire for her. He cocked an eyebrow. "Are you patronizing me, water sprite?"

Her eyes twinkled with mischief as she offered a coy smile. "Maybe."

As he tugged her onto his lap, a knock sounded at the door. He released her with a sigh and helped smooth her skirts before bidding the person to enter.

His mother eased the door open and frowned. "I hope I'm not interrupting."

"Of course not, Rosemarie. I was just telling Luke I was ready for bed. I'll leave the two of you alone." Vivian's mouth turned up slightly at the corners when she glanced at him. She wasn't thinking about sleep.

"I'm not long for bed myself," he said.

When Vivian quit the drawing room, his mother claimed a seat. "I won't keep you long. I just want to know what you make of Gabby accepting Lord Thorne's proposal."

Luke joined her on the settee. "She is adamant she wants to marry him. I thought her affections lay with Ellis, but I was mistaken apparently."

"Did you get any sense she is hiding something?"

He shook his head. His sister's emotions had always been easy to read, but her motivations often remained elusive. "She was upset, but I didn't know if it was because she felt bad for hurting Ellis, or if she doesn't really want to marry Thorne."

His mother's shoulders drooped. "I understand the conversation between her and Anthony didn't go well. I simply can't accept that they are not meant for each other. Your father and I used to comment on how compatible we thought they would be when they became adults. Anthony is levelheaded, which is what Gabby needs, and she would bring some liveliness to his life."

Luke put his arm around his mother. She was a tiny woman, but her will was strong. "Only Gabby can know which gentleman feels right for her. We should trust her judgment."

"Perhaps if they spoke again, Gabby would see she is mistaken."

He sighed. He didn't want to become embroiled in a battle between his mother and sister, but he had a soft spot for his mother. "I could encourage Anthony to call on her once more, but then we must accept whatever decision Gabby makes."

"Very well, so long as you promise to allow her to cry off if she changes her mind."

"Of course, Mother. She is free to choose her husband. I won't stand in her way."

❧

Gabby wanted to do nothing more than to hide away at Talliah House until her wedding—that is, besides not marrying Lord Thorne at all. Nevertheless, she had a role to play and if she didn't act the part of happy bride-to-be, her family would figure out the truth. At least Thorne had kept his distance the last few days and given her time to lick her wounds in private.

More than once she had considered telling Luke what had really transpired in the drawing room the day Mama and Lady Eldridge discovered her in Thorne's embrace. But she couldn't. Not when she watched

Luke and Vivian together and knowing he would make good on his promise to challenge Lord Thorne.

Her brother and his wife were either unaware she could see them through the conservatory windows as they strolled the gardens or else they didn't care. Luke had his arm around Vivian's waist, and when they stopped on the path, he tipped her chin up to kiss her gently on the lips.

Gabby's attention returned to her drawing, her heartache as fresh as it had been when she'd said her good-byes to Anthony. As much as she tried to accept her fate and tell herself she deserved what she had gotten, part of her rebelled against it. Her state of mind was reflected in her artwork. Dark slashes marred the paper where she'd pressed down hard, almost ripping it.

"Here you are, my darling girl."

Gabby startled at the sound of her mother's voice.

"Are you ready to visit the modiste? There isn't much time to prepare your wedding gown."

Ordering a mourning gown seemed more fitting, but she forced a smile. "I don't believe Vivian is ready to leave yet."

Mama came to sit beside Gabby on the settee and nodded toward Luke and his wife beyond the window. Vivian lifted her face as they shared a laugh. "All I have ever wanted was for my children to be happy in love. It does my heart good to see them together."

Gabby's nose tickled, a sign she might start crying again. She rubbed it furiously then went back to her drawing.

Mama smoothed her hand over Gabby's back. "I want all of my children to be happy?" Her inflection made it sound like a question that hung between them.

How Gabby would love to unburden her heart to her mother, and perhaps she would if not for the word "all." It was impossible for all to be happy now, so it was Gabby's duty to make certain *most* were happy. But she could pretend for her mother's sake.

"Oh, I quite agree. It's wonderful to be in love." At least she wasn't forced to lie to her mother on that account. Gabby had been gloriously happy during her short time with Anthony.

Mama sighed and took Gabby's sketchbook to study her drawing. "It's a spider's web."

"Yes." She pointed to a shrub close to the window where a web stretched between thin branches. Earlier, dewdrops had glistened on the strands, making it beautiful. She wondered if insects were more likely to be drawn to the web because of the light glinting off it. Perhaps they judged it harmless just as she had misjudged Lord Thorne. In the end, she was as trapped as they were.

Vivian and Luke were walking arm in arm back toward the house. "It appears Vivian is ready now," Gabby said.

"We should commission a few more dresses as long as we are at the dressmaker's shop. If you intend to go through with this marriage, you must begin to make appearances again. It isn't right to ignore invitations and then expect friends and acquaintances to attend your wedding."

She didn't care if anyone attended her wedding.

She would miss it if she could. But her mother had a point. A happy bride would not be hiding out after her betrothal, and she feared she wasn't fooling anyone, least of all her family.

"Yes, Mama. I would be delighted to attend whichever events you deem appropriate."

Her mother's lips curved down. "Are you certain you aren't still ill?"

Gabby chuckled for the first time in days.

❧

Anthony's gut felt rotted inside, as if he'd eaten rusted metal instead of the three-course meal Lady Sorin had served that evening. In actuality, he'd only been able to force down a few bites before his throat refused to work any longer.

Gabby had been placed far away from him at the table, so there had been no opportunity to speak with her. She'd looked up several times to catch Anthony staring, and a bright flush had colored her cheeks. As soon as dinner ended, Thorne had been at her side, cutting off any hope Anthony had of stealing her away for a private word.

Anthony had been certain everything wasn't rosy between Gabby and the baron, and he'd come to the dinner with the intention of uncovering the truth. But seeing them waltzing together was killing him. They seemed like any other happy couple.

Gabby smiled when Thorne smiled, she laughed when he spoke, and she spared him the dark looks he deserved when he held her too close during the dance. And as far as Anthony was concerned, one would think Gabby had never met him with the way she actively ignored him when they danced past.

Frustrated, he grabbed a glass of champagne from a passing footman bearing a sterling tray, then stalked onto the terrace.

Bollocks! Why am I here? Perhaps he was a masochist, because watching Gabby and Thorne together was torture. She wouldn't even meet Anthony's eye. Was this how things would be from now on? Never speaking to one another again?

A sharp pain ripped into his chest as if to shred his heart. Not only was he losing the woman he loved, it appeared he would lose the only family he'd ever known. The Forests may not be related to him, but they had accepted him as if he belonged. They were the reason he could accept Annabelle completely, because Gabby's parents had shown him the ability to love was not dictated by blood. If it were, he would have still had a mother after losing his father and brother.

Two shadowed figures strolled onto the terrace, the glow from the ballroom behind them hiding their faces.

"Ellis, are you all right?"

It was Drew and Luke. Anthony didn't want them to see him this way. "I've been worse," he lied.

Luke slapped him on the shoulder before embracing him as if they were brothers. "I don't believe that's true. I have seen you down and out, but nothing like this."

"Does it show on my face?"

Drew roughly grabbed him next. "No, but we know you. Perhaps it was a bad idea for you to come tonight. I thought you might have a moment to speak to Gabby, but Thorne has set up camp at her side."

"I don't think she would speak with me in any case. She wouldn't even look my way."

"Let's find a tavern and have an ale," Luke said, his pitying frown almost more than Anthony could take. "Just like the old days."

Drew's lopsided grin appeared. "Perhaps not too much like the old days. My sweet wife would demand my bollocks as payment, and I've grown rather fond of them."

Anthony offered a halfhearted chuckle for his friend's attempt to lighten the mood, but even halfhearted required too much effort. He didn't want to visit a tavern, but he wanted to go home even less. "Very well. Lead the way."

As they passed through the ballroom, Anthony couldn't take his eyes off Gabby. She stood with a group of ladies as they chatted together, but she had a faraway look to her gaze. Thorne was still at her side. When everyone laughed, Gabby's smile was delayed. Perhaps she wasn't as happy as she'd been pretending.

Thorne glanced in Anthony's direction and pulled Gabby closer. Every muscle in Anthony's body tensed and hatred flooded his veins. He and Thorne had never had a typical friendship, but they'd been far from sworn enemies. Until now.

❧

Gabby's rigid backbone dissolved the moment Anthony left the ballroom with her brothers. She knew Drew had told him where she would be this evening. Her brother had pulled her aside and told her as soon as she had arrived. At once, she'd experienced a surge of energy and her breath had come quickly. Then her betrothed had approached, and she'd realized she no longer had the freedom to speak with whomever she wished.

She would have no freedoms, except for the ones her husband would allow. How could it be that Anthony would no longer be part of her life in any capacity? The thought weighed her down.

Lord Thorne gently grasped her elbow; his touch was warm against her bare skin. "Would you like to take some fresh air, my lady? The ballroom is stuffy this evening."

She nodded and accepted his escort to the terrace. The outside air seemed as heavy to her as it had been in the ballroom, but it was quieter. He led her toward a corner of the terrace, away from the other couples. Torchlight danced across the stone when a slight breeze blew.

"How are the preparations for our wedding coming?" he asked.

"I was fitted for a gown yesterday, and Mama posted the last of the invitations today."

He turned her so she was facing him and frowned. "I do wish you were happier about the prospect of becoming my wife, even though I don't deserve your good favor."

She blinked, surprised by his statement.

"I never meant to force you into marriage, Gabrielle. I hope someday you might forgive me." His dark eyes shone with regret, and the anger bubbling under her surface receded a little. "I wanted you to choose me, and I thought you might if I showed you how caring and tender I can be. If I had known your mother would walk in when she did…"

"The kiss never should have happened."

He flinched and she regretted her sharp tone. It wouldn't do to start their marriage at odds with one another. He had never shown an inclination toward unkindness, but she didn't really know him either. The baron could be a different man behind closed doors, although in truth she doubted he would ever be cruel.

She sighed, wishing this entire affair didn't require so much energy. "I'm as much to blame as you, my lord. I should have called for a chaperone before receiving you."

His face fell. "You really want nothing to do with me."

"That's not true…" Well, perhaps it was, but since they were stuck in this situation together, it seemed unwise to admit it.

"If you want to cry off, I'll release you without consequence. I would never wish to marry a lady who doesn't want me." His offer seemed sincere, but they both knew crying off was not an option after what Lady Eldridge had witnessed. It did her no service to entertain possibilities that could never happen. Besides, this was her penance for stealing her parents' happiness. She knew she'd have to pay it eventually.

"I have given my word to marry you, Lord Thorne. I don't intend to break it."

He caressed her cheek with the back of his fingers, his glove soft against her skin. His touch didn't send her pulse racing, but it was nice enough. His smile was soft and made him appear more handsome in the flickering light. "I can't stomach the thought of you being miserable, love."

"Misery is a state of mind, my lord. I don't have to choose to live in that state unless I wish it."

Her father had told her that on more than one occasion when events hadn't gone as she'd planned. She had always thought Papa wise, and she hoped his sage advice held up through the years facing her.

"Do you think you will ever agree to call me by my name?"

She sighed. "One step at a time."

"Fair enough." His grin grew wider before he kissed her cheek; his scent made her think of pine trees. In fact, the man himself was like a tree, wild in some ways and yet steadfast. Definitely unmovable.

If nothing else, she supposed she could picture an amiable partnership in their future. But that seemed like enough steps to take for one day.

Twenty-one

ANTHONY STILL COULDN'T BELIEVE HIS RELATIONSHIP with Gabby was over. Her brothers had convinced him to call on her at Talliah House after the Sorins' dinner, but when she'd turned him away, the truth had knocked him over the head.

He'd lost her.

And he may have lost his sanity as well. He hadn't slept a full night in two weeks, food had become a tasteless lump, and the simple act of crawling out of bed sapped his strength, so he'd stopped bothering.

He hurt like hell. All over.

The only time he'd come close to experiencing this kind of pain was when he had fallen down the stairs at Ellis Hall when he was a lad. He had been trying to help his mother to her bedchamber so the downstairs maids wouldn't discover her passed out in the drawing room. The soured smell would have lingered in the room, however, so her drinking couldn't be hidden completely. Still, he'd tried.

Her brandy-soaked breath had made him want to retch, but he'd exerted his will to overcome the urge.

As they had reached the top step, his mother jerked, suddenly alert. "I can walk by myself," she'd screeched and shoved him. Her attack had come quite unexpectedly, and he'd tumbled down the flight of stairs and cracked his head on the solid post.

His tutor had doctored his cut, but Mr. Lynch hadn't been one for kind words. Then again, neither was Anthony's mother. The next morning, she'd had no memory of what she had done and considered it her motherly duty to berate him for his clumsiness. He'd never tried to cover up her weaknesses again.

On second thought, losing Gabby was worse than that incident. Maybe this was the reason his mother had wanted to be unconscious all the time.

"Dammit." He didn't want to become like her. Scrubbing his hands over his whiskers, he tried to calculate how long it had been since he'd shaved or taken a bath.

He caught a whiff of himself. *Too long.*

It was time to join the living, even if he would remain dead inside. Hauling himself from bed, he groped for the bellpull in the dark. He wasn't even certain if it was day or night with the curtains drawn.

When Pierce entered his chambers, Anthony heard the valet's sharp intake of breath. Not that Anthony blamed the servant for his reaction. He rarely allowed himself to reach this state of dishabille.

"I wish to shave and have a bath." His voice sounded gravelly.

"Very good, milord." The slight lilt to the valet's voice indicated Anthony's decision pleased him.

Pierce threw open the curtains, flooding the room with light.

"Bollocks!" Anthony squinted against the onslaught. "A little warning next time?"

"Perhaps a bit of fresh air will improve your mood, milord." The servant lifted the window sash and drew in a deep breath. "Ah, much better. I will have the footmen set up the tub."

Pierce had an added spring to his step as he left the room. *Gads.* The man possessed more bounce and cheer than one person should be forced to endure.

When everything was set into place for his bath, Anthony stripped down and sunk into the hot water with a groan. His valet returned moments later and made quick work of setting Anthony to rights.

Once he resembled a member of the human species again, he sent Pierce away with orders to bring coffee to his study. He should have been at the House of Lords that morning, but it was too late to make an appearance now. Instead, he would tackle the correspondence that had been piling up on his desk, although he'd prefer to toss it in the grate and forget about it.

He was in his study sorting through the stack when a light knock interrupted him.

"Enter."

He expected to see a footman with a coffee service, but it was his butler bearing a calling card. The feminine lettering caught him off guard.

"The Duchess of Foxhaven wishes to see me?"

"Aye, milord."

What the devil was Luke's wife doing calling on him?

The servant lowered his voice and lifted his brows meaningfully. "Her Grace has arrived with two young ladies in tow."

His heart jolted to life. *Gabby?* He leaned back in his chair and attempted a casual air. "Please show the ladies to the drawing room and have Mrs. Duffy prepare refreshments."

"Very good, milord."

Moments later, Anthony stood outside the drawing room doors, fighting back a smile. He inhaled deeply then barreled into the room. The air rushed from his lungs in a noisy whoosh.

"Good afternoon, Lord Ellis."

"Lady Elizabeth and Lady Katherine, it is you." Cringing at the inanity of his observation and the disappointment present in his tone, he schooled his features. "How kind of you to call."

The Duchess of Foxhaven had her head tipped to the side, studying him. Anthony smiled for her benefit. "To what do I owe this honor, Your Grace?"

"Lord Ellis, please forgive us for barging in on you this afternoon. I realize it is most improper."

Perhaps, but impropriety didn't often create an obstacle for the young duchess. The reason Luke had fallen for the lady was no mystery. Her daring was often a topic of conversation at society events, and yet her sweet nature had won her many friends who found her charming.

"My doors are always open, madame."

He took a seat opposite the ladies sitting on the couch and noted the duchess fiddling with a sealed letter. He nodded toward it. "A missive from the duke?"

She nibbled her bottom lip as if considering whether to give it to him. Appearing to have made up her mind, she held it out to him, but Lady Elizabeth snatched it from the duchess's fingers.

"Wait! That's not for you."

The duchess drew back, appearing as surprised as he was. "B-but Gabby wanted—" She sputtered to a stop, her eyes narrowing. Lady Elizabeth offered a dimpled smile.

"Oh, my molasses," the duchess said. "Gabby didn't request we deliver this, did she?"

"Not exactly."

Lady Katherine lowered her head, a pink stain upon her cheeks. "We're sorry, Vivian. We didn't know any other way to gain an audience with Lord Ellis."

The lady nailed Gabby's sisters with an imperious glower. It appeared Luke's mother had taught the new duchess a thing or two about how to put others in their place. "I demand to know what you are about, ladies. What do you have to say for yourselves?"

Lady Elizabeth didn't appear contrite in the least as she boldly met his gaze and ignored her sister-in-law's command. "She loves you, Lord Ellis. You do know that, don't you? She can't live without you."

The duchess gasped, but Lady Elizabeth wasn't deterred. "It's true, Vivian. Our sister is miserable. How can we look the other way knowing how unhappy she is?"

He looked to the duchess for confirmation. She nodded sharply. "Gabby hasn't been herself lately."

Because she still loves me. Lady Elizabeth's confident assertion sparked his hope. "Did she send you to tell me she loves me?"

"Not in so many words," Lady Elizabeth hedged.

She frowned at the duchess. "Vivian, you cannot say a word to Luke about what I'm about to reveal."

The duchess held up her hands. "Oh, no. No, no, no." Each denial was accompanied by a vigorous shake of her head. "Keeping things from your brother is a bad idea."

Lady Katherine reached toward her. "Vivian, please hear us out."

"I'm sorry, but I promised your brother there would be no more secrets between us." She bolted from the couch and gathered her reticule. "We should go. Thank you for your time, Lord Ellis, and we apologize for disturbing you."

She marched toward the door, but Gabby's sisters didn't budge from the couch. The duchess turned back at the threshold and her eyes rounded. "*Girls.* What are you doing?"

Lady Katherine offered an apologetic half smile. "We understand you can't keep secrets from Luke. It wasn't right to ask. But if you could allow us a moment alone with Lord Ellis…"

The duchess's eyes darted from one girl to the next while they gazed back at her like sad pups.

"Oh, sugar biscuits," she said with a soft stomp of her slipper. "Very well. I shall walk slowly to the carriage, and I expect you to catch up to me in a moment."

Gabby's sisters beamed.

"Thank you, Vivi. We knew you were the perfect one to help us," Lady Elizabeth said.

A flush spread over the duchess's face. "You mean I'm the only fool you know." There was a ring of affection in her words. "Don't be long, ladies."

As soon as the door closed, Lady Elizabeth arched an eyebrow. "Gabby needs you. She doesn't want to marry Lord Thorne, but she feels she must."

Anthony shook his head with a weary sigh. "Gabby has made her decision, and there is nothing I can do to change her mind. I tried."

Lady Katherine held up the letter her sister had taken from the duchess. His name was scrawled across the front. "Do you know what this is, my lord? It is your wedding invitation. Gabby stole it from Mama's pile, because she couldn't stand the thought of you suffering while she exchanged vows with Lord Thorne. Just like she suffered when you married Lady Ellis."

His breath lodged in his throat. Had his marriage ceremony truly hurt her so badly? She had seemed fine. Better than fine, actually. She had smiled brightly, laughed often, and wished him well with a vigorous hug.

"Oh, God," he mumbled. How had he not seen it? She had been too happy for the occasion. He had wanted to believe he'd made the right decision by discouraging her. He'd grasped on to the belief he had been nothing more than a passing fancy, and she would thank him for acting with honor.

Lady Katherine carried the invitation to him. "If she didn't care for you, why would she spare your feelings?"

Anthony took the envelope and trapped it in his fist.

"There are only two days left until she marries the baron. You must do something, Lord Ellis. Our sister has suffered too much in her life already. She deserves to be happy."

He looked up into Lady Katherine's unwavering gaze. She possessed the wise eyes of a person four times her age.

"She won't listen to me," he said.

Lady Elizabeth bounded from her seat. "You must *make* her listen. And if she won't, you need to make the correct decision for her."

His hollow laugh echoed off the ceiling. "What would you have me do? Abduct her?"

Lady Elizabeth's thin brows lifted suggestively.

"You are joking."

When he glanced at Lady Katherine, she slowly shook her head. "Some situations call for drastic measures, my lord."

"This is insane," he said and pushed from his chair to pour a brandy for himself. "You should both go. The duchess will be waiting for you."

He kept his back to Gabby's sisters as the swish of their skirts indicated they were leaving.

"If you come to your senses," Lady Katherine said, "she is attending the theatre this evening. Lord Thorne sent word this morning that his mother and sister would collect her at eight, and he will meet her there. The session at the House of Lords is expected to run late."

"It can be difficult to tell carriages apart in the dark," Lady Elizabeth added.

With that being their final words, Gabby's sisters quietly slipped from the drawing room and left him to wrestle with his thoughts.

Difficult, my arse. As soon as Gabby spotted the coat of arms on his door, she would know the carriage didn't belong to Thorne. And Thorne's servants wore old-fashioned blue livery while Anthony's dressed sharply in gold. Apparently the baron and Anthony's grandfather shared the same tired tastes, for he recalled his grandfather's footmen wearing almost the same livery.

The door swung open and Pierce entered with a silver coffee service. "The footman is bringing the tea as we speak." His eyebrows drew together as he looked around the room.

"The guests had somewhere else to be."

"Do you still want coffee, milord?"

He waved his valet into the room and waited for him to close the door. "I have a different task for you."

"Yes, milord?"

Damnation, was he really considering this? Anthony plowed his fingers through his hair, noticing Pierce's horrified expression. Anthony didn't care. Ruffled hair was the least of his concerns.

How had time slipped away? In two days, Gabby would be lost to him forever. Unless he did something drastic. Something that could cost him the best friends he'd ever had or at the extreme, could get him killed.

But life without Gabby made him feel dead already.

"Search the trunks in the attic and find the old blue livery my grandfather preferred."

Twenty-two

GABBY AND HER MOTHER WERE ENTERTAINING LADY Thorne and Sebastian's sister when the butler interrupted. He stood uncertainly inside the threshold, tossing a quick glance at the guests.

"Is something the matter, Wesley?" Mama asked.

"I don't believe so, Your Grace. I have a message for Lady Gabrielle."

Gabby blinked. "Oh? Has Lord Thorne sent another note?"

His mouth turned down as he eyed Lady Thorne and her daughter. "No, milady."

Mama reached for the silver teapot and smiled politely. "Perhaps you should step out with Wesley, my dear. Lady Thorne and I have much to discuss about the wedding."

"Of course, Mama." Gabby caught Eve Thorne's eye, but the lady looked away as she fidgeted with her reticule. This evening would be the poor girl's first venture back into society since her abandonment at the altar, and it seemed her nerves were a bit frayed.

Sebastian—Gabby had finally capitulated and begun

using his given name, even though it still sounded odd to her—had been exceedingly grateful to Gabby for inviting his mother and sister to tea and for agreeing to accompany them to the theatre that evening. His praise had been lavish indeed. It had been the only time during their betrothal that she felt truly good about something.

It warmed her heart to think she might be able to help Miss Thorne. And if Gabby were to be bound in marriage to the lady's brother, she preferred to begin on good footing with his kin.

"I won't be long," she said then followed the servant from the drawing room, closing the door quietly behind her. "What is it, Wesley?"

"Lord Ellis is requesting a word with you, milady."

Her stomach dropped. She hadn't seen Anthony since the Sorins' ball, and she hadn't spoken with him since the night she had gotten herself into this mess with Thorne. "Where is he?"

She mentally scolded herself for sounding too eager.

"I showed him to the blue drawing room. He insisted I retrieve you or he threatened to barge in on your tea."

High-handed man. She frowned. What could he possibly have to say that they hadn't already discussed? A wise woman would send him away without an audience, but she wouldn't put it past him to make good on his threat. "Thank you, Wesley. I will see what it is Lord Ellis wants. You may go."

The butler nodded and left her alone in the corridor. She made her way to the second drawing room, stopping outside the door to rub a palm over her heart. It knocked against her breastbone, proving it still had life in it.

When she had gained composure, she yanked open the double doors and glided inside, exuding as much confidence as she could manage.

"You are interrupting a lovely tea, Anthony."

He was standing with his arms crossed over his broad chest and a mutinous scowl on his face. "Are you truly planning to marry that twit in two days' time?"

Her answer caught in her throat.

"And you didn't invite me to the wedding." He dropped his arms and strode over to her. "I have known you all your life, and I've been excluded from the guest list."

A blanket of heat wrapped around her. It was stifling and too heavy. "I—I didn't think you would want to come."

He stood too close. His scent beckoned her closer, but she resisted. His mouth twitched up at the corners. "I don't want *you* to go either."

A shocked laugh burst from her. "It's customary for a bride to be present at her wedding. Of course I'll be attending."

He cupped her elbow and drew her to him. He looked down at her through thick golden lashes, his eyes a deeper shade of blue-gray. Her lips were suddenly dry and she licked them.

He groaned under his breath. "You should be marrying me, my love, not Thorne. *We* belong together. Why can't you admit it?"

Her legs quivered. Oh, how she would love to toss aside her honor and throw herself into his arms, but she couldn't. She had made a promise to Lord Thorne, and her stance on putting her brothers' lives before her happiness hadn't altered.

Reluctantly, she pulled away. "I am marrying the baron. I'm sorry, but I can't go back on my word."

"At least have the courage to tell me the reason. Tell me you prefer him. That you love him and want to spend your life with him."

She shook her head and took another step back. If she said those things, she would be lying.

Anthony's hand on her stopped her retreat. Dizziness kept her from pulling away again. His touch kept her from sliding to the floor.

"Do you have any feelings for him, Gabby?"

"I—I'm fond of him."

"Fond? Just fond of him? That is the most asinine thing I've ever heard from you."

His insult snapped her out of the spell he'd woven. Her hands landed on her hips. "Yes, I *like* the man I'm to marry. That is more than many ladies can say."

"You're not like other ladies. Your heart rules you; it always has."

And therein lay the problem. In all her memory, she couldn't recall a time when following her heart had ever led to good.

He tipped up her chin. "How long do you think you'll be happy when you are only fond of your husband?"

"What does it matter? Fondness is enough for now. Perhaps I can learn to love him as I—" She caught herself before she blurted out the truth.

He caressed her cheek and she fought the urge to

turn into his palm. Her skin tingled in the wake of his touch. "As you love me, sweetheart? Say it. Admit you love me. It's not too late to cry off."

A horrible pain seized her heart. It had been a mistake to grant him an audience. She was too weak. "I can't. I have given my word. Please, leave me in peace."

His hand dropped from her face and she was left wanting. "Then I'm afraid you leave me no choice."

She blinked, alarmed by the stubborn tilt of his chin. "No choice? What is your meaning?"

"Thank you for seeing me, Lady Gabrielle. This has been an enlightening conversation."

She called after him to wait, but he stalked from the room like a man marching to war.

❧

Anthony decided to join Annabelle and Miss Teague for an early dinner. He had more than a few misgivings about leaving his daughter for several days, but he'd spoken with his butler and had confidence in the man. No one would be allowed to enter Keaton Place during his absence, not that he truly expected Annabelle's sire to show his face in London.

His bigger concern was being absent from his daughter's life again. He was already furious with himself for hiding in his chambers these past days. He'd despised his mother for isolating and shutting him out, and yet he had done the same thing in his grief.

Hell. He'd wanted to be better than his mother, to rise above his childhood circumstances. And he would. No more feeling sorry for himself.

Annabelle and Miss Teague were already seated at the small table in the nursery when he arrived. For his daughter's comfort, he'd thought it best to enter her territory rather than dragging her to the dining room. Annabelle clung to Miss Teague's side as she did every time he came within shouting distance.

Miss Teague offered a smile. "Good evening, milord." She had taken more pains with her appearance this evening, dressing in one of the nicer gowns he had purchased as part of her wages. Their arrangement involved a roof over her head until Annabelle was married, food, a decent wardrobe, a modest allowance for her personal use, and a pension when her services were no longer required.

Everything he'd done was with Annabelle in mind. To her, Miss Teague was her mother. It didn't seem right to treat her as a servant, although jealousy from the other servants might have caused tongues to wag. How else would Thorne know about the circumstances of Annabelle's birth?

"Miss Teague, have you any knowledge of anyone on staff holding a grudge against you?"

She blinked, her blue eyes clouded by confusion. "No, milord. Has someone made a complaint against me?"

"Nothing like that. I didn't mean to alarm you." He pulled out the tiny chair and eyed it. Oak was a sturdy wood. It would hold his weight, he hoped. His confidence faltered when the chair creaked and groaned.

The corners of Annabelle's cupid-bow mouth turned up slightly. "Papa is too big."

His heart leapt at hearing her refer to him without

being prompted, even if she was pointing out a glitch in his plan to dine with her. He grinned. "You are an observant young lady, Annabelle."

Her smile slid from her face and she leaned against her aunt again. Perhaps sitting on one of her chairs was acceptable, but speaking to her was not. Duly noted.

Miss Teague picked up her fork and smiled sympathetically. "She is still a bit shy, milord. Please don't take offense."

He shrugged it off. "I don't take it personally." But he did. He wasn't proud of the fact, but he didn't see how rejection could be taken impersonally.

Snatching his fork, he dug into his buttered carrots. His knees nearly up around his ears made eating with grace a difficult feat. Annabelle smothered a giggle with her tiny hand when he bumped his elbow and spilled on his lap.

Her green eyes sparkled in her perfect little face as she whispered something to her doll, Lady Poppy. Her reaction made him even more eager to please her, so he purposefully fumbled his fork and turned dining into quite the spectacle. He was little more than a trained bear when treated to her laughter.

At one point, she even inched toward him and glanced up in expectation. Suddenly his napkin flew off his lap, landed on his head, and rendered him unable to see. Of course, that led to more silly antics, because how was one to eat when one couldn't see properly?

Her belly laughs were the sweetest sound he'd ever heard and filled him with expanding warmth and the insane desire to giggle too. Instead, he grinned until his jaws began to ache.

Miss Teague sighed happily as she patted Annabelle's back. "A few more meals such as this and I'm certain she will be putty in your hands, milord. Perhaps you would like to break your fast with us tomorrow?"

His merriment faded. How could it be that he was on the verge of breaking through Annabelle's walls only moments before he was to leave? He cleared his throat. "I'm afraid I will not be available tomorrow."

A pink blush infused Miss Teague's cheeks. "Of course, milord. Forgive me for being presumptuous."

"Not at all, Miss Teague. If I didn't have pressing matters, I would be honored to breakfast with Annabelle. This is partly my reason for coming tonight. I'm leaving town for several days, and I wanted to inform you of my absence and reassure you and Annabelle that you will be safe here."

Her smile returned. "I'm not worried, Lord Ellis. Even if my brother knew where we were, he doesn't have the means to travel to London."

Anthony had suspected as much, but he appreciated having his beliefs validated. "And I should probably inform you that when I return, I'll have a wife."

◆

Gabby's sisters gushed over her newest ball gown as she checked her reflection in the looking glass. Her mother slowly nodded her agreement. "You look lovely, darling."

The muted red and the off-the-shoulder style were bolder than her mother typically allowed, but Mama had reluctantly agreed. After all, Gabby was to be a married woman soon.

She wished the prospect didn't make her want to cry.

As if sensing her sadness, Mama grew misty-eyed. "I know I must let you go, but it's harder than I expected."

"Oh, Mama." Gabby went into her open arms and allowed her mother to hold her. For a moment, she surrendered to the security of her mother's embrace like she had when she was a child. She didn't want to leave her family either, but this was her fate. Once she spoke her vows, she would belong to Sebastian's family.

Fear squeezed her heart. He had promised to let her visit Mama and her sisters any time she wanted. He seemed honest and kind, but what if she'd misjudged him?

Gabby clung to her mother and tried to catch her breath. Her sisters crowded around them, their arms circling her and their mother.

"Everything is going to be fine," Katie whispered in her ear. "You will see."

Her sister's sensitivity nearly broke her, but she managed to quash her tears. She'd been hiding her sorrow from everyone and she intended to keep it hidden.

She eased from their embrace with a breathy laugh. "I had best gather my wrap. Lord Thorne's carriage will be here any moment."

Her mother pursed her lips. "Perhaps I should accompany you."

Katie hugged Mama's arm and tugged her away. "Now, Mama. This is Gabby's chance to become better acquainted with Lady Thorne. Besides, you promised to play whist with Lizzie and me tonight."

Mama sighed and smoothed a hand over Katie's hair. "I suppose you're right. It won't be long until I must say good-bye to all of my daughters. I shouldn't allow the time to go to waste."

She gave Gabby one more hug and allowed Katie to draw her from the bedchamber.

Lizzie lifted an eyebrow as she ran her gaze up and down Gabby. "You should take a heavier wrap."

"It's plenty warm enough for this one," she said as she draped the thin material around her shoulders.

Lizzie marched to the wardrobe and grabbed a wool shawl. "I sense the weather changing. You won't be warm enough."

"I'll be fine." She refused her sister's offering and left her chambers. Lizzie followed to press her argument.

"But what if you aren't? What if you are wishing later you had listened to me?"

Gabby was willing to take that chance.

Her sister scrambled to keep up. "Wait a moment."

The front door creaked open as Gabby descended the stairs. "Thank heavens," she muttered.

Sebastian's footman stood just outside of the door, waiting to escort her to the carriage. "I must go, Lizzie."

"Please, take it just in case." Her sister dogged her heels outside, trying to force the wrap on her.

"Really, Elizabeth. You are being a pest."

Grateful to escape her sister, she accepted the footman's assistance and clambered into the carriage. The inside was blanketed in darkness when the door closed, and she hadn't even sat down before the coach jerked, tossing her back against a hard body. A large hand clamped over her mouth as she drew in a breath to scream.

Twenty-three

"YOU'RE SAFE, LADY BUG."

Anthony tightened his hold on Gabby as she flailed on his lap. If she broke free, he would have a hell of a time keeping her safe.

The coach careened around a corner and threw them to the left. Anthony's shoulder banged against the wall, and an explosion of pain sent shock waves down to his elbow. Righting them on the bench, he planted his feet in preparation for the next sudden turn. Gabby continued to thrash, making his task more difficult than it needed to be.

"It's me, Anthony. Be still before we become injured."

Her reply was muffled, but he didn't need to understand her words to know what she thought of his surprise. Her heel connected with his shin and he dropped his hand from her mouth with an incredulous yelp.

"Anthony, what do you think you're doing? I'm expected at Drury Lane."

"You are missing tonight's performance." He loosened his grip enough for her to swivel on his lap, but he refused to release her until there was no more danger. A wheel hit a rut in the road and she slammed against his chest.

Her fingers dug into his shoulders as she clung to him. "Egads! Is your driver trying to kill us?"

"Once we have cleared London, there won't be sharp turns, but we really must press on if we don't want to be caught."

"Where are you?" She groped his face and her finger rammed into his eye.

He jerked and almost unseated her. "Blast! What is it with you and your kin trying to blind me?"

"I can't see a thing. At least open the curtain so we have a little light."

She grasped the curtain's edge, admitting a sliver of light from the carriage lamp. He slapped her hand away before she could fling it open.

"Not until we're out of town."

She huffed and dropped the curtain back into place. "Where in God's name are we going, and why must we remain in the dark?"

He managed to capture her chin and pressed his mouth to hers, partly to stop her questions, but more so because he had missed her beyond words. She held herself rigid, her lips unyielding.

"I love you, sweetheart," he whispered.

She laid her hand against his cheek and sighed. "Oh, Anthony." The wistfulness in her voice called to a part of him that longed to protect her.

"I love you," he repeated. Tenderly, he kissed the corners of her mouth, her chin, the tip of her nose, each eyelid. Her breath quickened as her hand splayed on his chest, and she leaned into his kiss. She wanted him as much as he wanted her, but something kept her from surrendering.

"Please, love me back, Gabrielle."

She whimpered softly and placed her divine mouth against his. Her sweet taste flooded his senses as her lips parted and allowed him access. Warm tingles raced over his skin. She twined her arms around his neck, and her tongue brushed against his lips.

His heart was lighter and larger with her wrapped in his embrace. Thank God, taking her had been the right thing to do. Doubt had hounded him all evening.

Gabby's ample bottom nestled into his crotch and her lush breasts pressed against his chest as she wiggled closer. She was the perfect amount of plump in all the right places. He covered her breast and marveled at how well it fit his hand. His thumb circled her nipple until it stood erect and ready for his mouth if not for the clothes in his way. Her heart drummed against his fingertips.

She moaned into his mouth. Blood raced through his veins, causing a low rumble in his ears and a throb in his cock.

He wanted her. Badly. *Painfully*.

But he had promised to make her his wife before he took her to bed.

Curse oaths, honor, and friendship.

Ignoring his body's demands for satisfaction—or trying, at least—he broke the kiss, but he couldn't resist nibbling a trail down her neck, across her bare shoulder, and over the tempting mounds spilling from the neckline of her gown.

She inhaled sharply, and he nearly ignored his good sense and laid her out on the bench beneath him. The cut of her gown made for an irresistible display of her charms. Realization doused him like a bucket of cold water, and he set her away. The coach was moving at a steady pace now. They had cleared the city.

"What the hell are you wearing?" He jerked the curtains aside to allow a shaft of light from the carriage lamps to thrust inside. Her ivory skin glowed in the lamplight. And there was too much showing. He hooked a finger inside her dress and tried to hike it up to cover her better. "Did you dress this way for Thorne?"

The very idea made him shake with anger. Had the blackguard touched her like this?

She tensed, the atmosphere chilly once again. "I am marrying him. Why shouldn't I dress to please him?"

How could she burn so hotly with Anthony's touch and dare to speak of marrying another man? He grabbed her shoulders so she couldn't turn away. If she wanted to lie, let her lie to his face.

"In case you haven't noticed," he said through clenched teeth, "you are here in *my* arms. Not Thorne's. And the way you were responding to my kisses says this is where you want to be. I think it's fair to assume the wedding is off."

Her eyes gleamed in the scant light. "It most certainly is not, because you are signaling your driver to turn this coach around and take me home."

He scoffed and captured her chin. She didn't pull away, but met his gaze boldly as if daring him to kiss her again.

"There's nothing on this earth that will make me take you back, Gabby. You belong with me."

She jerked from his hold. "You're incapable of reason."

She had to know he spoke the truth. She belonged to him and him to her. Nevertheless, she wouldn't like him pointing it out again. He released her so she could retreat to the opposite bench and sulk a moment.

"When you are ready to rest, I brought a blanket," he said. "It's a long drive to the border."

An outraged sputter came from her side of the coach, but since she seemed incapable of words, he decided the discussion had run its course.

He smiled, partly to irritate her, but mostly because he was genuinely happy to see her.

"I'm only doing this because I love you, Lady Bug."

"Oh, sod off!"

⤛❦⤜

Gabby crossed her arms and fumed over Anthony's deception. He had bested her again, and blast if she knew how he had managed it. Yet, in spite of her anger, a small thrill passed through her. He was taking her to Scotland to marry her. She would become his wife, something she had desired since she was a girl.

The implications of eloping with Anthony quickly crushed her excitement. It would be the biggest scandal of the Season, and there would be no way to cover it up. Sebastian and his family would be humiliated. Her family would be ashamed.

Oh, dear heavens. No! Her sisters' prospects next Season would be ruined. She couldn't do this to them.

"Have you considered the consequences of what you're doing?"

Anthony opened the curtains fully now that they had left the city. Lamplight bathed one side of his face in a golden glow. His eyes appeared as if they were black jewels, his lips set in a thin line. "I am betraying your family's trust, a family that has welcomed me as one of their own. I'm aware of what this means."

She hadn't thought about how her brothers would react to Anthony abducting her. This was even worse than she'd first imagined. Her throat squeezed and she gulped in deep breaths to fight the feeling of suffocating. If they would challenge Sebastian for stealing a kiss, what would they do to Anthony for ruining her?

Switching back to his side of the carriage, she grabbed his hands. "It's not too late. There's time to turn back. My brothers will forgive you."

He wrapped his larger hands around hers, the warmth of his touch coaxing her toward him. Meeting her halfway, his lips grazed her forehead. His kiss was tender and she closed her eyes to savor it.

"We can't turn back," he murmured. "This has been our destiny all along."

This is our destiny? This path would only lead to heartbreak. Her sisters' futures destroyed. Gabby an outcast to her own family. And most distressing of all, Anthony could be lying in a field bleeding to death. What would become of his daughter if he were to die? He clearly hadn't thought this through.

"How does Annabelle fit into this destiny you think exists?"

His fingers tensed, then he released her hands. When

he didn't answer, she wanted to shake him. Anything to unravel this ridiculous fantasy he had weaved. He had to see how valuable his life was. How could he even think to risk it for her?

"I asked you how Annabelle—"

"I heard you." He leaned across her to snatch a blanket from the bench and plopped it on her lap. "Rest."

His abruptly barked command made her jump. He moved to the opposite bench, crossed his arms, and closed his eyes.

She stared at him, slack-jawed. His actions could ruin the lives of everyone they cared about and he was refusing to talk about it?

With a huff, she unfolded the blanket to spread it over her lap.

"You stubborn mule," she spat.

He grunted in response but didn't even bother to open his eyes. He was the most infuriating person she'd ever known, and yet she couldn't stop herself from loving him. She had been trying for as long as she could remember.

❧

Anthony's heart was battering against his ribs. Damn him for listening to Gabby's sisters. What did two chits know about love? Of course, *he* was the simpleton who had taken their advice. He had wanted to believe them when they had said Gabby loved him, and perhaps she did. Still, love wasn't always enough to overcome obstacles.

How did Annabelle fit into their destiny? What

options were there except to find a place for her in their lives? He wouldn't send his daughter away, which left him and Gabby at an impasse.

A pulse beat at his temple, keeping time with his heart. What a mess he had created. Despite Gabby's belief that he hadn't considered the consequences, he had. He knew he was risking his friendships with her brothers, close friendships that had kept him going when his home life had left him hopeless. And they had been there for him as his heart was breaking over their sister.

After the visit from Gabby's sisters, he had convinced himself her family would forgive his rash decision, but perhaps they wouldn't. He had taken her two days before her wedding. There was no way to avoid a scandal. Perhaps Thorne would even sue for breach of contract, which would only make the affair more scandalous. Anthony would pay whatever settlement was reached, but no amount of money would erase the memory of Gabby stealing away with another man so close to her wedding. Her brothers wouldn't take kindly to her name being dragged through the muck.

What concerned Anthony most, however, was how her family would react toward her. If they believed Gabby was a willing participant in their flight to Gretna Green, her brothers could be put out with her. Perhaps they might even turn their backs on her. He didn't judge it likely, but it wouldn't be the first time a lady was disowned by her family.

Anthony could take care of her. That wasn't a worry. But Gabby loved her family dearly. Her heart would be shattered if they disowned her.

And she would hate Anthony.

Then again, if her brothers believed he had taken her against her will, he was as good as dead. He wouldn't raise a hand against any of the men he thought of as brothers, not even to defend himself.

This was a mistake. As soon as the thought appeared, he fought against the logic. The feel of Gabby in his arms hadn't been a mistake. Her lips beneath his weren't a mistake.

He raked his fingers through his hair. Why did his head and heart have to be in conflict? He blew out an exasperated breath. Turning back was not an option, because living without her was impossible. Therefore, he would take his chances with her brothers, and he and Gabby must come to an understanding about Annabelle.

"We need to talk." He opened his eyes and discovered Gabby had fallen asleep. Her head listed to the side and jostled with every bump. She appeared bloody uncomfortable, and yet she slept on. He smiled, their troubles receding for a moment. The chit could sleep anywhere.

He and Drew had often used her uncanny ability to sleep through a raiding horde to their advantage. His backbone became slack and he dissolved against the cushion as he recalled those less complicated days.

It had been the best summer of his life. He'd been a guest at Twinspur Cottage, the duke and duchess's summer home. His days had been filled with swimming in the lake, horseback riding, and exploring the land with Luke, Richard, and Drew.

And then there had been Gabby.

She'd been a skinny, shrill little nuisance. No matter how early he and his friends had risen in the hopes of evading her, she had been dressed and waiting to join their adventures. Anthony had become adept at losing her that summer. Her wide-eyed trust had made the task easy, and his ploys to send her to retrieve different items so she could join them earned him much admiration from her brothers. Still, she had been determined and often found them despite their efforts to lose her. Therefore, Anthony had taken it upon himself to make her as miserable as she made him and his friends by playing a prank on her.

Because she was such a sound sleeper, she hadn't known anything about the toad he slipped into her bed until she woke the next morning. When she saw the toad's vapid eyes staring back at her, she had screamed so loudly he'd heard her at the other end of the corridor where he had been allotted a bedchamber. The duke's scolding had been a small price to pay to get back at the pest.

Little bug. His heart filled up his chest. He had loved Gabby in some form most of his life. There had to be a way to convince her they were meant to be. Once she believed it, he knew she would come around with Annabelle. Gabby wasn't judgmental or unkind. Perhaps she would even forgive him some day for forcing her hand. She did love him. She had never denied her feelings.

A rut in the road tossed her to the side, and her head bumped against the coach's wall. Still, she didn't wake.

He chuckled under his breath and slid onto the bench beside her to draw her into his arms. His bride would be well rested when they reached Gretna Green, but she would also be black and blue.

She didn't stir as he settled her head against his chest, tucked snugly under his chin. Her steady breath and heartbeat infused him with calmness. All would be well. He refused to believe anything else, because whether or not she chose to believe, they were each other's destiny.

Twenty-four

SEBASTIAN DEPARTED FOR TALLIAH HOUSE THE MOMENT Mother and Eve returned home to report Gabrielle was missing. Apparently, there had been a bit of confusion when his mother and sister arrived to collect her for the theatre. The butler had insisted Sebastian's coach had already taken her to Drury Lane. Valuable time had been wasted sending a footman to the theatre only to have the servant return with the verdict everyone should have already realized: Sebastian's coach had never arrived.

"Because it wasn't my bloody coach," he growled to no one in particular as he approached the duke's front door. He raised his fist to knock and the heavy door swung open.

The butler balked. "Lord Thorne, we were not expecting you."

Sebastian charged inside, the servant shuffling aside to avoid being trampled. "My betrothed has been abducted and no one was expecting me? Take me to Foxhaven, now."

He stalked across the marbled floor en route to the drawing room.

"His Grace hasn't yet returned from this evening's entertainments, milord. I thought you were the duke arriving just now."

Sebastian halted, fists forming at his sides. Turning on his heel to face the incompetent fool, his voice took on a dangerous edge. "It has been over an hour since you discovered her ladyship was abducted. You should have sent for the duke the moment my mother arrived to collect her."

"We didn't realize anything was amiss, milord."

Sebastian shook with a repressed desire to thrash the dolt. What in the devil's name was wrong with this household? None of Sebastian's staff would have hesitated to summon him if there was any hint of danger to Eve.

He strode toward the butler, stopping just inches from the servant's face. "Lady Gabrielle's chaperone arrived a quarter of an hour after *someone else* took her, and you didn't realize something was amiss? How could you mistake her abductor's coach for mine?"

The servant backed away. "Please, milord. His Grace will be home soon."

The sound of slippers padding across the foyer penetrated Sebastian's furious fog. "Please don't yell at Wesley. He didn't know."

One of Gabrielle's sisters came to stand beside the servant. It was the prettier one, the one with dimples. "My apologies, Lady Elizabeth, isn't it? I didn't mean to disturb you, but a situation has arisen and this numbskull"—he jabbed a finger toward the butler—"doesn't seem to grasp the seriousness."

Her eyes expanded with each word he bit off.

Damnation. He pinched the bridge of his nose and exhaled, trying to regain control of himself. What was wrong with him that he would speak so plainly in the girl's presence?

He was frightened, that was what was wrong. Anyone could have taken Gabrielle. Perhaps one of the riffraff that frequented the Den wanted revenge against him for cleaning out his pockets. If any harm came to her, Sebastian would never forgive himself.

"You may go, Wesley," Lady Elizabeth said then captured her bottom lip between her pearly teeth. She remained that way until the servant quit the foyer. "It is I who should apologize, my lord. Wesley didn't notice the coach because I was causing a distraction."

Sebastian's brows shot up. "Did *you* see the coach? Were there any unusual features?"

She dismissed his question with a wave. "The only thing that matters is Wesley isn't to blame. Perhaps you would like to wait in the drawing room for my brother's return. I'm certain you will have much to discuss. Given the circumstances, I can't imagine he would deny you a generous settlement."

"A settlement?"

Lady Elizabeth nodded, her big blue eyes earnest. "That is customary when a betrothal is broken, isn't it?"

His gut clenched. "What gives you the idea our betrothal has been broken?"

"Well, it's only logical that you and Gabby cannot marry once she has exchanged vows with Lord Ellis."

It took but a second for her meaning to sink in. "Your sister has eloped?"

"Well…" A pink flush spread over Lady Elizabeth's cheeks.

No, of course Gabrielle hadn't eloped. She was no coward. Had she wanted to end their association, she would have come to him and cried off. Over the past two weeks she had begun to accept their union, and he had vowed to make her happy every day of their life together. It was the least he owed her for the sacrifice she was making to help his sister.

His chest squeezed as he realized what had happened. "Ellis abducted her."

"No! It isn't like that, Lord Thorne."

If Sebastian didn't stop Ellis, Gabrielle would be ruined. She would have no choice but to marry the damned blackguard.

Just like you gave her no choice? He ignored the meddlesome voice at the back of his mind. A conscience was a bloody nuisance. The point was Gabrielle had agreed to marry him and Ellis had taken her. Sebastian would lose the only challenge ever worth winning unless he caught them tonight, and he needed Gabrielle.

"I'm going to kill him," Sebastian muttered as he stormed from Talliah House.

It wouldn't take long to catch them on the Great North Road if Sebastian went by horseback, but a visit to the mews was just one more blasted delay in bringing Gabrielle safely back home.

❧

Luke, the Duke of Foxhaven, pressed his fingers against his temple and blinked at his twin sisters. They sat side by side on the brocade settee in the drawing room, their hands punching the air to emphasize points he couldn't follow. Making out anything his sisters were saying was impossible with them talking at the same time.

"Slow down," he said, but their rapid chatter continued. He suppressed a groan.

After a pleasant evening out with his wife, he had been looking forward to a pleasant evening in bed with her. Apparently this wasn't to happen any time soon, unless he got to the bottom of what had agitated his sisters.

So far, the only parts of their story he could understand had to do with his butler, a livid baron, and true love.

He waved his hands as if he could clear the confusion from the air. "Please, you must take turns."

Liz and Katie snapped their mouths closed, exchanged a look as if to determine which one should go first, then started in again at the same time.

"Stop," he commanded. Quiet descended over the room. He glanced toward his wife and found her nibbling her bottom lip. Vivian appeared as lost as he was.

"If I were to piece together anything from what you've told me so far," he said, "I might conclude Lord Thorne and Wesley are in love."

A chuckle burst from Vivian, but she sobered quickly when the girls shot incredulous looks in her direction. "I fear it may be more dire than that, my love," she said. "From what I can gather, Gabby and Lord Ellis have eloped and Lord Thorne is none too happy about it."

How had she garnered *that* from his sisters' garbled words?

Liz clutched a hand to her chest. "And Lord Thorne has gone after them and plans to kill Lord Ellis."

That got Luke's attention. "Like hell he will."

His sisters gasped.

"Forgive my foul language, but I won't allow Gabby's life to be placed in danger by some idiot bent on revenge." He wasn't in favor of harm coming to Anthony either. He stood and shooed away the girls. "Off to bed, both of you, and don't fret. I'll not let anything happen to Gabby or Lord Ellis."

A part of Luke knew Anthony was as equally deserving of his displeasure as Thorne, but a man in love was known to do irrational things. Luke had never doubted his friend's devotion to Gabby. He just hadn't realized she returned Anthony's feelings. Any time Luke had questioned her decision to marry Thorne, she had reassured him she was following her heart.

The girls hopped up from their seats and came to throw their arms around him, thanking him for going after Gabby. He ruffled their hair and placed kisses on their foreheads. "I don't want either of you getting it into your heads I enjoy this part of my brotherly duties. I expect *you* to be good girls."

"Yes, sir," Katie responded while Liz rolled her eyes.

"I saw that, Elizabeth."

She ducked her head and hastened to escape the room, likely before a lecture ensued.

He rang for Wesley and ordered a message to be sent to Drew before discussing his plans with his wife as he hurried up the winding staircase. Vivian was close on his heels, keeping pace with him as always.

"If Drew and I give chase tonight, we may be able to stop Thorne before he catches Gabby and Ellis."

"Are you certain Drew is your best choice?"

At the landing, he captured his wife around the waist and planted a kiss on her sweet lips. "You know you can't go this time, Viv. My brother is most suited for this task."

She may have swayed him in the past to play rescuer to his mother's companion, but this was a horse of a different color.

Vivian smiled ruefully. "I hadn't expected you to allow me, but there must be something I can do to help."

"If you could tell Mother what has happened and reassure her everything will be all right, I would be grateful. She will need to begin penning letters at once cancelling the wedding."

"I can assist her." His wife kissed him once more before heading in the direction of his mother's chambers.

As he watched her walk down the dimly lit corridor with a sensual sway to her hips, he reconsidered thrashing Anthony. Being madly in love was no excuse for ruining another man's pleasure.

❧

Gabby woke contented and warm. Her eyes drifted shut on a sigh. It was nice waking snuggled against Anthony's broad chest.

Good heavens! Her eyes flew open again. Before she'd fallen asleep, he had been across the carriage.

How had they ended up cuddled together? The evening's events came rushing back, making her head spin.

Anthony's chest rose and fell steadily under her cheek. She lifted her gaze to confirm he was sleeping. Early-morning light filtered through the window and created a golden haze on his strong jaw where his whiskers had grown.

Green pastures beyond the window didn't provide a hint of where they were. Somewhere between London and Gretna Green, she assumed, but she had no idea how far they had traveled. How had she slept through the changing of horses? Now there was no hope of returning before anyone learned she was missing.

She tried to ease from Anthony's embrace without waking him, but his lashes fluttered. He blinked several times, his blue eyes red and puffy. It appeared he'd had a rough night. He still had a smile for her, though.

"Back from the sleep of the dead?" he asked in a husky voice.

She ignored his teasing and pulled the blanket up to her neck. The air was much cooler than it had been in London. Now she wished she had listened to Lizzie and worn her wool shawl.

Her head snapped toward Anthony. "Did my sister help you plan this?"

"Your sisters may have suggested it."

"*Sisters?* As in both of them?"

He stretched like a giant cat instead of answering; his muscles rippled beneath his trousers and shirt. Sometime in the night, he had removed his outer clothes and untied his cravat, and he looked deliciously unkempt. A flash of heat made her too warm all of a sudden. She tossed the blanket aside, her gaze landing on a large black splotch on the crimson silk of her skirts.

"What is this?" She jerked the material up to examine the stain. "Is this paint?" There was a slightly hysterical ring to her tone.

Anthony rubbed the back of his neck, color rushing into his face. "I'm afraid so. There wasn't time for the door to dry fully."

She assumed he meant the coach door. She dropped her skirts with an unladylike growl. "And *why* was there paint on your door?"

"I wanted you to be comfortable, so it was necessary to bring the travel coach. But there was the little matter of the coat of arms."

He'd had the coat of arms covered with paint. No wonder she hadn't known she was climbing into his carriage. "You—you deceitful bounder!" She thrust a finger in his direction. "You always were a sneaky scoundrel, even when we were children. Well, not only have you ruined my reputation, you've wrecked my favorite gown."

Perhaps she was overreacting. After all, it was only a gown, but the permanent stain reminded her of what *she* was to her family: a dark blotch on their lives. She hurled a few choice words at him, peppered with the appropriate number of references to his lack of intelligence and honor, and finally ended her tirade with another frustrated growl.

"I'll buy you another gown," Anthony said, rubbing

the sleep from his eyes. "You may have five new gowns if you'll just stop screeching in my ear."

Of all the gall! Her hands landed on her hips. "Will you buy me a new reputation, too, my lord? How much money do you think it will take to erase my family's embarrassment? Do you think you can afford to make the entire *ton* forget that Mama and Papa brought fickle girls into this world, ones that run away two days before they are to walk down the aisle?"

He grimaced. "Your parents only had one fickle daughter. I'm sure the other two know their minds well enough."

She cried out. Of all the things he could have said to her, that had to be the most hurtful. "But *I* didn't change my mind. You took me and now I'll be held responsible. Everyone will be talking behind my back, which wouldn't bother me so much except I will be a disgrace to my family."

He had the decency to look chagrined. "Gabby, I'm sorry. I didn't see any other way."

"I told you—" She swallowed a sob, closing her eyes to regain control of herself. "I told you I wouldn't marry you. That's all you needed to see."

The coach slowed and she realized they were approaching the next stop. They passed several small cottages before the buildings became butted up against each other. A bakery, haberdashery, and a butcher's shop. None of the landmarks looked familiar. "Where are we?"

He reached for his waistcoat and jacket, avoiding eye contact. "Litchfield, I believe. We'll change horses here and you may freshen up if you are quick about it."

"We aren't traveling the Great North Road?" Her family always traveled the Great North Road en route to Northumberland.

Anthony shook his head as the coach rolled to a stop. "There wasn't enough lead time. We would have been overtaken in the night if we had traveled that route."

"Oh." Her eyebrows lifted. She hated to admit she was impressed with his thinking, especially after she had made such a scene and insulted his intelligence. In truth, she was relieved her brothers hadn't found them last night. Even when she was furious with Anthony, she couldn't bear the thought of any harm coming to him, and that is what she feared would happen if her brothers caught them before she had time to make an appeal on his behalf.

Anthony's manner was short as he escorted her into the small inn, arranged for fresh water and a room, then left her in the care of the innkeeper's wife. The woman was dressed in a plain gray gown with her hair pinned under a snow-white cap. Her tidy appearance was a reflection of the surprisingly well-kept room she led Gabby to above stairs.

"Is there anything else I can get for you, milady?"

"Perhaps a bite to eat?" Her stomach had growled twice on the stairwell.

"Yes, ma'am. I'll send something up at once," the woman said before leaving Gabby to fend for herself. She caught her reflection in the looking glass and gasped. Her hair stuck up at odd angles, and red creases from sleeping on Anthony's shirt crisscrossed her cheek. Add in her soiled gown and she looked a mess.

Gabby set to work on her hair and had just finished her toilette when there was a knock at the door. Anthony entered without waiting for permission. He leaned back against the closed door with a dark piece of material draped over his arm and tucked his hand into his pocket. He jiggled his fingers, an unbecoming habit he had developed later in life.

He smiled, but there was an air of sadness about him. "I couldn't find a suitable gown, but I managed to locate a cloak."

"Thank you." Her distress had little to do with her ruined gown, but he seemed incapable of understanding her position. Still, her heart warmed to him. He was trying to please her, even when she had treated him poorly.

She allowed him to drape the garment over her shoulders and tie it at the neck. His hands lingered on her shoulders, and tingles traveled to her fingertips.

"I've been thinking about what you said in the coach," he said. "You did tell me you wouldn't marry me. I should have listened, but I've been miserable without you. I can't eat, and I have no gumption to do anything. I thought if there was any chance to change things…"

Sympathy welled up inside her and urged her to reach out to him. Their fingers laced together. She had been just as miserable as he. No matter how wrong it was to put herself above her sisters, she loved him. She couldn't lie to herself or him any longer.

"I forced myself to eat when Mama started fretting, but I could have been eating mud for all the taste food had. Heartache is the worst kind of pain."

"Forgive me, Gabby. I don't want to be at odds." He wrapped her in his embrace, exhaling loudly when she sagged against him.

She didn't want to be angry either. It created a wall between them, keeping them apart when they had been separated long enough. Deep down she was grateful for what Anthony had done. If she had thought there was any way to get out of marriage to Lord Thorne without harming anyone, she would have done it. Now he'd taken the burden from her.

She'd reflected on their situation in these moments alone, and she had come to a realization. She and Anthony *were* getting married, and they would be better off facing the fallout together. Another revelation was that her family would love her no matter what scandal became attached to her name. They had proven as much after her ill-fated assignation with Lt. MacFarland. Her nose tickled and she blinked away her tears. She wished someday to prove herself worthy of her family's devotion. There would still be consequences to pay when they returned to London, but she would have Anthony by her side.

He kissed the top of her head and hugged her tighter. "In light of your distress, I have decided we'll turn back. There's still a chance no one outside of your family and Lord Thorne knows."

She broke his hold with a loud protest and glowered up at him. How could he even consider returning her to London after she'd admitted how she too had been miserable during their separation?

"*Now* you want to turn back? For heaven's sake! Lord Thorne will know we spent the night together, and if he has any sense at all, he will break the betrothal on the spot. Are you trying to destroy my life?"

Oh, no. It was too late for Anthony to back out now. With a huff, she marched for the door. "I hate to disappoint you, Lord Ellis, but you are saddled with me now. You will marry me good and proper. And you had best feed me soon, because I can become churlish when I'm hungry."

A shocked laugh sounded behind her. "As you wish, my lady."

Blasted right, as I wish.

Once they were settled in the coach and on their way again, she avoided looking at him. Of all the insufferable things he had done to her, this was at the top of the list. Take her back, indeed.

Anthony cleared his throat. "I think you misunderstood me."

She raised an eyebrow.

"I have no desire to return you to Thorne, but if that's your wish, I will do it. Even if it kills me," he added softly. He pulled a bundle from his jacket and passed it to her. "The innkeeper's wife wrapped this for you. It isn't much, but perhaps it will keep starvation at bay until we reach our next stop."

She accepted the offering with a thank-you and unwrapped the bundle. Inside was a hunk of bread, a slice of ham, and two small apples. Her stomach grumbled loudly. "There's enough to share. Would you like to split it?"

"That's all for you. Can't have you wasting away to skin and bones." He smiled smugly, pulled another apple from his jacket, and bit into it. Juice dribbled down his chin and he swiped at it with his sleeve.

"Neanderthal," she grumbled, but she couldn't hold back a slight smile. "You should inform your driver to keep up the pace. I'd like to reach Gretna before I become an old woman."

He beamed and took another hearty bite before opening the trapdoor and calling out for the driver to increase their speed. For some time they traveled in silence, except for the occasional crunch of his apple. The emptiness in her stomach was fading by the time she popped the last bite of bread into her mouth and started on the ham. Her mood was much improved, too.

"Thank you for the food."

"I'll always take care of you, Lady Bug."

She studied him, letting go of her temper fully. Anthony had always been dutiful. He may have had his moments of engaging in tomfoolery with her brothers, but there had been an air of seriousness about him for as long as she could recall. "What was it like inheriting the earldom at such a young age?"

He flinched and she wished she had thought before she'd spoken. She didn't want to bring back bad memories for him.

"I'm sorry. We can talk about something else," she said.

"I don't mind." His slight frown told her he was lying. "Honestly, I don't remember what it was like before I became earl. I have vague recollections of my father and older brother, but I'm never certain if my memories are real or based on stories my nurse told me about them."

"Your nurse? Didn't your mother ever talk about them?"

He shook his head. His eyes glazed over as he stared at something beyond her shoulder; perhaps he was seeing another time. "Sometimes I thought Mother wished she had died with them. I think that's the reason she avoided the living."

An image of a young boy with golden locks and short pants rambling around Ellis Hall alone made her throat scratchy with unshed tears. She forced herself to swallow the bite of ham she had taken, then set her food aside.

"I tried to live up to expectations, but I never quite knew what those were." He smiled wryly, suddenly back in the present. "Someone forgot to hand me a list of instructions. I supposed I muddled through well enough, though."

He was being modest. She had overheard her father speaking proudly of how well Anthony had managed his properties, much better than the former earl had.

"I don't believe there was any muddling involved."

He shrugged, his smile growing wider. "Don't tell me you're getting sweet on me now?"

She shrugged too and picked up the second apple. There had never been a question of her holding a *tendre* for him. He had been the reluctant one.

Questions bubbled up in the back of her mind, and she settled on the one that had been haunting her for years. "Why did you marry Camilla?"

His grin faded as he turned his gaze to the landscape outside. "Looks like we might run into rain."

The sky had darkened, and from Gabby's vantage

point, she could see voluminous clouds churning in the distance. Their shapes were changing and expanding at a rapid rate.

"More like a thunderstorm," she said.

He craned his neck to see what she had spotted behind him. The sky lit up, outlining the angry black clouds on the horizon. He turned back to her with a frown. "We should find shelter before long."

It seemed far enough away to her. They might even avoid it entirely.

"Shouldn't we press forward? Luke can't be too far behind. As clever as it may have been to take a different road, my brother is no dimwit."

"I told you I would always take care of you, and it's safer to find shelter."

She could argue her oldest brother was as dangerous as anything Mother Nature could dole out, but Anthony had squared his jaw. Any further discussion was pointless.

She suppressed a sigh. Her worry was likely for naught. Luke would listen if she told him she had changed her mind and wanted to marry Anthony. Having her brother think her a fickle twit didn't sit well with her, but she had no other option.

She looked out the window and chuckled.

Anthony narrowed his eyes.

"I'm not laughing at you. Come see." She waved him over to her side and pointed out the window. "In the clouds, there's a man laughing and a little dog leaping from his mouth."

"I don't see it."

She rolled her eyes. "Really, Anthony. How can

you be so blind?" Drawing an outline of the figures in the air with her finger, she provided verbal cues of where to look. His head brushed against hers as he bobbed to make out what she saw. He too burst into laughter.

Wrapping his arm around her, he placed a kiss at her temple. "Only you, Gabby. Only you."

She laid her head against his shoulder and closed her eyes. They continued in silence as she savored his heat. His cologne had worn off long ago, but his scent was familiar and comforting.

His hand made slow passes over her arm from shoulder to elbow. "I was at the age when a man took a wife. Camilla wasn't the most-sought-after debutante, but she was accomplished enough."

Gabby held still, praying he would continue.

"There were times during our courtship that I found her petulant and difficult, but I ignored the signs that we didn't suit. Her father was pleased she was marrying into the upper ranks, and I assumed she was happy with the match as well."

Gabby swiveled on the seat to face him. "Camilla didn't want to marry you?"

"It seems not," he said with a grimace. "Perhaps that answers your question, but I suspect what you really wish to know is the reason I chose her over you."

Her breath caught in a noisy wheeze.

He smiled ruefully and pushed a wayward strand of hair from her face, his hand lingering on her cheek. "I didn't mean to shock you, but that is what you wish to know, isn't it?"

"Yes." It seemed pointless to deny it.

"You were still a girl."

She had been fifteen. "I was old enough to know my mind."

"And young enough for me to think you didn't. Your likes and dislikes changed frequently. One day you preferred Mozart. The next Beethoven was your favorite. Besides, dangling after your best friend's little sister isn't right. I thought it was best if I found a lady closer to my age."

Even now, his words cut deep. He hadn't even acknowledged her letter. "And was it for the best?" she asked, a note of bitterness creeping into her tone as she eased away from him.

His arm tightened around her back and pulled her back in place. Lifting her chin up with the tips of his fingers, he traced her lips with his thumb. "You already know the answer."

A crack of thunder echoed on the air, but it barely registered as she stared into his eyes.

"I never meant to hurt you, my love. Had I known my wedding would bring you pain, I would have arranged for a private ceremony."

She frowned. "But you still would have married her."

"I was young and stupid, Gabby. I can't change the past." Another loud boom startled them. His hand fell to his side. "It doesn't appear we'll make it to the next village in time. I'll have Geoffrey look for someplace close to wait out the storm."

Twenty-five

EVEN FROM A DISTANCE, THE FORBIDDING STRUCTURE on the hill appeared abandoned. Lightning reflected off remnants of broken glass left standing in the windows of the crumbling walls as the carriage bumped along the overgrown road. Charring marred the ruins.

"Fire," Anthony mumbled.

They might not find shelter in the castle, but perhaps an outbuilding would keep them dry and out of harm's way. As the carriage rounded the last curve, a second wing came into view, the roof still intact.

Hopefully, the fire damage hadn't spread beyond the west wing.

The carriage rolled to a stop outside the iron gate and Anthony climbed out. He needed to determine if it was safe before bringing Gabby inside.

She shivered when he assisted her from the carriage. "It's eerie to see a place like this abandoned. What do you think happened to everyone?"

Anthony playfully tweaked her nose. "Don't let your imagination run wild. It's hard to maintain a home this size. I'm certain it made more sense to leave than try to restore it."

Unruly shrubs scraped against the walls as the wind kicked up, and dark clouds rolled like ocean waves, bearing down on them. There wasn't time to stall. "Wait here while I determine if it's sturdy enough to enter."

He and the outrider pushed through the gate and headed for the intact wing, passing through a large arch to reach the weathered door. A quick walk around the outside revealed no cracks in the stone exterior.

"Let's look inside."

After a couple of good pushes, the sticky door gave way with a loud crack. Inside, debris littered the bare floors and a smoky smell hung on the air, but at a glance the wing appeared to have been untouched by the fire. Anthony made a round of the lower floor, looking for sagging ceilings or defects in the rafters. When he was satisfied the structure wasn't going to cave in on them, he returned to the carriage to collect Gabby.

The wind whipped her skirts at her ankles and a strand of ebony hair blew across her face. She pushed it aside, her eyes questioning.

"It will do," he said.

She shuffled closer to him as they approached the front door, but her death grip eased once they passed through the threshold. "It's not as bad as I expected. Just a bit chilly."

"An imagination can be a dangerous thing," he said with a wink. "Come this way. The drawing room is warmer and there's a place to sit."

He led her toward the room he'd discovered on his prowl through the first floor. Dim light trickled through the bank of smudged windows to cast the area in shades of gray. Dingy sheets draped the furniture as if someone expected to return when the home had been abandoned, but the thick layer of dust suggested no one had been there for a long time.

She released his arm and moved farther into the room. "Do you know who owns the house?"

"No, and I didn't see evidence of anyone living in the caretaker's cottage."

Gabby wandered the room, inspecting the contents. "What do we do now?"

Anthony ripped a sheet from a fainting couch, slumped down on the lumpy piece, and rubbed his gritty eyes. "We wait."

Gabby may have gotten a good night's sleep, but he hadn't. Every rut in the road had jostled her against him and kept his body alert and at the ready. The blasted traitor.

She glanced over her shoulder. "You look tired. Perhaps you should rest."

"And what do you propose to do?"

"I'll find something to entertain myself." She opened a drawer to the writing desk and dug inside. "Aha! Paper." The single sheet was curled at the edges and yellowed, but she beamed as if she'd uncovered treasure. She rifled through the other drawers, frowning. "But I don't see any ink."

Anthony lugged himself from the couch to search the fireplace. Finding a stick that hadn't burned all the way, he retrieved a letter opener and whittled one end. "In lieu of charcoal," he said as he handed it to her.

"Thank you." She held up the stick for inspection and wrinkled her nose. "I suppose I can't afford to be choosy. I'll sketch while you rest. Go lie down."

Needing no further encouragement, he stretched out on the couch and closed his eyes. Gabby's skirts rustled as she moved around the room until she finally settled.

His arms and legs were as heavy as lead, but despite his exhaustion, sleep didn't claim him. Rain pelted the windows; just a few pings at first, soon followed by the steady drumming of a downpour. Thunder shook the ground, but nothing to cause him concern.

An odd sensation, as if he were being watched, made his eyes flicker open. Gabby's gaze slid over him, a fine line of concentration between her arched brows. She pressed her lips together as she turned her attention to her paper and made light, careful strokes.

Was she drawing him?

His heartbeat sped up. He closed his eyes and lay still so she wouldn't stop working. The crude charcoal scratched against the paper, each sound vibrating in the room. His breathing shifted, becoming as volatile as the weather outside.

To have her gaze on him, knowing she took in every detail of his form, was arousing. How long would it take her to notice that rather telling detail? Well, he could do nothing about it. He imagined her hands exploring his body instead of her eyes, and his fingers itched to touch her. When he could no longer resist looking, he found her staring back with stormy blue-gray eyes.

He cleared his thick throat. "Are you sketching me in the nude?" he teased.

She answered with a sly smile and abandoned her drawing. "Perhaps." She lowered beside him on the couch and wound her fingers in his cravat. Her thigh pressing against his hip made his blood simmer. "It would be easier"—she untied the first knot—"if you had on fewer clothes. For the sake of art, of course."

His laugh sounded gruff. "For art," he agreed.

He forced himself to stay still while she fumbled with his cravat. Her inexperience made him smile, even as she tried to hide it behind a flirtatious smile. When she moved to the fastenings of his waistcoat, a low groan escaped him.

"Do you really intend to draw me in the nude?"

She shrugged one shoulder, shyness showing in the hesitation of her fingers. "Shouldn't I at least be afforded a peek? We are to be married soon."

No, she most certainly shouldn't be allowed a peek. That was for their wedding night. Her brothers would kill him otherwise. At this point, he was only risking permanent maiming for stealing away with her. But she looked so damned alluring with her mussed hair and flushed cheeks.

Oh, hell. He could hold his own against her brothers.

Capturing her at the nape, he pulled her down to cover her mouth with his. Her lips moved with his, returning his attack with vigor. She shifted on the couch and climbed atop him to work more furiously at unfastening his waistcoat.

He breathed her in, her essence filling him and giving him new life. Her taste and sweet scent always felt like coming home. This was how it was with Gabby. No one else had ever measured up.

When she finished with his waistcoat, he sat up, cradling her bottom so she didn't tumble from the couch. She grappled with his coat and pushed it down his arms. He shrugged out of it and his waistcoat, then tore his shirt over his head.

"Oh," she said on a breath. Her eyes roamed over him with an appreciative glint. "I'd forgotten how magnificent you are."

He'd never been a vain man, but her admiration made him hungry for more.

He eased back on the couch as she traced his muscles. Fire followed in the wake of her touch. It felt good to have her hands on him again.

His abs twitched as her exploration traveled lower. She slid a finger into his waistband and caressed him from one side to the next. He swallowed against the lump forming in his throat. He should stop her journey here, but he was so hard and the promise of her hand around his cock was difficult to resist. Still, a gentleman wouldn't allow it.

Three more fingers nestled into his trousers, her knuckles brushing against the pale hairs she couldn't yet see. God, why couldn't he be an unapologetic rogue like most gents he knew? She wanted him. It was clear in her swollen lips and smoky gaze.

He gently circled her wrist. "Not this time, my love."

She sat back on her haunches, her bottom snug against his groin. A deep blush rose up her chest and neck, and she didn't seem to know where to look. "I'm s-sorry."

He didn't want her embarrassed by her desires any more than he wanted to keep his word to wait until they married to bed her. "Don't apologize. If our circumstances were different, I wouldn't stop you."

When he'd given his word to Drew, he hadn't anticipated this moment. She would be his wife by now if their courtship had run its course, and they would be in London, not seeking shelter among castle ruins in the middle of nowhere.

If Thorne had stayed the hell away from her.

He let loose a string of curses in his mind. Why had she accepted Thorne's proposal? It made no sense. Before he could ask, her hand landed on his pocket where he kept his lucky talisman. His heart tripped.

Her brows arched as she probed the hard lump. "What is this?" She dug into his pocket.

"No!" He grabbed her wrist, but she already had the rock entrapped in her hand.

"Is this what you're always fiddling with?" She uncurled her fingers, and her eyes expanded.

∽

Gabby blinked, unable to believe what she was holding. The surface was worn smooth, but there was no mistaking the heart-shaped rock.

Flashes of that day made her quiver. Anthony flinging away her gift. His sneer. But there was more to her memories this time. His mournful gaze fixed on the ground. His fist shoved into his pocket.

She licked her lips. "You kept it?"

He gently took the rock and cradled it in his palm. "Yes."

A thousand thoughts swirled in her head, disputing what she'd always considered the truth. "But I saw you throw it away."

"You saw me pretend to throw it away."

She blinked back tears as the hurt she'd known that day returned in a flood. "But why?"

He sat up halfway and captured her face. His eyes drilled into her. "I never wanted to hurt you. I swear it. But Drew would have harassed me the whole ride back to school, and I didn't want him teasing you for the kindest gesture anyone had ever shown me. I'm sorry, Gabby. More than I can ever say."

"Why didn't you ever tell me you'd kept it?"

"When I saw how stricken you were, I hated myself. I meant to tell you I'd kept it, but by the time I saw you next, it had been months. You seemed to have forgotten everything, and I would have felt daft bringing it up. I thought it had only been important to me. I didn't see the truth until now."

She hadn't forgotten, but she had learned to cover her hurt feelings with happy chatter.

His thumb traced the curve of her jaw, sending warmth radiating down her back and spiraling in her lower belly. His touch drove away the doubts that had plagued her for too long. He'd kept her gift. All these years, it meant something to him. *She* meant something.

"Do you always carry it with you?"

His Adam's apple bobbed as he rubbed the rock between his thumb and finger. "I've kept it in my pocket every day since you gave it to me. It was a little piece of you—of your heart. You were the closest I ever had to family that cared about me."

His image blurred like a watercolor painting. How long had he felt unloved and alone? Probably most of his life. The thought made her want to weep.

"Anthony, *I* love you."

He shrugged and slipped the rock into his pocket. "I know."

Did he really? Had he felt so unloved in his life that he didn't believe her?

"I don't think you do." She placed a tiny kiss on his lips. "I love you. There is nothing you can do that will drive me away, so stop trying."

"I haven't been trying to drive you away."

"Haven't you been? You ignored my letter, pretended you'd never received it. You hid the fact that you had kept my gift. You don't have to be afraid I'm not going to love you back. I have loved you all my life and I'll never stop."

He blinked, perhaps shocked that she saw through his bravado. Why had it taken her so long to notice his vulnerabilities? Because she hadn't been seeing *him*, not really. She had looked at him with a girl's eyes and placed him on a pedestal next to God himself, then suffered when he hadn't lived up to her expectations. Suddenly, her world felt right. Anthony wasn't above her and out of her reach. He was here, flesh and blood, flawed just as she was, and she loved him even more.

Cupping his face, she leaned toward him. "From this day forward, I take you as my husband. You are mine and I am yours forever."

A broad smile broke across his face. "You do realize you'll have to wait until we are in Scotland before we can be married."

"Not in my heart."

When she pressed her lips to his, a loud crash of thunder rattled the windows. Or perhaps it was simply the effect of his kiss. Together, they were combustible. He could anger her beyond reason or incite her passion until she couldn't think, but sometimes not thinking was the biggest gift someone could be given.

Their mouths moved together hungrily, driven by a need for more. She'd meant every word. She was his. Surrendering to the desire that had been pulsing inside her for years, she parted her lips and welcomed his tongue. Each languorous sweep was incredibly erotic as they shared every breath and thundering heartbeat.

She buried her fingers in his golden hair. The skies outside were dark and furious, but he was her sun. How could she have ever thought herself capable of turning away from him?

He held her tight against him and wriggled them around until she was beneath him. His lips touched the corner of her mouth, her chin, and her neck.

"I love you too," he murmured, his breath hot against her skin.

Her heart nearly burst. Although he'd said the words in the past, it was different this time. He'd risked everything to have her.

His hand wrapped around her ribs, his thumb brushing the underside of her breast as his mouth slid down to her shoulder and along her collarbone. Scrumptious shivers raced down her back.

When he kissed the swell of her breast, she gasped softly. It was a most wicked place to be kissed, and she was certain it was wicked of her to like it.

Anthony drew back. His chest rose and fell in jerky motions. "Th-that's enough of that, then."

She smiled and urged his head lower. "It's not nearly enough for me."

He pulled back again and laughed, stirring a lock of hair that had fallen on his forehead. "Not for me either, Lady Bug. But a man must have some honor."

She rolled her eyes. "That would make you the only man I know who has any."

A dark scowl greeted her comment. "What is that to mean? Has another gentleman taken liberties?"

When he tried to sit up, she grabbed his shoulders to keep him close. "Not with me, ninnyhammer. But I'm not ignorant of the ways of men. Ladies talk."

His frown disappeared and he returned to cuddling her.

She smiled, perhaps a bit smugly. He wasn't as determined to release her as he'd indicated. "I know for a fact my brothers weren't always on their best behavior with their future wives."

Anthony kissed the tip of her nose. "It's one thing to forgive yourself a misstep, but there are different sets of rules for one's sister."

"Good thing I'm not your sister," she teased.

He laughed. "Yes, or this would be very awkward."

She swatted him on the shoulder, chuckling despite herself. "And now you've spoiled the mood."

Offering her a hand up, he settled on the couch beside her then bumped her with his shoulder. "Tell me the truth. You were drawing me as a jackass again, weren't you?"

She wrinkled her nose and pursed her lips, trying

not to smile as she recalled the caricature she had drawn the day after he snuck a frog into her bed. "No, but it would serve you right if I did, especially after insisting on upholding your honor."

He hugged her. "Don't be upset with me, sweetheart. Look at this place. I want everything to be perfect when we lie together our first time."

She glanced at the dusty furnishings and cobwebs coating the ceiling with a dawning sense of disgust.

"You deserve flowers and pretty linens." Lacing their fingers, he brought her hand to his lips to place a soft kiss. "You deserve the vows that will bind us together."

"I already gave you my vow," she grumbled, but with less conviction. He was right. She did want flowers, pretty linens, and candles, even though the only thing that should matter was love. Glancing up at the peeling wall covering, she admitted their surroundings mattered more to her than she'd first thought.

"As you wish," she mumbled.

He chucked her on the chin. "I *wish* this room could be transformed with the snap of my fingers, but since it can't, we should continue to the border as soon as the storm wanes. Only two more days and we'll be married."

Two days seemed like forever.

Twenty-six

SEBASTIAN CURSED THE RAIN AS HE LEFT THE RED STAG Inn on a fresh horse. The storm had forced him to take shelter until afternoon, and even though he'd needed the sleep, the delay increased his frustration.

He had ridden hard for hours last night before realizing Ellis hadn't taken the Great North Road like any other sane gent. Not that Sebastian should be surprised. Sebastian had rarely known the earl to do anything that implied good sense. Their first encounter at Eton had been a testament to Ellis's lack of judgment.

Sebastian had been a new student and different from his classmates. He hadn't come from generations of pampered aristocrats, and it showed in his manners and bearing. His father had been a soldier in the King's infantry, where fancy words didn't keep men alive.

Sebastian and Eve had been given all the advantages their father never had, but their sire's influence had still been present in their home. No amount of instruction had been able to change the fact their father's blood wasn't blue and their attitudes were bourgeois.

Hard work and determination reaped rewards, and one couldn't sit around waiting for fortune to fall into one's lap. That little tidbit of advice from his father hadn't made him many friends among a class of lads who'd done nothing besides enjoy a leisurely existence with the full knowledge fortune *would* land in their laps.

Yet it was Father's strange spells at the most inopportune moments, believing he was still at battle, that set the Thornes apart. Apparently, his father was the talk of the *ton*, because every boy at Eton had heard tales of his madness. Sebastian's teeth ground together as he recalled the taunts, and he still wanted to fight, but how could he defeat a memory?

There were three boys in particular who'd tormented him. Bullies, all of them. It soon became clear Sebastian wouldn't be rid of them until he fought his way free. *Hard work and determination reap rewards.* He'd known he would suffer a beating against three of them at once, but he'd planned to get in enough licks to prove he was not a victim. He had been holding his own, too, until Ellis interfered.

Sebastian had been knocked down for the fourth time, but he was struggling to his feet when the bloody earl entered with fists swinging. He took out the leader in one lucky punch and soon the others turned tail. Within moments, Ellis was a hero and Sebastian became a weakling in need of protection.

When the taunts and beatings continued, Sebastian knew the only way to escape was to prove himself superior to Ellis. So, he'd set on a course to challenge the earl and come out the victor. As Sebastian grew in size and strength, the mocking and fistfights had ended. His rivalry with Ellis had become a game in time, more a source of amusement for Sebastian. Until Lady Gabrielle's hand became the prize.

If Sebastian could have caught the earl's coach before dawn and rescued Lady Gabrielle, no one would have been wiser. Now there was no hope of keeping her abduction a secret. Her family was likely cancelling their wedding, which would make Sebastian a laughingstock again.

Worse. A bloody cuckold! Abandoned at the altar just like his sister.

Perhaps he wasn't the most upstanding gentleman in London, but Eve was a saint. She deserved better than life had doled out, and Sebastian couldn't fail her.

Ellis's coach must travel through Penrith to reach Gretna Green, and Sebastian would be waiting. He would rescue Lady Gabrielle, save her reputation, and somehow convince the *ton* she had eloped with *him*. He didn't know what reason they would supply since their wedding had been only a couple of days away, but his future wife was a clever girl. She would help him create a believable story.

First he must deal with Ellis, however, and Sebastian hadn't yet discounted a lead ball for the earl.

❧

Night fell, but the carriage didn't stop except to change horses and allow Gabby a chance to freshen up from time to time. At their last stop, Anthony had procured a basket of food, and she was greedily devouring a chicken leg. The savory meat was like a taste of heaven after the meager meal she'd had much earlier in the day. Juice dripped on her décolletage, and she felt a warm flush rising into her cheeks.

Anthony wiped the juice with his handkerchief and chuckled. "I had hoped your dowry would offset the cost of feeding you, but I don't suppose there is much chance your brother will allow us to have it now. Abduction is a messy business."

She laughed, forgetting to be embarrassed by her poor manners. "You could hold me for ransom."

He hugged her and placed a kiss on her forehead. "A ransom implies I'm willing to give you up, and I'm not."

She was unwilling to be given up, too. The warm glow that had enveloped her earlier that afternoon had settled in her heart. "Then I shall try not to drain the coffers with my appetite, but I can't make any promises."

"Fair enough."

She captured her bottom lip between her teeth and studied him. Dark shadows had formed under his eyes, and his movements had grown more sluggish throughout the journey. How long could he go without sleep?

"You look exhausted. And you've barely eaten anything," she said.

"I ate."

Not enough for a grown man. Their hurried pace was taking a toll on him. And she could use a bath.

She packed the remainder of her meal into the basket and wiped her mouth. "We're taking a room at the next inn."

He shook his head. "We have to keep going if we want to reach the border before nightfall tomorrow. We won't be able to evade your brothers much longer."

"What makes you think they would bother giving chase?"

He scoffed.

"I'm serious," she said, facing him. She'd been giving their situation thought this evening. "If Lizzie helped you make arrangements to whisk me away, she wouldn't hide it from Luke. Well, perhaps she would hide *her* part in everything, but she wouldn't want to worry Mama."

"And you believe your sister told your family we eloped rather than the truth."

She caressed his jaw, stubble rough against her palm. "We *are* eloping."

"How short your memory is, love. Only this morning you were taking me to task for deceiving you and stealing you away from Thorne."

She dropped her hand to her lap and frowned. She hadn't given Sebastian any more thought beyond her initial concern. "I feel horrible for the embarrassment I've caused him. You and I will have each other to weather the scandal together, and I know my family will stand behind me. But the Thornes may not fare as well since this is the second scandal to touch their family."

Anthony slowly raked his fingers through his hair, then slid his hand to the back of his neck and squeezed. "I would hate to see his family suffer more than they already have. If there was a way to spare them…"

She pulled the blanket up to her chin and snuggled

against his chest. In her momentary happiness, she had forgotten about the people who would be hurt by their actions. Liz. Katie. Miss Thorne. Sebastian. Perhaps even her mother would face displeasure from lifelong friends who had traveled to London to attend a wedding that wasn't going to happen. Yet Gabby could do nothing to stop the inevitable, even if she wanted to.

She closed her eyes as a shield against the shame she'd managed to keep at bay so far. She was the most selfish person on earth, because not even the threat to her sisters' futures made her want to change anything.

"We should stop for the night," she said. "My brothers aren't chasing after us, not if they know I'm with you."

"But if they are—"

She pushed back enough to make eye contact. "They aren't. I know my brothers."

His lips thinned. She thought he was going to argue, but he surprised her. "We may stop for a couple hours. Just long enough for the servants to rest."

She laid her head against his chest again to hide her smile. Once she had him in bed, he would be fast asleep. They would be going nowhere until morning.

She was still awake when they arrived at the next coaching inn some time later. As Anthony helped her alight from the carriage, he asked his men where they were.

"Penrith, milord."

"We'll stop here until first light."

"Yes, milord."

Warmth chased away the chill as Gabby and Anthony

entered the inn. The taproom rumbled with voices and the sweet yeasty smell of ale reached her nose, reminding her slightly of the breads served at home. Tankards clinked together as they were set upon the long tables overflowing with men.

A drunken fellow howled with laughter, causing Gabby to jump. Although she knew it was unreasonable to think she was the source of his amusement, she was still mortified by her disheveled state. She lowered her head and stuck close to Anthony's side.

The innkeeper wore a bemused frown as they approached; his gnarled fingers tapped against the bar and betrayed his nervousness.

Anthony pulled a small purse from his jacket. "My wife and I would like a room above stairs."

The man's frown deepened and he nodded toward the packed tavern. "Many travelers stopped for the night, sir. Afraid there's no rooms left."

Gabby sagged against Anthony. "Is there no place we may rest? Perhaps there are other rooms available in the village?"

"No, ma'am. Least that's the word."

She shouldn't have gotten her hopes up about a bath.

Anthony dug several coins from the purse and dropped them on the counter. "Is there a private dining room we may use?"

The innkeeper scooped up the money and displayed a toothless grin. "Aye. That I can provide."

He motioned to a buxom woman across the room, then gave instructions to lead them to the dining room. Once they were alone, Anthony slumped onto a chair.

In the lantern light, she could see red streaks crossing the whites of his eyes. He appeared ready to drop dead.

"Would you like to lie with your head in my lap?" she offered.

A halfhearted smile eased across his face. "Tempting, but this isn't the time or place."

"Suit yourself."

The serving wench returned several moments later with a tankard of ale and pot of tea.

"We didn't request anything," Gabby said, certain the young woman had entered the wrong room.

"It's from a gentleman in the tavern. He thought you both looked like you could use refreshment."

She set the ale in front of Anthony and carefully placed the teapot on the table, along with a small dish of sugar just as Gabby liked.

"Please extend our thanks to the gentleman," she said.

"Aye, madam."

Anthony sipped his ale while Gabby poured a cup of tea. He grimaced and pushed the tankard aside. "I appreciate the gentleman's hospitality, but this ale is hideous."

"You're welcome to share my tea."

Before he could respond, there was a knock at the door. The innkeeper entered with a broad smile. "Bit of good tidings, I have. The gentleman who sent refreshments says he don't need his room after all. He said I'm to give it to you."

Anthony frowned. "Who is this generous benefactor?"

"He didn't give a name, sir."

Anthony was already rising from his seat. "Then take me to him so I may extend our appreciation."

"He left the tavern. Said he had a ways to travel yet, and he didn't want to take a room when there was a lady in need."

"How kind," Gabby said, genuinely surprised by the gentleman's generosity. "I wish he'd given us a chance to thank him."

"Please, enjoy your ale and tea," the innkeeper said, "then Penny will show you above stairs."

Anthony's frown remained even after the innkeeper left.

"What's the matter?" she asked.

"No man is that generous. I want to know his scheme."

She rolled her eyes as she dropped two sugar cubes into her cup. "There are kind strangers in this world."

He lowered to the chair, his gaze still on the door. "Not in my world."

Really, he was being too paranoid by half. People were kind to her all the time. He just failed to recognize the truth that most people were good at their core. "Then I'm sad for you."

He smirked over the top of the tankard as he prepared to take another draught. "Somehow I doubt the sincerity of your sympathy."

She stuck out her tongue, then laughed when he did.

Anthony had finished half his ale, and she had drained her teacup when the serving wench, Penny, returned to show them to their accommodations. Gabby requested a bath the moment they reached the room.

Penny bobbed her head, then bustled from the room.

With a groan, Anthony dropped on the bed. "How do you expect me to sleep when you are nude only a few feet away?"

Gabby sat on the bed beside him and brushed aside the hair covering his heavy eyes. "I don't think that will be a problem. You look done to a cow's thumb."

"Men are never too tired to bed a fine wench."

"A wench?" She playfully tugged a lock of his hair. "You'd best mean me, although I take issue with the reference."

He placed a kiss in her palm, then grinned. "Of course I mean you, wench."

Striking before she knew his intentions, he grabbed her around the waist and tossed her back on the bed. He was above her in a flash, his fingers tickling her ribs.

"Stop, you blackguard," she said between laughter as she kicked and wiggled to break free.

He ceased his teasing and bent down to kiss her. When he drew back, his eyes twinkled. "I love you, Gabby. There's nothing I wouldn't do to make you happy."

A knock sounded at the door and Anthony pushed off her. He offered her a hand up before bidding the person to enter.

Two young men carried in a tub and placed it close to the fire, then left quickly with a promise to return with buckets of water. Anthony reclined on the bed again and closed his eyes.

She rolled her shoulders and moved to the cloudy-looking glass in the corner. The embroidered hem of her beautiful gown had become splattered with mud, not that it mattered. She would never get the paint out of the skirts. Her middle ached as if her waist was encased in a corset made of dull knives. She groaned softly as she stretched.

"Corsets are a blasted nuisance. I refuse to wear it to bed." Turning away from the mirror, she sighed. It was too bad Lizzie hadn't planned her abduction a little better and packed a valise. She didn't look forward to dressing in her dirty gown after her bath.

After a while, the young men returned with steamy buckets. It took several trips to fill the tub halfway, but Gabby would have been happy with less. She only needed enough to wash away the grime.

Once their task was finished and they had gone, Gabby glanced at Anthony still stretched out on the bed. His chest rose and fell with regular, deep breaths. She nibbled her bottom lip, trying to figure out how she could undress without his help. She hated to wake him, but she didn't have much choice. Softly, she cleared her throat.

"Yes?" His voice sounded husky, but more alert than she'd expected.

"I need assistance with my gown."

He lifted to his elbows to run his lazy gaze over her. "Perhaps the serving wench could be persuaded to help you."

"Don't be silly. I'm certain she is busy running for the other guests. You heard the innkeeper. They have no vacancies." She turned her back to him. "Now, do hurry. The water is growing cold."

With a low growl, he dragged himself from the bed. She met his disgruntled expression in the looking glass and her temper flared.

"I wouldn't have awakened you if it wasn't necessary."

"I wasn't sleeping." He roughly tugged at the fastenings down the back of her gown.

"Well, you should be. You are as surly as a Cob."

And she should know since she'd once been assaulted by a flock of geese. "Nasty creatures."

He finished with the fastenings and practically ripped the dress over her head, catching her hair on his ring.

"Be careful!"

"I'm not a lady's maid, Gabby. I can't undress you without thoughts of tossing you on the bed and taking my fill." His eyes flamed in the looking glass. "Either I hurry or I abandon being a gentleman."

Her heart slammed against her breastbone, and a pink flush covered her chest.

He tugged her corset strings in the same rough manner, but she didn't dare complain again. She'd had no idea when she ordered up a bath that he would be troubled by it. She had truly thought him too tired to be tempted. Her corset fell away and she inhaled deeply.

Her petticoats crumpled to the floor. His hands settled on her hips, his touch burning through the thin chemise, and slowly the hem began to rise. Inch by inch, her bare calves were exposed. She couldn't look away as her thighs came into view.

"Beautiful," he murmured as her dark curls peeked below the hem.

There was a lovely tingle between her legs. She had never looked at herself without clothes, and it felt naughty and exciting. Her breasts began to ache as the fabric slid over her flat stomach marred by crimson marks from her corset. Two hard peaks formed beneath the thin garment when his thumb brushed the sensitive underside of her breast.

His heart pounded against her back.

As the bottoms of her breasts came into view, he

slid his hands over the mounds so that all she could see was almost bare and Anthony touching her. His tan fingers splayed over her ivory skin were the most erotic vision she'd ever encountered.

"Someday I will sketch us like this."

He buried his face into her neck with a low groan and kneaded her breasts. She closed her eyes and laid her head back on his shoulder as another delicious current traveled from her nipples to her core.

He slowly peeled the chemise over her head, leaving her in nothing but stockings. He pressed a kiss to her shoulder. Hot breath feathered over her skin and made her shiver. His seductive gaze traveled over her, seeming to pause on her breasts.

"You are perfection, my love."

Her stomach pitched and there was a quick pulse between her legs. "You…" She licked her dry lips. "You would make a perfect lady's maid."

He smiled. "I look forward to undressing you often. Now, get in the bath before your water grows cold." He swatted her bottom, the soft pop echoing in her ears. His withdrawal left her shaking.

"Has anyone ever told you that you're too honorable?"

"Never," he said with a chuckle.

She scowled as she climbed into the metal tub, but her irritation faded as soon as she sank into the warm water.

Anthony moved to the washbasin and splashed water on his face. Grabbing a towel, he rubbed it furiously before raking his fingers through his hair. "I'm going to see about something clean for you to wear after your bath. I won't be gone long."

He strode out the door before she could protest.

Twenty-seven

GABBY SIGHED AND WIGGLED LOWER IN THE TUB WHEN Anthony closed the door behind him. She'd been so close to feeling those wonderful sensations he'd introduced her to months ago at Ellis Hall, and now *she* was a little on the surly side.

Honor was a horrible taskmaster. When Gabby next saw Drew, she was going to box his ears. Her brother was the last person who should be placing demands on anyone to mind their manners. He never had minded his.

She fished in the water for the sliver of soap she'd dropped, then dunked her head as best as she could in the short tub. She had just rinsed her hair when a knock sounded at the door. Her heart leapt into her throat. Anthony wouldn't knock. What if one of the men from the taproom had wandered upstairs by mistake?

"Uh…" She snatched the towel from the stool beside the tub as she stood and hurriedly tried to dry herself. "One moment, please."

Searching frantically for something to cover herself better, she scrambled from the water and nearly slipped in a puddle before catching herself against the side of the tub.

Another urgent knock rattled the door.

"Just one more moment," she called. Grabbing the cloak draped over a chair, she threw it around her shoulders. She still wasn't decent, but she was covered enough to peek through a crack in the door and send the person away.

She opened the door just a little to see who was disturbing her bath and startled. "Sebastian!"

"Let me in. We haven't much time." She hopped out of the way as he barged into the room. "Where are your clothes? I saw Ellis leave the inn, but he could return any moment."

She froze inside the threshold. "What are you doing here?"

He lifted an eyebrow as he snatched her soiled gown from the floor. "Rescuing you, of course."

When he returned to yank the cloak from her shoulders, she squealed and scooted out of reach.

Sebastian's jaw dropped. "I only meant to help you dress. There isn't time to summon a girl."

She wrapped the cloak tighter around her body. The hurt in his eyes made her stomach turn, but she couldn't do as he wished. After allowing Anthony to undress her, it felt like a betrayal to bare her body to Sebastian.

Deep lines formed at the corners of his mouth. "Today was our wedding day, Gabrielle. I think any impropriety can be overlooked, given the circumstances."

He was her betrothed. Not Anthony, the man she loved. The man she had pledged her fidelity to earlier that morning and promised to love forever. The room swayed.

Sebastian put his arm around her waist and held her up as her knees wobbled. "Are you all right? Did he harm you?"

She shook her head. "What is it you mean to do?"

"We'll continue to Gretna Green and marry. No one must know anything about this. Once we return to Town, I'll make certain Ellis knows if he speaks a word of this misadventure, he will pay."

Her mouth was too dry to speak. How could Sebastian still wish to marry her? For heaven's sake. He'd just discovered her barely clothed and sharing a room with another man.

He gently urged her farther into the room and reached for the tie at her neck, speaking in soothing tones as if she were a frightened animal.

"Sebastian, wait."

"Take your bloody hands off her!" Anthony's command boomed inside the small room.

Sebastian's eyes expanded before he shoved her behind him and whipped a pistol from inside his jacket. "Stay where you are, Ellis."

Anthony came up short and raised his hands. "Put away your barking iron. What are you thinking? There's a lady present."

Lamplight glinted off the gun barrel and her breathing ceased. Suddenly, their voices sounded muffled and far away, as if she was stuck in a dream.

"I don't want to distress her," Sebastian said, "but you've left me no choice. If you will allow us to leave peacefully, there's no need for bloodshed."

Anthony's face hardened, and nausea swept over her. "You aren't leaving with Gabby. You'll have to shoot me before I let you take her."

Gabby's heart seized. "No!"

Sebastian lowered his pistol a fraction in response to her anguished cry. Anthony's glower frightened her. He wasn't surrendering and he was going to get himself killed.

"I don't want to harm you, Ellis. Don't force my hand."

Only giving her actions a fleeting thought, she launched at Sebastian and jumped on his back. He fumbled the pistol, and it clattered to the floor. They careened toward the window, but he recovered his footing before they crashed through the glass.

She clung to him, her arms and legs locked around his body, while the room circled and shouts filled her ears. Fingers like steel clamped around her wrists and broke her hold around his neck. Next she was flying through the air over Sebastian's shoulder. She braced for impact and gasped when she landed on the bed. Her cloak gaped, revealing her nakedness.

His eyes rounded. Her breath caught. Time froze and neither of them could move or look away.

Anthony's hand clamped on Sebastian's shoulder and whirled him around. "Stop eye-shagging her, you bastard." His fist slammed into Sebastian's cheek with a crack and squish that made her shudder.

Sebastian stumbled but kept his feet. He ducked Anthony's next swing, then came up with fists flying. Blood exploded from Anthony's nose.

Gabby scrambled to her knees. "Stop!"

They locked their arms around each other and staggered as if they were engaging in a primitive dance. Baring his teeth, Sebastian shoved Anthony backward. He banged into the tub, sloshing water onto the floor. His boot slipped in a puddle, slowing down his counterattack.

Sebastian leapt at him, and they both flew over the tub, slamming into the floor.

Gabby covered her scream with her hands.

They rolled, each vying for the dominant position and getting closer to the open hearth.

Good heavens. They were going to set themselves on fire. "Stop at once!"

Neither man listened as they continued to throw punches. Anthony rammed his elbow into Sebastian's face. His head jerked back from the impact. His howl made her tremble.

She had to stop this now. Gabby clambered from the bed. Her gaze shot wildly around the floor, her heart hammering in her chest. Where was Sebastian's pistol?

She dropped to her knees to search under the bed. It had slid to the far side against the wall. Lowering to her belly, she wiggled underneath, her bare skin sticking to the floor. Her fingertips grazed metal. Her first grab missed, so she stretched farther to close her fingers around the barrel.

With the pistol in her grip, she shimmied her way out. A nail head scraped her thigh, and she banged her head on the wooden frame.

She growled, frustrated and in pain. Holding her head, she struggled to her feet and paused to study the pistol.

Drat! Why hadn't she learned how to use one of these things? Well, she knew how to hold it, but that was the extent of her knowledge of firearms. She shouted once more for them to stop, but they continued to roll around on the floor.

"You blasted dimwits!" She shook the firearm at the men. "This is your last warning."

They didn't listen.

She moved a few steps closer. "I say, I have a pistol and I've no idea how to use it. I could shoot either of you by accident."

Her words penetrated their thick skulls this time. Their fighting ceased as they whipped their heads toward her. They sat up, both of them battered messes. Anthony's nose was bleeding profusely, and Sebastian's eye was swollen and red.

"Just look at yourselves. You should be ashamed. Heathens, the both of you."

Anthony slowly drew his sleeve across his nose to staunch the flow of blood. "Lower the gun, sweetheart. You're going to hurt someone."

"*I* am going to hurt someone?" She looked down her nose at them. "Why, I've never seen such a ridiculous display in my life. Two grown men acting like animals."

"Gabby, lower the firearm now."

She did as Anthony demanded for two reasons: the gun was heavy and her arm was so shaky she feared she might actually discharge the pistol by accident.

The men released their breath at the same time when she placed it in Anthony's hand. With their eyes on her, she recalled her nudity beneath her cloak and jerked it tighter around her.

Sebastian pushed to his feet with a soft groan and kept his distance. "You're correct, Gabrielle. This is undignified. Please accept my apologies."

"Apology accepted, Lord Thorne. But nothing like this should ever happen again, do you understand?"

He nodded, but Anthony still had murder in his nearly black eyes. She raised her brows at him, but he didn't bat a lash. *Stubborn man.* "I mean it, Anthony. My heart can't handle this type of brutality."

The hard lines around his mouth softened. "I promise to control my behavior in your presence."

That would have to do, she supposed.

He tucked the pistol into his waistband. "You didn't have it cocked. You wouldn't have shot anyone."

Sebastian glowered in Anthony's direction. "It hardly matters. Had you not abducted her, she never would have been faced with this situation."

"You're the one who brought a firearm into our room."

"*Your* room? You would have had the lady sleeping in a tavern if I hadn't given up my room."

Gabby threw her hand up, palm out. "Stop bickering. You two are worse than children."

Anthony narrowed his eyes but held his tongue.

"You were the kind gentleman from the tavern?" Gabby asked.

Sebastian nodded sharply. "I did it for you. I would do anything to see you comfortable and safe."

"Like waving around a loaded pistol," Anthony scoffed.

"To protect her from you."

They were impossible. Gabby pressed her fingers

against a spot above her eyebrow where a slight throb had begun. "No more arguing. You both gave your promise."

The men lapsed into sullen silence. No doubt, if she gave the word, they would return to tearing each other to pieces. What a mess!

Shouts and loud footsteps sounded in the corridor. The door flew open and the innkeeper and the two young men who had carried water for her bath charged inside, one holding a shovel. They skidded to a halt, the innkeeper's mouth gaping.

Anthony stepped in front of her to block her from view. She peeked around him, not wanting to miss anything.

"My lord, I thought you had left," the innkeeper said to Sebastian.

He employed one of his charming smiles, although it lost some of its appeal with his battered face. "I'm afraid there has been a misunderstanding. I left something behind and surprised the young woman when I came to retrieve it. We have cleared up the matter now."

She admired his quick thinking.

The innkeeper looked to Anthony to confirm the baron's story. "Yes, everything is settled. Lord Thorne was mistaken. There's nothing of his in the room."

Sebastian's dark eyes flared.

"I will pay for any damages," Anthony added.

The innkeeper's toothless grin returned. He shooed the young men out the door. "Very good, sir. Is there anything I can bring you?"

Anthony assured him there was nothing, and they

were left alone again. He faced Sebastian with his arms crossed. "I should have had the man clear out the vermin."

Sebastian didn't rise to the bait. He held his hand out to her. "Let's go, Gabrielle. I've hired a coach to take us to the border."

She didn't move. Her gaze shot from Anthony to Sebastian.

Anthony's arms dropped by his sides, his golden brows arching as if surprised she hadn't already declined. She licked her dry lips. The prospect of hurting Sebastian created an icy knot in her belly. Her fingers shook as she gripped the rough edges of the cloak.

A dark shadow passed over Sebastian's face when she didn't take his outstretched hand. "I'm offering a chance to save your reputation. Your *heart*. Don't be foolish."

She lowered her head, unable to look him in the eye as she delivered her answer. "Your offer is more than generous, Lord Thorne, but I'm staying with Anthony."

"I don't believe for one moment you came with him freely. Not after what you learned about him. Why would you choose to stay?"

"What did you learn about me? What does he mean?"

She shook her head. "Nothing. He's mistaken."

The air was thick and hard to take into her lungs. She chanced a quick glance at Sebastian. His teeth were clenched and his face, scarlet. "You would choose a liar over an honorable gentleman?"

"I have never lied to her." Anthony put an arm

around her, trying to shield her from this unpleasant-
ness of her own making.

She eased from his embrace, because as comforting
as she found him, this was something she had to
face alone.

Sebastian jabbed the air with his finger. "He's lying
even now." His feral gaze landed on Anthony. "You
told Gabrielle that Miss Teague is your daughter's
nanny, and yet she is your mistress, is she not?"

"No! Never." Anthony swung an incredulous look
on her. "Is that what you believed?"

"No… I—I don't know."

His eyes flared.

She reached for his arm. "She and Annabelle are
duplicates of each other. Perhaps I thought it for a
time until you told me different. Tell us what relation
she is to Annabelle, so Lord Thorne's mind is put
at ease."

Anthony flinched. Barely, but she'd seen his reaction. "I care nothing about his state of mind."

He was hiding something. She didn't know what,
or the reason, but he had a secret he was unwilling
to share. Her stomach pitched as doubt began to
creep up behind her. Was she playing the fool for
him again?

Sebastian gently took her hand. "Listen to me,
Gabrielle. Miss Teague is the girl's mother. *That* is her
relationship to his daughter."

"That's untrue," Anthony said quietly and slipped his
hand into the pocket where he kept her rock. His blue
eyes bored into her, pleading with her to believe him.

Her heart filled with compassion for the young boy

who had suffered from loneliness, and admiration for the strong man he was. She had accepted him as family long ago and pledged her heart to him today. Whatever he was hiding, she had to trust he had his reasons. She eased from Sebastian's hold and placed her hand in Anthony's. His warm fingers curled around hers.

"I'm sorry, but this is where I belong. Anthony holds a piece of my heart and always will. I can't walk away."

The baron's eyes blazed, scorching her with the heat of his anger.

"Sebastian, please understand." She tentatively laid her hand on his arm.

"Don't." He jerked away and stalked toward the door. At the threshold, he swung around. His cool smile seemed controlled and yet brittle. "Allow me to be the first to wish you luck, Lady Gabrielle. You're likely to need it."

When the door closed behind him, Gabby released a tremulous breath.

Anthony wrapped her in his embrace, grounding her. "God, I love you."

She held on tight, the shock of the encounter making her shake. "I love you, too, Anthony Keaton. And I want you to tell me what you're hiding."

He pulled back; lines crisscrossed his forehead. Blood was smeared over his upper lip and cheek. "I'll tell you whatever you wish to know."

"You'll tell me *everything*. But first, I'm doctoring your nose. Sit down."

His Adam's apple bobbed. "Perhaps you should get dressed." He pointed to a wrinkled nightrail lying on the floor. "The baker's wife was willing to part with one for a price."

Twenty-eight

ANTHONY ANGLED AWAY WHEN GABBY TOUCHED THE wet handkerchief to his busted nose. Not because her ministrations hurt, but because he wasn't accustomed to this type of tenderness. If he got knocked down, he was expected to drag his sorry arse up again, without assistance or compassion.

"I'm trying not to hurt you," she murmured, her nearly lavender eyes shimmering with sympathy.

Perhaps that was the problem. He'd never had a woman taking pains not to hurt him. He hissed when she gently swiped the handkerchief across his cut lip.

"Would you rather do this?"

"No," he snapped, then cursed under his breath. He was being an arse. Before she could retreat, he captured her hand. "I haven't let go of my anger over Thorne. I don't mean to take it out on you."

Her face softened, causing his stomach to churn again. "It's all right. I'm not offended." He wanted to accept her tenderness as she intended, but the only time he'd ever been the recipient of a woman's soothing touch was in bed. He wasn't sure what to do with the urges her care was stirring up. Having her stand between his thighs wasn't helping matters, either.

She dabbed at the rivulets of sticky blood that had dripped down his neck. Her dark hair was still damp and hung loosely around her shoulders. She looked sweet in the virginal nightrail that was too big for her. Yet, he couldn't block from memory what was underneath the voluminous material or stop his cock from standing at attention. Her hips brushed against his inner thighs, sending shock waves through his body. She rattled him and threatened to shatter his fragile restraint.

He circled her wrist with his fingers. "Sit beside me. I promised answers and I can't concentrate with your hands on me."

Her breath hitched. "I didn't realize..."

"I know." Her kindness was not meant as a sexual gesture, but it didn't temper his lust. He reached for her hair, savoring the softness as strands tangled around his fingers, then released it with a resigned sigh.

She climbed onto the bed and sat cross-legged facing him. "It seems like you don't want to talk about Annabelle."

He didn't. Admitting to his failures was humiliating.

"Why do you close off to me every time I ask about her?"

Flames licked up his neck and face. After her unequivocal faith in him a moment ago, he was ashamed to doubt her. "I don't trust easily. Experience has proven it's unwise, so I learned the only person I may count on is myself."

She pursed her lips.

"Until now," he amended, taking her hand. He had to have faith in Gabby too if there was any hope for them. "Thorne was correct about one thing, but he had the details wrong. Annabelle is illegitimate, but she isn't the result of an affair with Miss Teague or any other woman of my acquaintance. Camilla was unfaithful to me."

"Oh." Her eyes narrowed. "Then Lord Thorne was correct about another thing. You lied to me at the Norwicks' party."

"In a sense."

She tugged her hand from his hold and frowned.

Bollocks! He was botching everything. "I don't want to quibble over words. Yes, I lied about the circumstances of her birth, but Annabelle is mine. Legally, she belongs to me. She was born during my marriage, and I have laid claim to her. I'll not punish a child for her mother's doings, and I won't send her away, no matter who is asking it of me."

"Do you truly think that's what I'd want? To send your daughter away?"

He scrubbed a hand down his face, his body and spirit weary. "I hope not, but when you said you would be bothered by the circumstances of her birth…"

"How would you like it if I told you *I* had a child out of wedlock?"

"I wouldn't care for it in the least."

"Well, neither did I," she said with a toss of her head, "especially when I thought you still had feelings for the woman."

He'd felt the same when he had discovered his

wife's affair. How hurt Gabby must have been when she'd thought Miss Teague was his mistress.

He captured her chin and stroked his thumb over her smooth skin. Her eyes lost their hard edge. Her cherry lips parted.

"I only have feelings for you, Gabrielle. That will never change." He would never fail her or their marriage. "I had planned to share my daughter's secret when I returned to London. I wanted you to know before we married. When I learned you were on the marriage mart, I wasn't certain if we had a future anymore."

"But you knew we would be married when you brought me north. You've had many opportunities to tell me today."

"I should have told you, I know. I was wrong."

Her lashes fluttered and she licked her lips. "You were no more wrong than I was for seeking answers from Lord Thorne. We could spend all night tallying our mistakes, or we could agree to forgive each other."

He smiled softly. "Agreed."

She reached for his hand, placed a kiss on his palm, and then laced their fingers together. "Tell me what happened with your wife."

He took a deep breath. It was likely best to stick to the facts. "When I married Camilla, I had no idea she was in love with another man. He was a servant in her father's home, a footman. Obviously, Camilla couldn't marry him, but that didn't stop them from becoming lovers. Nor did marriage interfere with their amorous sport."

Gabby's eyes expanded, but thankfully, she didn't

say anything. It was humiliating enough to admit he couldn't please his wife. He couldn't take Gabby's pity, too.

What a dimwit he had been employing James Teague at his wife's request. But Anthony had wanted to please her, just as he'd tried to please his mother when she was alive. He'd entered marriage in good faith and had intended to be a first-rate husband. The memory of his gullibility was similar to a kick in the head. He rubbed his forehead to ease his mental pain.

"When Camilla told me she was with child, I viewed it as a new start. Ellis Hall was going to become a home again, like it was before Father and Byron died. No more covered windows or tiptoeing through the corridors. We would have house parties like your parents, and children's laughter would fill every room. Perhaps we would get a dog or two."

Even now his heart ached for his fantasy, as silly as it was. He didn't see how everything would ever be as he had imagined, especially when his daughter trembled anytime he came near.

Gabby squeezed his hand, bringing him into the present. "*I* like dogs."

He couldn't help but smile at her kind reminder that she was part of his future now. Perhaps there was still hope for his dreams. "What kind of dog do you like?"

"Anything fluffy that I can spoil."

"Not a useful breed that can earn its keep? I was considering a sheepdog."

She shrugged, a wide smile on her pretty lips. "A sheepdog is fluffy."

He chuckled. "I don't deserve you, Lady Bug."

"You didn't deserve that horrible woman you married, and if I may be frank, I was never very impressed with your mother, either."

"You're a welcome change." He pulled her into his arms, realizing how true his statement was. He couldn't imagine anyone more perfect to share his life.

She circled her arms around his waist and buried her face against his shirt. "I take it the footman sired Annabelle?"

"Yes," he said on a sigh. "Camilla went missing weeks before she was to give birth, along with her lover. One of the other servants came forward and shared her suspicions about my wife's involvement with the help.

"I was convinced Annabelle was mine, and that Camilla's affair began after she was with child. I've never been so furious with another person. An investigator eventually tracked them to Wales, but it took a year." The worst year of his life. "Only when I arrived in Crickhowell did I learn Camilla had died in childbirth. Her lover had fled, leaving Annabelle with his sister."

Gabby lifted her face. "Miss Teague?"

He nodded. "The poor woman didn't know who Annabelle's mother was. Her brother arrived with an infant bearing the same shocking red hair inherent to their family, and left the babe in her care. The first time I met my daughter, she was already crawling. Miss Teague was the only mother Annabelle had ever known. I couldn't bring myself to tear them apart, even though I wanted my daughter home with me.

Instead, I chose to provide for her and visited as often as I could, but I fear it wasn't enough. My daughter barely knows me."

"I'm so sorry I doubted you, Anthony." Gabby gently touched his bruised cheek, her beautiful gray eyes filled with remorse and compassion.

He kissed the tip of her nose. "I should have been honest from the start about Annabelle, but I never anticipated people believing Miss Teague is my mistress…" He released her and blew out a forceful breath. "I'm sorry too, Gabby. I knew there would be a scandal when I took you from London, but this is worse than I imagined. My failure with Camilla shouldn't reflect on you."

"Your wife failed *you*, and I don't wish to hear another word of this nonsense. We'll face any scandals together." She sat up straighter. "You know, I rather like the idea of being known as the Notorious Countess of Ellis."

"Notorious?" He laughed, grateful to have this beautiful, generous, and rather dotty woman in his life. "And just what kind of notorious do you intend to be?"

She cocked an eyebrow. "I don't know. The interesting kind, I suppose. Much like Lady Norwick. Ladies with sterling reputations pale next to her. No one can accuse her of being dull."

He brushed a strand of hair behind her ear. "You could never be dull either."

Her gaze dropped and a pink blush stained her cheeks. "Anthony, people are going to talk about us for more than one reason. Everyone is going to think we have… Well, I think you know what people will believe."

One more scandal heaped upon her shoulders. He really should be flogged for being this selfish.

"It seems unfair to be accused of something we didn't do." She adjusted her weight to her knees so she was kneeling on the bed. Her hesitant fingers moved to his stained cravat. She nibbled her bottom lip and glanced up at him shyly. "If we are already judged guilty, we should at least enjoy the deed. Don't you agree?"

Damn, but he was tired of fighting temptation. He tugged her against his chest. Her cry of surprise turned to a soft moan as his mouth covered hers. Plump, moist, and sweet, her lips intensified his hunger. Unleashed at last, lust surged through his veins. Pounding echoed in his ears and invaded his cock.

He tangled his fingers in her damp hair and angled her mouth where he could taste her fully. He was driven to taste her everywhere, but he couldn't tear his mouth from hers. Not yet.

Her tongue twined with his, beckoning. He wanted to be inside her, to possess her body, heart, and mind as she did him. She'd had him tied in knots, hopelessly bound to her for so long. And yet she had been beyond his reach until now.

She gripped his cravat, urging him closer, but he resisted. A small protest was on her lips. He kissed it away.

"Untie my cravat." His voice sounded rough.

Her hands shook as she fumbled with the knot; her stormy gray eyes flicked to his face.

Grasping handfuls of her nightrail, he eased the hem over her legs, his fingers forging a path along the silky skin of her inner thigh. His knuckles brushed against her curls, and she sucked in a breath.

He glanced up to gauge her reaction. Her bottom lip trembled and she captured it between her white teeth. He kissed the corner of her mouth. "We don't have to do this." Next, he kissed the other corner.

She melted on an exhale, her head rolling back. He accepted the invitation to nibble down the column of her neck, his tongue dipping into the hollow of her collarbone when he reached journey's end.

"I want to," she whispered and arched into his hand as it covered her breast.

The intermittent quaking of her limbs hinted that she might be conflicted about her decision.

"Are you frightened?"

"A little."

He smiled against her neck. Her honesty showed how much she trusted him, and strengthened his resolve to deserve her trust.

"We may stop at any time." It wasn't a lie, per se, but *any* time might be a stretch. Still, he would do his best.

"I won't stop you. I don't want to." She finished untying his cravat and slid it from his neck. "What would you have me do next?"

He removed his shirt and grinned. "Let's remove your nightrail."

❧

Gabby's heart battered her ribs until she was certain her insides would be bruised. Anthony peeled her nightrail over her head, then drew back slowly. A soft light shone in his eyes. Pleasant warmth enveloped her as his blue gaze slid leisurely over her curves. Had she not seen herself in the looking glass earlier, she might have been embarrassed. Instead, the memory of her body being revealed inch by inch and his hands touching her caused a sudden pull between her legs.

Anthony kicked off his boots and stood to drop his trousers. Her breath caught at the sight of him naked. Yes, she'd seen marble statues of nudes and several paintings, but nothing had prepared her for *this* flesh-and-blood male form. Muscles shifted beneath warm skin as he laid her back on the bed and kissed her. The sweet scent of ale lingered on his breath, the aroma heady.

He nudged her thighs apart and settled between her legs.

Ceasing his lovely assault on her mouth, he eased back, his weight resting on his elbows. Candlelight shimmered in his eyes. He swept a lock of hair from her face before touching his lips to her forehead.

"Gabrielle Forest, I take you as my wife. I pledge my faithfulness and love for all time. I promise to protect your heart until my last breath and ask—" His voice broke, and he looked away as if embarrassed. "I ask that you take care with mine, too."

His vulnerability brought her tears. Opening himself up to rejection pained him, but he had nothing to fear from her. Her fingers splayed upon his chest, the light sprinkle of blond hair soft beneath her palms. His heart beat steady and constant against her hand as if she truly held this tender part of him. "Your heart is safe with me always."

His smile reached his eyes, and he captured her mouth again, nipping and licking until she parted her lips and welcomed the sweep of his tongue. His kiss was loving, but a driving urgency lurked in the shadows. Sensing his barely restrained desire lit a fire in her belly. The flames fanned upward into her chest; her breath turned heated and fast.

Her breasts grew full and tingled. She brushed her fingers over the swell.

"Touch me," she whispered.

He plumped her breast, then circled his thumb around the peak. Vibrations traveled through her, culminating between her legs. Adjusting his position, he drew his tongue slowly across her nipple and she dissolved into the bedding. Her fingers tunneled into his hair, cradling his head as he took her in his mouth. Each draw on her breast carried her away from the turmoil of the day and closer to him. She couldn't look away as his lips closed around her flesh. The sight sent blood speeding through her veins.

An insistent throbbing began between her legs, and she lifted her hips, trying to ease the ache. She had heard there was pain with losing her innocence, but she hadn't expected it to be a pleasing kind. Anthony's hand slid into her curls and caressed her. A pleasing tingle radiated into her lower belly and down her legs. She sighed.

He teased her flesh until she shifted restlessly on the sheets. Then finding her special spot, as she had come to think of it, he gently flicked his finger over it until her body reached the limits of its ability to contain her pleasure. It burst from her in a husky moan, her back arching as he continued to caress her. Once he had carried her beyond the brink with one last cry, she collapsed against the bed, her breath deep and slowly evening out.

Anthony lay beside her and wrapped her in his arms. She snuggled against his firm chest and placed her lips against the pulse beating at his neck.

"There is more, isn't there?"

"Yes." His hand caressed her back and circled her bottom until his touch made her hungry for more. "But we will take it slow."

He rolled her to her back and gazed down with blue-black eyes. "Open your legs. I haven't gotten my fill."

Her heart paused then took off at a gallop, but she followed his command. Instead of preparing to enter her, however, he kissed his way down her body. His lips pressed to her trembling thigh, his breath skating along her skin.

"Lie back and take your pleasure again. It will make everything easier."

She closed her eyes and smiled. Who was she to argue? But when his hot mouth touched her instead of his fingers, her eyes flew open. His head was nestled between her legs, his mouth creating new sensations. He looked up at her as his tongue slid along her flesh. She stifled a groan. Now *this* was the most erotic vision she'd ever seen.

His lips played over her flesh, his tongue circling her spot until her thoughts became fuzzy. Her breath escaped in long, deep exhales. She closed her eyes. Her fingers curled into the bedding and she held on, attempting to maintain control. His hands cradled her bottom and provided her with a sense of security. Even as she lost her senses, he was there loving her, holding her while she moaned.

A quiver originated from somewhere deep inside her. The currents traveled over her body, teasing. Promising something more. More than what she'd received in the past.

Pleasure seized her and she tensed. Her release came fast and unrelenting, her cries becoming louder with each driving pulse until she slipped over the edge, tumbling back to the small chamber and Anthony's gentle embrace. She sank into the bed, her arms and legs limp. Even her eyelids had become too weak to stay open, but she could smile.

Anthony chuckled as he covered her body with his. He lifted her arm and it flopped back on the bed. "Have I killed you then?" His voice held a teasing note.

She cracked an eye open. "There are worse ways to go."

His brilliant smile warmed her like the sun.

He kissed her tenderly once more. His hips pressed her into the bed, his shaft a hard ridge against her lower belly. "Are you certain you want to do this?"

"Yes," she murmured.

❧

Anthony released the breath he'd been holding waiting for her answer. He stroked the length of his cock before positioning to enter her. Gabby's face was tipped up toward him, her eyes wide and yet trusting. He gently probed her dewy skin and kissed her as he eased into her. When she tensed, he stopped to wait for her to adjust. His muscles trembled as he held himself back.

She took a deep breath and grew lax beneath him. He pushed deeper. Her nails dug into his shoulders, but she didn't utter a sound. Her body surrounded him, slick and hot. He closed his eyes. This was heaven, wrapped in her arms, his heart bursting.

He moved carefully, aware of the sting of her nails easing. Her body no longer resisted, but he still made love to her slowly. His mouth touched hers and her tongue flicked across his top lip. Each tender thrust was accompanied by a deep kiss, their tongues stroking together. His blood thrummed through his veins, filling his ears with a rushing sound.

The world closed around him until there was only her and him and an overwhelming love flowing between them. When he came, he was at her mercy, forever connected in a way he'd never been with anyone else.

He kissed her once more before collapsing on the bed beside her. His eyes drifted shut and he surrendered to sleep, confident his heart was safe in Gabby's hands.

Twenty-nine

"HELL'S TEETH. DID *SHE* DO THAT TO HIS FACE?"

The voice in Anthony's dreams sounded vaguely familiar, but it took too much effort to place the owner so he drifted under again.

The jab of cold, hard metal under his chin woke him in a hurry. His eyes flew open and Drew's even colder glare greeted him.

"What the hell did you do to our sister?" Drew said through clenched teeth.

Luke's dark glower wasn't any friendlier, but at least he didn't have his pistol aimed at Anthony.

Gabby murmured in her sleep and rolled toward him, her bare breast brushing his side beneath the covers. He swallowed hard.

Bollocks! This was a fine mess to find himself in the morning after a perfectly lovely night.

"Gabby. Wake up, sweetheart." He nudged her, relieved when she stirred. Her arm flopped across his chest, just missing contact with her brother's pistol. She nestled against his side with a sigh, not waking as he'd hoped.

Luke frowned at Drew. "Disarm yourself. Do you want to make our sister a widow before she's even married?"

Drew narrowed his eyes and holstered his pistol. "You're lucky he is here to protect you."

If Anthony were truly lucky, neither brother would be threateningly lurking over his bed.

"Thank you," Anthony spat, then clamped his lips together to keep from ordering them out of his room. Until Gabby was his, he'd be wise not to antagonize them more than he already had.

Drew looked around the room, the muscles shifting in his jaw. Evidence of Anthony's fight with Thorne was present everywhere. The bellows had been kicked across the room, dried blood splattered the wood plank floor, and the curtain rod hung askew. Diffused light trickled through a split in the curtains.

"Gads. It's barely dawn," Anthony complained.

Drew leaned closer and bore his teeth. "If I learn you've hurt her in any way, you will meet me on a field."

"I didn't hurt her." At least no more than Anthony could help it. And he'd tried to make up for any discomfort by pleasuring her again in the middle of the night. The memory of her throaty voice calling his name made his cock twitch.

Damn, but this was a bloody unpleasant way to wake up.

"A little privacy, please," he said on a growl.

Luke gave a sharp nod. "We will wait below stairs. When you're decent, there are matters we need to discuss."

Anthony pushed up to his elbows. "How did you get in here?" He'd turned the lock last night as a precaution against Thorne returning to finish him off in his sleep.

"There was a pretty little wench more than happy to retrieve the key for us." Anthony wanted to knock the cocky grin from Drew's face.

"I'm telling your wife," Gabby grumbled, her eyes still closed. She was awake after all.

Her brother's scowl returned. "You utter a word to Lana and I'll share with Mother every detail of what we've stumbled upon this morning."

Gabby gasped and struggled to sit up while keeping herself covered with the sheet. "You wouldn't dare! I would never forgive you."

Luke clapped Drew on the shoulder and shoved him toward the door. "He won't say a word. He's only needling you. I paid the girl to unlock the door, so there's nothing to report to Lana."

"Perhaps I was needling *him*," Gabby said under her breath. When her brothers didn't leave at once, she lifted her brows and adopted a haughty tone. "My betrothed has asked for privacy, so please see yourselves out."

Luke chuckled as he turned on his heel. "Don't be long or the food will turn cold."

Even after her brothers left, she glowered mutinously at the door. "They have some nerve barging in, acting as if they are saints. And threatening to call you out is beyond the pale. I have a few words for my brother once I'm decent."

She was hellfire and retribution when she was angry, just as she'd been since she'd learned to talk.

Anthony grinned as he smoothed her mussed hair and kissed her cheek. "Drew is nothing but bluster. A duel would interfere with his beauty sleep."

"From the looks of it, he has missed a couple of nights already."

"Gabrielle Forest, you wicked girl. You had best not say the same about me. I've missed a few nights myself."

She wrapped her arms around his neck and pulled him closer, her smile dazzling. "Yes, but you don't require beauty sleep. Rugged looks attractive on you."

When she pressed her lips to his, he wanted to lay her back and fill her again. But they had a little problem waiting in the tavern. At least he hoped it was a minor complication. Since Gabby hadn't reached her majority, it was within her brother's rights to deny his suit. He didn't anticipate Luke would do any such thing, but Anthony didn't want to cross him.

"We'll require Luke's permission to marry. I shouldn't keep him waiting."

She rolled her eyes and snuggled closer. "It's a little late to worry about obtaining his permission."

"Still, I may be able to salvage the situation, but only if I don't fall further into his bad graces." Anthony gently extracted himself from her hold, his stomach churning as he climbed from bed.

Gabby's family meant everything to her. In truth, they were important to him too. He couldn't regret what he'd done—losing Gabby hadn't been an option—but he would miss his friendships if her brothers were unwilling to forgive him. If nothing else, he would implore Luke to continue to welcome Gabby into his home. She really was innocent in everything.

"Shall I send up breakfast?" he asked, pulling on his trousers.

"I'm coming with you. You will have to play lady's maid again." She climbed from bed and stretched, not seeming the least bit self-conscious of her state of undress.

He smiled and returned to dressing. "Perhaps you should wait until I have spoken with your brothers."

She snorted. "And leave my future up to those lackwits? I think not."

He didn't argue since she had as much say in their future as he did. "All right, but no goading Drew. He's no match for your wits."

"Fine, but only because you have requested it." She gathered her wrinkled gown from the floor, humming off-key.

He set himself to rights before assisting her. When he finished with the last fastening of her dress, he wrapped his arms around her waist and nuzzled her neck.

"I love you, my perfect match."

She beamed at him in the looking glass. "And I love you, *my* perfect match."

The tavern below stairs was empty except for a woman with a valise resting on her lap and a young boy at her side. Likely they were waiting to catch the post coach.

As Anthony and Gabby made their way arm in arm to the private dining room, he felt invincible. They still had tough days ahead, but neither of them would be alone. Luke and Drew were sitting across from each other at the scarred table. They barely looked up and continued to shovel food into their mouths as he and Gabby entered.

"Must be a family trait," Anthony mused.

Gabby's brows shot up to her hairline. "Pardon?"

He just smiled and shook his head. He would never again tease her about her appetite, not when he was fortunate enough to have it extend to the bedchamber. "Are you hungry, Lady Bug?"

"Ravenous," she said and joined her brothers at the table.

Drew plucked the sweet roll from his plate and handed it to her. She accepted it without question and tore off a piece, her plans to call him on the carpet apparently forgotten.

"Have a seat," Luke said to Anthony and passed them plates. "There's more food coming."

Anthony's shoulders relaxed as he slid into the seat next to Luke. "Shall we have it out now?"

Her brother grunted and bit into his roll. Anthony would take that as a no.

He expected nothing in the way of financial compensation from Gabby's brother under the circumstances. It didn't matter anyway. Anthony was far from destitute and in need of a wife's fortune. He'd had nothing to do for the past few years except improve upon his estate. The only thing he required was her brother's blessing.

A serving wench entered the dining room with a platter held aloft filled with ham, fruit, and bread. Once she quit the room, Luke glanced up with his fork halfway to his mouth.

"I expect my sister will enjoy a comfortable existence as your wife."

Anthony nodded. "Of course she will. I'll see that she is loved and well cared for always."

Luke set down his fork and extended his hand. "Then welcome to the family."

Anthony grabbed his hand, pumping it vigorously with what he suspected was a ridiculous smile on his face. Her brothers were grinning too.

"We can discuss her dowry when we return to Town," Luke said.

Gabby bolted upright on her seat. "Return to Town? Do you think that's wise?"

Luke sent a sympathetic look in her direction. "The rumors will be worse if you don't. I would advise you and Ellis to accept any invitations you receive. Allow the gossips to see you have made a love match, and the scandal will die away eventually."

"How long is eventually?" She looked too pale of a sudden, her meal forgotten.

Anthony reached across the table for her hand. Her fingers were cold and he rubbed them between his palms. "You mustn't worry overmuch. We'll weather the storm together."

Drew cocked an eyebrow. "We will *all* weather the storm, Ellis. The Forests never abandon one of their own."

Unfortunately, eloping with another man before her wedding wasn't the only scandal facing them, but Anthony didn't want to dredge up everything now when she was already fretful.

Gabby grew misty-eyed as her gaze shot from one brother to the next. "Thank you. I can't tell you how much it means to have your support, but we must consider what is best for Liz and Katie. If Anthony and I distance ourselves, perhaps their prospects next Season won't be affected."

Drew draped his arm around her shoulders. "I hardly think our sisters would agree to such an arrangement."

"Put your mind at ease," Luke said kindly. "Elizabeth and Katherine are accomplished, beautiful young ladies and they will make good matches. I wouldn't be surprised if they, too, have gentlemen competing for their attentions."

Gabby nibbled her bottom lip. "I hope nothing to the extremes I witnessed last night. Lord Thorne scared the wits out of me."

Drew narrowed his eyes at Anthony. "Is that what happened to your face? I take it you were the victor since there's no sign of Thorne today."

"The win goes to your sister actually."

Her brothers looked to her for confirmation, and she nodded, her eyes wide. "I rescued my future husband."

"That sounds like something Vivian would do," Luke said with a laugh.

Drew's lips thinned. "Or Lana."

Apparently, he still hadn't forgiven his wife for risking her life to save his. When Anthony recalled how frightened he'd been for Gabby when she'd jumped on Thorne's back, he could understand his friend's position perfectly. She glanced up, caught him staring, and frowned.

He smiled in return, not wishing to inadvertently share his fear last night with everyone. It was one thing for her to know about his vulnerabilities, but he preferred to keep some things just between the two of them.

They needed to address the situation concerning Thorne, however. He experienced a slight pang this morning when he considered how badly their friendship had deteriorated. Anthony cleared his throat. "The baron will expect to be compensated. I will bear the costs."

"She isn't your responsibility," Luke argued.

"She will be as soon as we make it to Gretna Green."

"True." Luke ran his gaze over his sister. "I hope you don't expect her to exchange vows in a soiled gown."

Gabby returned his sour look before popping a grape into her mouth.

"Fortunately, Mother had the foresight to send a perfectly acceptable gown with me," he said.

She shuddered. "I'm not wearing the gown I was to marry Lord Thorne in. It seems like bad luck."

"No one would expect you to wear it. Mother sent the gown she wore when she married Father."

"Oh." She didn't appear as happy as one would expect.

"Mother wanted you to have it, Gabrielle. She said it marked the beginning of many years of happiness for her and Father. She wishes you the same."

Her fingers covered her mouth as tears filled her eyes.

Drew dug into his jacket. "Now don't start crying, princess. Unless they are tears of joy."

She accepted his handkerchief and shook her head as she dabbed at her tears. "I don't deserve to wear her dress. If not for me, Papa would still be alive."

Her brothers' frowns mirrored Anthony's own. "I

thought you had given up that ridiculous idea," he said. "You're not responsible for your father's death."

"You most certainly are not," Drew said. "How could you think such a thing?"

She shook her head as her tears streaked down her cheeks. Anthony wanted to round the table to gather her in his arms, but he stayed put. She needed to speak her fears aloud to her brothers. She'd been holding on to her guilt for too long.

"My attempt at running off with Lt. MacFarland stressed Papa's heart. It was impulsive and stupid, and if I could go back and change everything, I would. That's why I can't wear Mama's dress."

Luke smiled sadly. "She used to say she thought you blamed yourself. I didn't see how that could be possible when I believed I was at fault."

Gabby's head came up sharply.

He reached into his jacket to pull out a folded piece of foolscap and slid it across the table. "As it turns out, neither of us caused his death. He had been having chest pains for years, but he hid it well. Mother said she tried to convince him to slow down, but he refused. He wasn't happy unless he was pushing himself to his limits." He nodded to the note. "Mother wanted you to have her blessing on your wedding day since she couldn't be with you."

"And she made us swear to remember every detail to recount later," Drew added.

Gabby hugged the note to her chest. "I never thought we would have family present when we exchanged vows. Thank you."

Luke set his napkin aside and pushed back from

the table. "We should depart soon, but first, I need to freshen up. Could we share your coach, Ellis?"

"As long as you don't mind me making cow eyes at your sister."

Drew snorted. "As if you haven't been doing that for years already."

Gabby's smile was brilliant, and Anthony's heart expanded, filling with so much love for her it might burst. If it was possible to die from happiness, he was doomed.

⌘

Gabby read her mother's letter for the fifth time as the young maid placed a wreath of heather on her head. Mama's words were encouraging and congratulatory, but her letter was so much more.

She had filled it with stories about Gabby's father: his reaction when he had first laid eyes on her as an infant; how he had loved her passionate nature; his regret over his severity after that *unfortunate* situation with Lt. MacFarland. Gabby chuckled at her mother's choice of words, and longing tugged at her heart. How she wished her mother could be with her today, but her spirit was present, as was Papa's.

> *Your papa said he had been afraid you still might defy him—he most admired your determination—so he had been very stern. He berated himself for the things he had said, but he could not bring himself to apologize. He knew you deserved someone who understood and accepted your nature. He rather liked the notion of Anthony becoming his son*

some day and had hoped you would make a match with him.

Gabby tucked the letter into the bodice of her mother's gown to keep it close to her heart, then went to meet Anthony and her brothers. Happiness bubbled up inside her as she descended the stairs to find the love of her life waiting.

He was handsome in his gray trousers and black jacket, and the sky blue of his waistcoat set off his eyes. But what made him most appealing was the light radiating from him. His love wrapped around her, making her feel safe and content for the first time in a long while.

She held her hand out in invitation and he took it, his warm fingers closing around hers.

"You look lovely," he murmured.

She returned his smile. "It's hard to imagine I looked like a street urchin only an hour ago."

"You're always beautiful to me." He tucked her hand into the crook of his elbow and grinned at her brothers. "Can you believe your sister has accepted me at last?"

Drew clapped him on the shoulder. "Don't count your chickens just yet, Ellis. We still have to make it to the blacksmith without incident."

Gabby wrinkled her nose. "If there is any *incident* involved, it is likely to be my half-boot making contact with your derriere."

Drew gave a mock gasp. "Lord Ellis, what have you taught my sister?"

They all laughed and continued teasing each other

as they walked to the smithy's shop. Several of the villagers stopped to stare at their boisterous entourage, some with smiles and others with pinched faces. Gabby called out greetings to everyone they passed and wished them well.

In all her girlish fantasies, she had never pictured marrying over an anvil, but there had been one constant in all of her dreams. *Anthony.*

She held him back as her brothers walked into the weathered building.

He frowned. "Is something wrong?"

"No, everything is right for once." She wrapped her arms around his waist and looked up into the face she had loved for as long as she could remember. "I always knew you were meant for me."

His smile was a glorious sight. "I'm forever yours, Lady Bug. Be gentle with me."

"Always," she promised then sealed it with a kiss.

Their ceremony was brief, and likely mundane to the blacksmith, but Gabby tried to memorize every moment to hold in her heart forever. The robust smell of a wood fire. The clarity with which they spoke their vows. Anthony's soft smile and glittering blue eyes reminiscent of the North Sea.

Her wedding was nothing like she had ever imagined, and perfect just the way it was.

Thirty

ANTHONY VIEWED THEIR ARRIVAL BACK IN LONDON with mixed emotions. He missed his daughter more than he imagined possible and he couldn't wait to see her, and yet her possible reception caused a flutter in his chest. What would Gabby think if his own daughter burst into tears when she saw him?

He took his wife's hand as the carriage turned onto Charles Street. "I'm not certain how Annabelle will behave when she sees us."

Gabby squeezed his hand. "I imagine she will be pleased to see her papa. I wish we'd had time to find a nice gift. My papa always brought home trinkets for my sisters and me when he had to be away."

Anthony frowned. He should have thought to bring something back from Scotland, but their stay had been brief since everyone in the traveling party had been eager to return to their loved ones. Their pace home had been only slightly less harried than their flight to Gretna Green.

He hugged Gabby. "I'm proud to bring you home. Annabelle will like you even without trinkets."

He held out no hope of improving his standing with his daughter with or without presents. Having tried that path, he knew it led nowhere. Still, he'd like to live up to Gabby's image of what a father should be.

When the carriage rolled to a stop outside his town house, he placed a hand on her leg to halt her exit. "There is a chance Annabelle won't be pleased when she sees me. I—I thought you should know so you aren't caught unaware."

Gabby pursed her lips. "You mentioned once before that Annabelle is frightened of you. There must be an explanation that makes sense."

"I'm sure you're right." He forced a laugh to hide his doubts. "Would you like to freshen up before we visit the nursery?"

Her brows arched. "Won't you have her come downstairs to greet us?"

His jaw clenched. Gabby was already finding fault with his parenting. "She'll likely be playing this time of day."

His wife's ivory skin flushed. "I hadn't thought of that. I'm afraid I have a lot to learn about being a mother. Please, be patient with me."

Tension drained from him, making his bones go soft again. Gabby had that effect on him. He cupped her cheek and kissed her sweet lips. "We have a lot to learn together. I'm still figuring out this father business myself."

Gabby opted to freshen up before he introduced her to Annabelle and Miss Teague. Her mother had arranged to have her belongings brought to Keaton

Place and his butler had placed her in the rooms adjoining the master's chambers. He left her to set herself to rights, but no sooner had he entered his rooms to change than the doors connecting their spaces swung open. She stood in the threshold, smiling.

"There! That's much better. No walls to keep us separated."

He returned her smile with a ridiculously wide grin. He hadn't even had time to miss her, and here she was making herself comfortable in his space. After so many years of solitude one might think it would be annoying, but he found her intrusiveness endearing.

"Well," she said. "I suppose I'll order up a bath now."

"Lady Ellis, I don't think you are disheveled enough yet." He sauntered toward her, his body eager for a reunion.

Her eyes flared, but she held her ground as he advanced. "I didn't know that was even a possibility."

He swept her into his arms to carry her toward his big bed. "Appearances can always be made worse, sweetheart, and I'm going to muss you up splendidly."

She squealed when he tossed her on the bed, but then reached her arms out in invitation, her gray eyes smoldering. "Do your best, Lord Ellis."

&c&

Gabby sensed a tremor race down Anthony's arm as they neared the nursery, and she squeezed reassuringly. She didn't understand the cause of his anxiety. Annabelle was just a girl, and certainly too small to engender this much trepidation.

Entering the bright rooms brought a smile to her

face. Shelves were loaded with angelic-faced dolls, a porcelain tea service complete with a tiny creamer and sugar dish, hand-carved carousel horses, and every other exquisite toy a little girl could imagine. A book lay open on the miniature table along with an abandoned slate.

A tinkling laugh, reminiscent of a fairy, floated through the doorway of the other room. She glanced up at Anthony to ask if they should announce their presence before entering and her heart melted. His eyes shone with a soft light she'd never seen, and a gentle smile played on his lips.

"You are smitten," she teased, enamored by how loving a father he was.

His smile stretched ear to ear. "You could say that. I almost feel I'm dreaming having you both under my roof."

"You're not dreaming. We are here and we're staying, so grow accustomed to it." She lifted to her toes and kissed his cheek before tugging him toward the doorway. "Come make introductions."

Annabelle was sitting on a plush carpet with Miss Teague, her back to the entry. The little girl chattered happily as she stacked colorful blocks one on top of the other.

"And the tower was very, very high," she said in her lyrical voice. Gabby could listen to her talk for hours. "So, so high and the princess had a—uh…"

Miss Teague smoothed a hand over the girl's copper curls. "A ladder?"

"No." She turned and wrinkled her nose at her aunt as if she'd posed the most ridiculous question

Annabelle could imagine. "The princess had a chick-adee to fly her to the tower."

"But isn't a chickadee too small?"

She flung her arms out to her sides. "A big one." She drew out the word *big* in such a cute way that Gabby couldn't help chuckling.

Annabelle and Miss Teague swung their heads toward them, their mouths hanging open.

"Sorry to interrupt your play," Anthony said as if disturbing the girl's activities were tantamount to barging in on a session in the House of Lords. The situation hardly required the amount of seriousness displayed in his expression.

Gabby smiled at Annabelle to put her at ease. "Good afternoon, Lady Annabelle. May I say your idea for a giant chickadee is the most brilliant solution I've ever heard?"

The corners of Annabelle's mouth eased up as she tipped her head to the side. "Are you Papa's wife?"

"Annabelle," Miss Teague scolded, placing a staying hand on the girl's shoulder when she started to stand. "Impertinent questions won't make your papa happy."

Gabby opened her mouth to correct the woman's mistake, but thought better of it. Having never been around Anthony when he was with his daughter, she really didn't know what made him happy and what displeased him. She supposed she should ask about his rules before she asserted her beliefs.

Annabelle's smile had disappeared, and she stared up at her father with large eyes.

Anthony snapped out of whatever spell he'd been

under. "Er, yes. This is my wife, Gabrielle, and she will be living here as mistress of the house."

The girl's green eyes flicked to Miss Teague, Gabrielle, and then back to her aunt. Her little brow wrinkled as if trying to puzzle something out.

Gabby leaned down so she was on her level. "You may call me Gabby if you like."

Annabelle nodded.

"Well," Anthony said with a slight clap of his hands that startled Annabelle, "shall we join you in playing blocks?"

She inched closer to Miss Teague and the woman wrapped her in a tight embrace, smashing the girl's rosy cheek against her side. "Annabelle is still a bit shy, milord. Perhaps another day would be better."

Annabelle's eyes rounded even more before she buried her face into her aunt's skirts. A tiny whimper slipped from her.

Gabby glanced at Anthony to see what he made of the strange display, and her stomach pitched. His long face and the defeated look in his eyes broke her heart.

"Very good," he said before spinning on his heel and walking away.

Gabby remained a moment longer, unsure of what she should say. Annabelle peeked at her and Gabby smiled. "It was nice to meet you, Annabelle. Perhaps in the morning you will visit the park with your papa and me."

She didn't answer, but neither did she shy away. Gabby bid her and Miss Teague a good evening and left. She paused in the adjoining room to take inventory once more. The space would make a good schoolroom for Annabelle and any siblings Gabby and Anthony created. She hoped it wouldn't take too long for her to get with child, because it would be nice if Annabelle had a brother or sister somewhat close to her age.

Studying the blank wall, she began formulating an idea for a mural, similar to the one she'd grown up with at Foxhaven Manor. Miss Teague's crooning voice interrupted her daydreams of re-creating a fairy world complete with pixie dust, gossamer wings, and blue bells.

"There, there, my precious girl. Your papa is gone. You are safe."

Her words sparked Gabby's ire. While it might appear Miss Teague was trying to reassure the girl, she was essentially telling Annabelle she was in danger when Anthony was near.

Gabby had a good mind to march into the other room and set the woman straight, but she didn't yet know her place in Annabelle's life, and overstepping her bounds might upset Anthony. Instead, she went in search of her husband.

She found him in his study behind his desk. "May I come in?"

His head snapped up; the paper he was holding fluttered to the desk. "Is something wrong?"

None of the distress she'd seen sweeping across his face earlier showed now. Not that she believed he was no longer hurt by his daughter's reaction. He was simply a master at hiding his feelings.

"There's nothing wrong." She wandered into the room, intrigued with exploring his private sanctuary.

"I told Annabelle we would take her to the park tomorrow. She appeared rather interested."

He grunted in response. They were back to primitive communication. She wondered if she should hop on his desk and beat her chest in order to get anywhere with him.

"Anthony, has Annabelle always been a nervous child?"

"Nervous? I don't think so." His jaw twitched as he returned to his work. "She has never fully warmed to me, but I can't blame the girl when I've only seen her a few times a year ever since she was born."

"Why did you leave her in Wales? Couldn't you have seen her more if she'd come to Ellis Hall?"

He glanced up. "Her aunt lived in Crickhowell and I already explained how Annabelle had formed an attachment with her. I didn't think it was right to split them apart."

"And Miss Teague wasn't in favor of moving to England until recently?"

He dropped the paper on the desk again with an exaggerated exhale. "Why are you questioning me about Miss Teague? I thought we had cleared up the matter of who she is to Annabelle and what she is *not* to me."

His tone stung, but she decided to let it go. He was hurting even if he didn't realize it himself. She moved beside him at his desk and smoothed his hair back from his forehead. "I was simply curious about Annabelle's past. I didn't mean to irritate you."

"And I didn't mean to be surly." He closed his eyes, melting under her touch. "Not long ago Miss Teague's brother came to her home demanding money. He'd gotten himself into debt, and he was not above using Annabelle as leverage to extort money from his sister. He threatened to take Annabelle unless she came up with six hundred pounds."

"Where was she supposed to get that kind of money?"

When he glanced up, his eyes were hard. "From me. But instead of writing to ask for money, Miss Teague wrote to inform me of his demands. I left for Wales as soon as I could."

The reason for his sudden journey and brief message. If he'd been open with her from the start, they could have been spared a lot of heartache. Nevertheless, she'd offered her forgiveness and couldn't allow herself to feel bitter. She propped a hip on the edge of his desk, waiting for him to continue.

"When I arrived at the cottage, Annabelle and her aunt were missing. The home had been ransacked. A neighbor said Miss Teague's brother had been there several days earlier. A ruckus had ensued and Miss Teague was later seen with a blackened eye. I feared something horrible had happened to Annabelle, but the woman said she thought Miss Teague had taken her to stay with a distant relative the morning after her brother's visit.

"Unfortunately, she had already fled to a different location by the time I found her cousin's farm. I spent the better part of my time chasing after my daughter and fearing the worst."

Gabby pressed her lips together in a frown. How childish she had been, expecting him to profess his love to her in letters when he was likely out of his mind with worry for Annabelle. "I'm sorry you went through something that scary."

"Annabelle and Miss Teague suffered more," he said with a shrug. "That's the reason I don't press my company upon Annabelle. Miss Teague has reassured me that my daughter's response isn't to be taken personally."

His blue eyes misted over. He blinked and picked up his paper. "I really should finish with this correspondence. It has been piling up for weeks."

Gabby smiled sadly, then leaned forward to kiss his forehead. "I'm sure Miss Teague is correct. Annabelle will warm to you soon, you'll see."

And Gabby would do everything she could to ensure her husband's heart healed fully, which meant helping him smooth the way with Annabelle.

Thirty-one

ANTHONY WOKE THE NEXT MORNING WITH A RENEWED sense of optimism with Gabby curled against his side and thoughts of a walk in the park with his daughter in his head. He eased Gabby from his embrace and slipped from bed to summon his valet, excited to start his day.

Pierce found Anthony in his dressing room rummaging through his jackets and gasped. "Milord, I will select your attire."

The man nearly shoved Anthony aside in his eagerness to fulfill his duties. One might think Anthony was in danger of being blown to bits if not for his valet throwing himself on a bundle of explosives. This was how seriously Pierce saw his responsibilities.

Anthony backed away with his hands up and chuckled. "Don't you wish to know where I'm going this morning before you decide what I should wear?"

"You go to the club every morning." His valet selected a gray waistcoat.

"But today I'm accompanying my bride and daughter to the park."

Pierce held up the waistcoat, wrinkled his nose, and put it back. "Too drab for the ladies, I fear."

"Yes, choose something cheerful." An outfit to match Anthony's mood. Annabelle had never accompanied him on a walk, and he looked forward to spending the morning with the two most important people in his life.

Gabby began stirring in the outer room. He went to greet her with a kiss and arranged to meet her in the breakfast room. They would enjoy a nice meal, then he would summon Annabelle.

He hadn't been at the table long before his wife swept in wearing a yellow walking dress and looking as radiant as a beam of sunlight. She bypassed the chair at the other end of the table where his footman had placed a plate and slipped into the seat adjacent to Anthony. The servant scrambled to accommodate her, a light sheen breaking out on his forehead.

Anthony sent him a sympathetic smile. They would all have adjustments to make, but adjustments must always be made any time there were improvements.

Gabby shook out a napkin and draped it over her lap. "Later today I wish to call on Mama. Would you give permission for Annabelle to join me?"

He blinked. "Are you certain you want a young child underfoot?"

"If you think Mama will welcome me without her newest grandchild, you don't know her very well."

Anthony's heart inflated and threatened to burst. His daughter had a grandparent. Well, a grandparent who wanted to know her. Camilla's parents had turned their backs on Annabelle once they learned her sire had been a member of the servant class. They did, however, give their word to keep the truth hidden. Too bad their promise had nothing to do with protecting their granddaughter and everything with avoiding the taint of their daughter's sins touching them. It was their loss and his gain. Annabelle was a beautiful child.

When the front door creaked, Gabby's eyebrows lifted.

"I must remember to tell Cooper to oil the hinges," he said and dug into his eggs, happier than he'd ever recalled being.

Annabelle's ecstatic squeal and running footsteps echoed from the foyer. He smiled, waiting for her to enter the breakfast room.

"Annabelle," Miss Teague scolded. "No running inside. Your papa will hear you and become very cross with you."

He balked. Had he truly presented as a brute to the woman and Annabelle?

Gabby's wide-eyed gaze locked on him, and hot prickles traveled the back of his neck. Surely she didn't believe his daughter running in the house would anger him.

He motioned to the footman. "Please let Lady Annabelle and her nanny know they may join us."

He schooled his features and avoided eye contact with Gabby as he waited for Annabelle and Miss Teague. The nanny could barely walk with his daughter wrapped around her legs. Large tears filled Annabelle's pretty green eyes and her bottom lip quivered.

"Good morning, milord and lady." A blotchy flush covered Miss Teague's skin. "I didn't realize you were awake already. We just returned from a stroll in the park."

Gabby's delicate eyebrow arched higher. "Lord Ellis and I had planned to take her for a walk this morning. I mentioned as much last evening."

"Aye, milady. But Lady Annabelle was up with the chickens this morning and terribly restless. I was at my wit's end, so I thought to try a walk to settle her."

Annabelle sniffled and peered at Anthony from across the room. Her tiny fingers gripped Miss Teague's skirts as if clinging for her life.

"I'm not certain your remedy was successful," Gabby said, sounding more than a tad snippy. "She still seems upset."

Miss Teague hugged Annabelle close. "A nap may be in order. If we may be excused, your lordship…"

Anthony sank against the seat back, defeated. "Of course. Keep me informed if she doesn't settle soon. Perhaps she needs a doctor."

Once the nanny had ushered Annabelle from the room, Gabby touched her napkin to the corners of her mouth and placed it beside her plate. "Does Miss Teague often warn Annabelle against angering you?"

His stomach roiled. He didn't want to have this conversation. "I may have been on the surly side a time or two during our courtship, but I never took it out on Annabelle. No doubt Miss Teague heard tales of my temper. I'm sure she means well."

Gabby sniffed but said nothing more on the subject.

After breaking their fast, she refused to release him from his promise of a walk in the park. "The fresh air will do us both good."

It wasn't until she had him strolling along the Serpentine that he learned their conversation wasn't over.

"I hope you will forgive me for speaking plainly, but I don't care for the manner in which Miss Teague coddles Annabelle. She is not a baby any longer and shouldn't be treated as one."

He stiffened at what he saw as a slight to his daughter. She'd been traumatized in Wales, and therefore a few tears on occasion were not out of the ordinary.

Gabby flung her hand to the side. "And then there's the matter of her taking Annabelle to the park when you and I were already planning to take her."

"I think it's best if we look to Miss Teague for guidance. After all, she has been with Annabelle since she was born."

Gabby halted on the path, forcing him to stop too. "Perhaps it's time to consider a change."

He clenched his jaw, unsure he liked where this conversation was headed. He had already told her he wouldn't send Annabelle away. "Miss Teague has taken exemplary care of my daughter. Annabelle is a blessing."

Gabby nodded. "She's a darling girl, and I am blessed with having her in my life as well. I want her to have the best advantages—just as our other children will have. That is the reason I think we should consider finding a governess. Miss Teague is not equipped to fulfill the role, and Annabelle no longer needs a nanny."

"No." He'd not take away the only person who could make Annabelle feel secure.

"No? Is there to be no discussion on the matter?"

"She knows what she is doing with Annabelle." Clearly, he didn't. And what did Gabby know about caring for children? She'd been a mother less than a day. "Miss Teague is staying."

Gabby's hand landed on her hip, her eyes sparking with irritation. "I never said she had to leave, but a little distance wouldn't hurt. I think it's possible Miss Teague is interfering with your bond with Annabelle."

He blew out an exasperated breath. Although he appreciated his wife's generous thought, he knew Miss Teague wasn't responsible for his troubles with Annabelle. He was to blame. He didn't know how to talk to his daughter or behave as a father should. How *could* he know when he barely remembered his own father?

And Miss Teague was a league above his mother in the way of affection and nurturing. He would have died for one hug from his mother, and Miss Teague was being criticized for giving too many?

"Sometimes a child needs a bit of coddling."

The fight drained from her and her hand flopped at her side. "I know how important love is, and I'm certain Annabelle needs more than most after her ordeal. But a papa's love is special to a girl, and no one else can give that to Annabelle."

Anthony's heart softened as he gazed at Gabby. The duke had been a wonderful father and she had blossomed under the warmth of his affection. Anthony wanted to be that type of father for Annabelle, but he felt like a failure at every turn.

The truth was he didn't know what he would do

without Miss Teague's assistance, but he suspected he would muck up badly.

A gentleman appeared on the path ahead, his walking stick striking the ground with each step.

Anthony groaned. "Corby. The last person I wished to see."

The scoundrel was still far enough away to avoid if they turned back, but he spotted them and called out a greeting. "Ahoy, Ellis."

"Blast," he muttered and drew Gabby closer.

"I thought you and Lord Corby were on friendly terms. He opened his gallery as a personal favor."

"I later learned he and Ledbery had a wager on Thorne and me, which of us would throw the first punch because of you. Corby won the bet."

She huffed. "That explains the reason he told Sebastian about Annabelle."

His gaze snapped to her. "I beg your pardon?"

A pink blush stained her cheeks. "I meant, Lord Thorne."

"Not that, although I'd prefer you never speak his name again. Did Corby start the rumors about Annabelle?"

She shrugged.

He made a fist as Corby approached with a smirk. "I should plant a facer on him."

"Do what you must, but hurry. Lady Corby and her companion are not far behind."

Beyond Corby's shoulder, his mother and her companion walked arm in arm, their pace much slower than the viscount's.

Gabby tipped her face up to Anthony, her eyes

bright. "I may have an idea on how to put the rumors to rest, but I need to speak with Mama first."

Corby reached them before Anthony could question her; the man's smirk had turned into a full-blown leer as he looked at Gabby. Anthony raised his fist and took a step forward, but Gabby's grip on his arm reminded him they had an audience.

She fluttered her lashes and smiled coyly at the scoundrel. "Why, Lord Corby. How fortuitous to cross paths with you this morning. Lord Ellis was just telling me you have another art collection so rare and special, you keep it hidden away in its own room."

Corby's step faltered and his lascivious grin fell. It was all Anthony could do to hold back a triumphant laugh.

Gabby hugged Anthony's arm and bubbled with enthusiasm. "How I would love to view your rare collection, and I'm certain Mama would be thrilled as well."

"Uh—" Corby rubbed the back of his neck and grimaced as if he were in pain.

"Perhaps I could speak with Lady Corby about arranging a private showing?"

"No! I mean, I'm sure the collection wouldn't interest you, Lady Ellis. My father collected a few odd pieces. Religious artifacts and such."

His gaze darted to Anthony as if pleading with him to support his claim. Anthony said nothing. He rather enjoyed watching Corby squirm.

Gabby clapped her hands. "Religious artifacts? How delightful."

Color drained from Corby's face and Anthony wondered if he might swoon. "Yes, well. We really must be going. Mother has a, uh…thing and she cannot…" He turned on his heel. "Good day."

As he marched away, Gabby lifted her hand and waved. "Next time Lord Ellis or I see you, we really must discuss a viewing."

She laughed when he flung his arms in the air to herd his mother and her companion in the opposite direction. "There. One problem solved. I don't think you will be seeing the viscount any time soon."

Anthony's optimistic mood returned and he held his arm out to her. "My, but you are a clever one, Lady Ellis. Shall we see if there are any other scoundrels lurking in the park you can make shake in their boots?"

She linked her arm with his and arched a brow. "Brilliant suggestion. I've only just begun to put ne'er-do-wells in their places."

Thirty-two

GABBY HAD INSISTED ANNABELLE AND MISS TEAGUE accompany her when calling on her mama later that day, refusing to hear any excuses from the nanny. Gabby took Annabelle's hand in hers as they climbed from the carriage at Talliah House and smiled when she didn't pull away.

"Now, Annabelle," Miss Teague said as she clambered down the carriage steps, "you can't touch anything. If you should break something…"

The threat hung unfinished on the air.

Gabby aimed a strained smile over her shoulder. "Miss Teague, you must be rather tired of being solely responsible for this darling girl. Consider this a day off from your duties and enjoy yourself."

She didn't pose it as a request, but rather a command. It was no wonder Annabelle was a Nervous Nellie with dire warnings being tossed at her every other moment.

Miss Teague pursed her lips. "Yes, milady."

Gabby's smile widened. "That's better. Now, come allow me to introduce you to Mama. I think you will get on well."

Mama got on well with everyone, and in actuality, Miss Teague was pleasant enough.

Gabby's mother and sisters greeted her with hugs and excited squeals. Then, as she'd expected, they turned their loving attention on Annabelle, fawning over her in a way that didn't make her shy away.

She readily climbed onto the settee beside Mama and accepted a sugar biscuit. "Look at this lovely hair, darling girl. You are the very image of your cousins, Chloe and Clare." Mama smiled at Miss Teague, including her in the conversation. "My youngest son has twins with their mother's red hair."

It took no time before Mama had Miss Teague engaged and sharing stories about Annabelle. Gabby sank into the plush cushions of the chair, allowing herself a moment to evaluate the other woman. Despite Miss Teague's tendency to feed Annabelle's anxiety, Gabby didn't believe the woman meant any real harm. She was tender with the girl, and she had devoted her life to caring for Annabelle. Gabby was grateful for all she had done for Anthony and his daughter, but now it was time to allow them to have a relationship.

And if Annabelle had any hope of being accepted into society, the rumors about Miss Teague being her mother had to be laid to rest. Gabby thought she had a solution, but she wasn't certain Anthony would agree with her plan. If Miss Teague sabotaged the attempt, Gabby feared Anthony would side with the girl's aunt.

When Katie and Liz offered to take Annabelle to the gardens, Gabby suggested Miss Teague enjoy a tour as well. She needed a moment alone with her mother.

Mama patted the settee. "I want to hear all about your wedding. Come. And spare no detail."

Gabby sat beside her and recounted every moment she could recall while her mother listened with a dreamy smile. "Now I have everything I want," she said. "Or I will as soon as Liz and Katie find their true loves and marry."

Gabby's smile faded. "Mama, there is but one thing keeping me from complete happiness. It's Anthony and his relationship with Annabelle. I need your help."

❦

Anthony perked up when he heard Gabby returning with Annabelle and Miss Teague. He leaned back in his chair and let their happy voices wash over him. The sound was foreign within the walls of Keaton Place, and yet it felt right.

He picked up his quill, intending to return to his work, when Gabby appeared in the doorway of his study with Annabelle.

"There is Papa," Gabby said, her voice infused with enthusiasm. "How happy he is to see his precious Annabelle." He chuckled at hearing his wife refer to him as Papa.

A small smile curved his daughter's lips. She was wary perhaps, but not frightened as she usually was. Gabby cleared her throat and raised her eyebrows at him.

He slowly pushed back from his desk so as not to spook her. "Happy is an understatement. I'm thrilled to have Annabelle visit my study. Please come in."

His daughter tipped her head to look up at Gabby, as if trying to determine how she should react. His wife's smile was radiant as she came toward him with Annabelle holding on to her hand.

Anthony stayed still, afraid if he moved an inch, Annabelle would burst into tears. As they drew closer, he noticed something clutched in her fist, a crumpled piece of paper.

Gabby placed her hand on his shoulder, then kissed him on the cheek. "We missed you this afternoon, Papa. Annabelle made you a present since you couldn't be with us today. She has a lot of promise as an artist, I believe."

His daughter watched him with luminous eyes. He gentled his voice, imitating Gabby's lilting quality as best as he could. "May I see?"

She looked to Gabby once more then hesitantly held out the paper. He took it and unrolled her drawing. It was a crude sketch of people—ladies mostly, he concluded from their dresses—and one man with a hat. "What a skillful drawing."

Gabby took the sketch and spread it on the desk. "Shall we tell Papa who everyone is?" Annabelle went into Gabby's outstretched arms and Gabby lifted her to the desk.

With one arm on Annabelle's back and a hand on his shoulder, Gabby formed a bridge. "Well, on the far right is Grandmamma. You can tell from her pretty necklace. And who is next to her?"

She looked expectantly at Annabelle. "Liz," his daughter said without hesitation.

"That's right. Beside her is Katie, then Miss Teague and I. And do you remember her name?" She pointed to the last figure wearing a dress.

Annabelle's smile spread, her little cheeks glowing. "Vivi."

"How wonderful your memory is."

Miss Teague appeared in the threshold but held back. He spared her a quick glance, but Annabelle's happy face occupied his attention.

He touched a finger to the man. "Then this must be the duke."

Gabby shook her head, her eyes shimmering. "This is you. Annabelle thought it would be nice if you could be with her and her new family."

A lump formed in Anthony's throat. He didn't know if he could speak, but Annabelle was watching and waiting for a response. He couldn't close down, not now. "I wish I had been there, too. It sounds as if you had a marvelous time."

Gabby hugged them close, so they were all three huddled together, Gabby and him grinning like mad hatters. "Well, you'll just have to make up for your absence by joining us for dinner in the nursery. I heard you put on quite the performance last time."

He laughed. "If Annabelle wants a show, she shall have a show."

His daughter smiled and then did something unexpected. She touched his shoulder briefly.

"Shall we leave Papa to his work and go speak with Mrs. Duffy about dinner?"

Annabelle hugged his wife as she set her back on the floor and then skipped away.

He captured Gabby's wrist before she left him alone in his study. "Come here, Lady Bug." He tugged her onto his lap and kissed her soundly.

When he released her, she sighed. "I wish I could stay, but there are preparations to be made for tonight."

"I don't know what you did, but thank you."

She shrugged as if what she'd accomplished today had been nothing, but to him it was a miracle. "I'm showing her how to love you."

He grinned. "Is it really so difficult?"

"I think it's easy, but I have been in love with you a long time." She winked. "Perhaps I've forgotten how challenging you can be."

He kissed the tip of her nose and reluctantly let her go.

The rest of his afternoon passed slowly, but at least a happy glow surrounded him. He dressed for dinner in a rush and arrived at the nursery just in time to join his lovely ladies.

That evening he was silly, clumsy, and very embarrassing, but his daughter's belly laughs were worth every antic. His valet might not agree when he saw the tomato stain on his jacket, but it had been an accident.

Gabby chattered about all the fun activities they would partake in the next day, and even hinted at a surprise that would be arriving in the next couple of weeks. No amount of cajoling by Annabelle or him convinced her to share the surprise.

At the end of dinner, Miss Teague helped Annabelle from her seat. The nanny had been so quiet throughout the meal, he had almost forgotten she was present. She rested her hands on Annabelle's shoulders.

"Milord, once I have put the little one to bed, may I have a word with you and Lady Ellis?"

"Of course. We'll be in the drawing room."

Below stairs, Anthony sat in his favorite chair with a brandy while Gabby sketched in her book as they waited for Miss Teague. He sighed, sublimely contented after the successful dinner with his daughter. "Do you know what Miss Teague wants to discuss?"

Gabby glanced up from her drawing. "Everything went splendidly this afternoon. I have no idea what's on her mind."

They didn't have long to contemplate before Miss Teague presented at the drawing room door. Anthony motioned her inside and stood until she took a seat. She sat at the edge of a hardback chair and fidgeted with her skirts.

"Did Annabelle go to bed without any trouble?" he asked.

"Yes, milord. She had an eventful day and was ready for her bed." Her gaze dropped and her lips turned down.

Anthony held his breath as he waited for her to speak. Had something gone wrong today?

Miss Teague pushed a strand of hair behind her ear. "I suppose I will be leaving soon, and I had hoped you might pay my travel expenses to Crickhowell."

"Leaving?" Anthony and Gabby asked at the same time.

Relief flooded through him upon realizing his wife was just as surprised as he was.

"Why would you leave?" he asked, sinking down into his chair. "Annabelle is especially fond of you."

"When I saw the three of you together today, I thought…" She laced her fingers together. "Well, I figured you would want me gone now that you have a wife, so you can be like a family."

Anthony didn't know what to say. He wanted Annabelle, Gabby, and him to be a family, but that didn't require Miss Teague to leave Town. "I'm sorry, but I can't allow you to return to Crickhowell. Not as long as your brother is free to visit you whenever he wants. He left you battered the last time you saw him."

Her gaze darted toward Gabby. "But I can't stay here either, can I?"

Anthony raised his brows. "Did I miss an exchange this afternoon?"

Gabby's head was tilted slightly to the side and fine lines appeared on her forehead. "This is the first I'm hearing of Miss Teague's wishes to go."

"I thought that would be best, milord."

"I disagree. Your place is with Annabelle."

Gabby aimed a sympathetic smile at the other woman. "I agree with Lord Ellis. You shouldn't return to Wales. Not only could it result in harm coming to you, but Annabelle would be devastated if she wasn't able to see you."

A rush of breath escaped Miss Teague. "Oh, thank you, milady. I didn't want to leave her, truly I didn't."

Anthony nodded once, the matter resolved in his eyes. "Then you won't go. You'll remain with her as we initially agreed upon."

Gabby lay her drawing aside. "Yet we don't want to be imprudent. Perhaps we should discuss the wisdom in Miss Teague remaining on as Annabelle's nanny."

Heat swept up Anthony's face. He drummed his fingers on the armrest, trying to control his temper.

He had already made it clear Miss Teague would be staying on as Annabelle's nanny. His wife challenging his authority did not sit well. "Explain yourself."

Gabby nibbled her bottom lip, glancing from him to Miss Teague then back to him. "I don't wish to anger you, but I feel I must speak up for Annabelle's sake. The rumors concerning her will continue as long as Miss Teague is under our roof. The family resemblance is too strong."

Miss Teague blinked. "What rumors? Are people gossiping about Annabelle?" She rose from her seat and clutched her hands at her waist. "What are they saying?"

He couldn't ignore the sinking of his heart. He hadn't given their situation appropriate consideration since their return, but Gabby was correct. As long as Anthony kept Miss Teague under his employ, people would believe the worst. Yet he didn't know what to do. If he sent her to live at another property, the rumors would likely grow, and there would still be the issue of Annabelle being heartbroken.

Anthony flicked his hand in a dismissive gesture. "We'll find a way to discredit the tales."

He sounded more confident than he was.

"I may know a way." Gabby changed her position on the settee, leaning slightly toward Miss Teague. "My mother is seeking a lady's companion. I spoke with her while you were on a stroll in the gardens, and she would like it if you would consider the position."

"But—"

She held up her hand to stop Anthony's interruption. "If you become Mama's companion, no one will question your past. They will assume you are a lady who has fallen on hard times. We could introduce you as Annabelle's distant relative."

Miss Teague's eyes brimmed with tears. "Then I would have to leave Annabelle after all."

"You could still see her every day," Gabby said. "I realize it wouldn't be the same, but as Mama said, if we all cooperate, we should be able to help Annabelle with this change." She looked to Anthony as if seeking his approval.

He nodded slowly, the wisdom of her suggestion sinking in. "Go on."

"Once we retreat to the country, you could spend even more time with Annabelle. We will be neighbors after all."

"I see." Miss Teague sat and swiped away a tear sliding down her cheek. "I do want what's best for Annabelle. She's like my own child."

The lines in Gabby's forehead deepened. "I'm afraid there is one more thing I must address. I think it would be best if we taught Annabelle to stop calling you Mama."

Miss Teague's head snapped up, and he could see the argument on the tip of her tongue.

"This is in Annabelle's best interest," Gabby said. "If anyone heard her, they might continue to believe you are Lord Ellis's—please, forgive any insult—*mistress*."

Miss Teague blanched; her hand fluttered to her throat. "Mistress? Oh, dear. Is that what people are saying?"

"Only the ignorant ones," he grumbled, then flinched when the women glared at him. In one sentence, he'd managed to insult them both by implying Miss Teague was undesirable and Gabby a dolt for believing he would take the nanny for a mistress. He grinned. "Sorry."

Gabby sniffed and resumed speaking with Miss

Teague. "There has been talk, but it seems to be limited to only a few. Still, we cannot take the chance of the rumors spreading."

"I understand, milady." A deep blush consumed the young woman when she glanced at him.

"There's no need to hurry. Mama says we'll need to prepare Annabelle for the change, and even once you move to Talliah House, we'll make certain you see each other every day." Gabby left the settee and extended a hand to Miss Teague. "Thank you for understanding. Annabelle is fortunate to have you in her life. I never want to take that away."

Miss Teague accepted her hand. "I believe you, Lady Ellis."

Anthony dismissed her before taking his wife in his arms.

"Ignorant, am I?" she said with a huff. "You're lucky I don't crown you with a candlestick."

He nuzzled her neck, showering her with kisses and making her squeal with laughter. Her hands splayed against his chest.

"It tickles. Stop!"

He pulled back, grinning. "I'm lucky I have you."

Her wide smile filled his heart. There were no more empty places inside him, no more loneliness or doubts. In his limited imagination, he'd never dreamed his life could be so perfect. He'd wanted a wife, a family, and noise. And he'd gotten more.

"I love you, Lady Bug."

She snuggled against him, her face lifted in invitation. "I love you, too. Now, do what you're best at and show me."

Epilogue

ANNABELLE SHRIEKED. "HE'S GETTING AWAY."

Gabby recovered the furry black-and-white bundle wiggling in her arms before he made an escape. "Shh," she admonished, laughing. "Remember, we're surprising your papa."

Although how Anthony could miss their arrival home, she didn't know. Her husband had gotten his wish. There was barely a peaceful moment these days since Annabelle had lost her shyness.

Gabby considered it a blessing that they'd scarcely received any invitations their first two weeks back in London, because it had allowed Anthony and her to spend evenings at home with Annabelle. She and Anthony were slowly being accepted into society again, but the time home had worked wonders with Annabelle.

Annabelle's parting with Miss Teague had seemed painless enough since she'd had time to grow accustomed to their presence. Of course, she still saw her aunt daily and had just seen her moments earlier when Gabby and Annabelle collected Anthony's gift. Gabby's brother, Luke, had found the perfect pup, even if he was being perfectly troublesome at the moment.

Annabelle bounded across the checkerboard floor, headed toward Anthony's study. Her copper curls bounced when she stopped with a hop and spin. "Come on, Gabby."

"I'm trying." The pup flailed until he turned in her arms and slurped his wet tongue across her lips and nose. She laughed again. "Ew. No more kisses, you naughty boy."

"Who's kissing my wife out there?" Anthony's teasing voice drifted from the study.

Annabelle's tiny hands captured her giggle. It was so good to see her positive response to Anthony. There was no more clinging or tears when he came near.

Gabby winked at her. "I could use your assistance, my lord. Unless you wish this rogue to keep taking liberties with me."

She looked up to find her husband lounging in the doorway. A grin stretched across his face. "Gabrielle, what have you done?"

"It's not my fault. This is all Annabelle's doing."

He faked a gasp, his eyes expanding. "You? Are you responsible for bringing this bundle of fur into my house?"

Annabelle's smile widened and she nodded. "It's a puppy."

"A puppy! You brought me a puppy?" He swept forward, scooped her into his arms, and rained kisses on her face as he often did with Gabby. Annabelle laughed like mad, her high-pitched scream ear-piercing and yet so pleasing. Anthony planted one more kiss on her cheek before settling her into the

About the Author

Don't let Regency romance author Samantha Grace's sweet smile fool you. She has a wicked sense of humor, and she's not above embarrassing her characters for a good laugh. Samantha writes what she enjoys reading: romantic comedies about family, friendship, and flawed characters who learn how to love deeply. Part-time hospice social worker, moonlighting author, and Pilates nut, she enjoys a happy and hectic life with her real life hero and two kids in the Midwest. To learn more about Samantha's stories, visit www.samanthagraceauthor.com.

into taking my ideas and making everything a reality. And a special thank-you to my editor, Leah Hultenschmidt, for her guidance and the wealth of knowledge she shares with me.

Lastly, thank you to my husband and kids for their support and patience, and for not complaining too much when we run low on groceries during deadline time.

Acknowledgments

Writing may seem like a solitary activity, but it takes many great minds to create a book. I'd like to take a moment to recognize just a few of the people who helped this book go from my imagination to print.

I'd be lost without my fellow writers, critique partners, and great friends. Plotting guru Jane Charles generously gave her time to brainstorm the story line with me; Ava Stone and Catherine Gayle gave me a kick early in the process so I could meet my deadline; Aileen Fish and Julie Johnstone were there every step of the way to provide invaluable feedback; Suzie Grant assisted with fight scenes, her specialty; and Robin Delany gave me great encouragement and feedback.

As always, thanks to my agent, Nephele Tempest, for her part in the creative process. I value her opinion and appreciate her willingness to talk through ideas, in addition to all the other technical things she does for me behind the scenes.

Thank you to Sourcebooks. Everyone I have contact with makes this a pleasant experience, and I appreciate all the hard work the entire team puts crook of his elbow. Her arms circled his neck. Her green eyes sparkled. "It's for you, Papa."

Gabby carried the pup closer so Anthony could see him. "He's a sheepdog. A useful breed just like you wanted."

He scratched behind the pup's ears, but the moment he stopped, the animal's pink tongue darted out and caught Gabby's chin.

She sputtered while Anthony chuckled. "Is he going to run around trying to lick the sheep then?" he asked.

Gabby wrinkled her nose. "No, he's going to run around Ellis Hall causing all kinds of havoc once we retire to the country."

She bent to place the pup on the floor and Annabelle clambered to be let down, too. The two tore across the floor and disappeared into Anthony's study; her happy giggles carried on the air.

A bang echoed from the other room, followed by another peel of laughter.

"He's simply getting a head start at Keaton Place," she said. "You do realize we'll never have a moment's peace again."

The pup yipped and Annabelle released a playful scream.

He placed his arm around Gabby and hugged her close. "Yes, I did get that impression. And *now* I have everything I've ever wanted."

"I'll have a devil of a time knowing what to give you at Michaelmas if that's the case."

Anthony placed a kiss at her temple, his arm so ⁿ and solid behind her back. "Somehow I think 'll manage, my love. You are full of surprises."